The Tale of Genji: Part Two

THE SACRED TREE

LADY SHIKIBU MURASAKI was born in 978 and, after a first marriage which ended with the death of her husband when she was still young, took up service in the entourage of the Empress Akiko in the year 1004. It is believed that she began to write *The Tale of Genji* before she arrived at court, and it is known from her diary that a large part of it was finished and was being read by members of the court by 1008.

The six parts of *The Tale of Genji* were published separately between 1925 and 1933, and the entire novel was published in 1933.

THE TALE OF GENJI: PART TWO

THE SACRED TREE

Lady Murasaki

TRANSLATED FROM THE JAPANESE

BY ARTHUR WALEY

1322

Doubleday Anchor Books
Doubleday & Company, Inc.
Garden City, New York
1959

COVER BY SEONG MOY

COVER TYPOGRAPHY BY REMY CHARLIP

TYPOGRAPHY BY EDWARD GOREY

LIST OF MOST IMPORTANT PERSONS

(ALPHABETICAL)

AKASHI, LADY OF	Daughter of the old recluse of Akashi.
AKIKONOMU, LADY	Vestal Virgin at Ise; daughter of Rokujo.
AOI, PRINCESS	Genji's first wife.
ASAGAO, PRINCESS	Genji's first-cousin; courted by him in vain.
CHUJO	Short for 'To no Chujo.'
CHUJO, LADY	To no Chujo's daughter by his legitimate wife.
CHUNAGON	Maid to Oborozuki.
EMPEROR, THE OLD	Genji's father.
FUJITSUBO	The Old Emperor's consort; loved by Genji.
GENJI, PRINCE	The Old Emperor's son by a concubine.
GOSECHI, LADY	Dancer at the winter festival; admired by Genji.
HYOBUKYO, PRINCE	Fujitsubo's brother; Murasaki's father.
IYO NO SUKE	Husband of Utsusemi.
JIJU	Maid to Suyetsumu.
JOKYODEN, LADY	Consort of Suzaku.
KI NO KAMI	Son of Iyo no Suke by his first wife.
KOKIDEN	Original consort of the Old Emperor; supplanted first by Genji's mother, then by Fujitsubo.
KOREMITSU	Retainer to Genji.

MURASAKI	Genji's second wife.
OBOROZUKIYO, PRINCESS	Younger sister of Kokiden.
OMYOBU	Maid to Fujitsubo.
REIKEIDEN	Lady-in-waiting at the Old Emperor's Court.
REIKEIDEN, PRINCESS	Niece of Kokiden.
ROKUJO, PRINCESS	Widow of the Old Emperor's brother.
RYOZEN, EMPEROR	Son of Genji and Fujitsubo; successor to Suzaku.
SHONAGON	Murasaki's old nurse.
SOCHI NO MIYA, PRINCE	Genji's half-brother.
SUYETSUMU, LADY (Suyetsumuhana)	Daughter of Prince Hitachi; the red-nosed lady.
SUZAKU, EMPEROR	Genji's half-brother; successor to the Old Emperor.
TO NO CHUJO	Brother of Genji's first wife, Lady Aoi.
UKON NO JO (Okon)	Faithful retainer to Genji; brother of Ki no Kami.
UTSUSEMI	Wife of Iyo no Suke. Courted by Genji.
VILLAGE OF FALLING FLOWERS, LADY FROM THE	Sister of Reikeiden; protected by Genji.

Contents

GENEALOGICAL TABLES

PRINCE ZEMBO, m. LADY ROKUJO, and died young.
— LADY AKIKONOMU.

THE OLD EMPEROR.
— SUZAKU (his mother was Lady Kokiden).
— GENJI (his mother was Lady Kiritsubo).

PRINCE MOMOZONO SHIKIBUKYO.
— PRINCESS ASAGAO.

PRINCESS OMIYA, m. Minister of Left.
— AOI.
  — YUGIRI.
— TO NO CHUJO.
  — LADY CHUJO.

MINISTER OF THE RIGHT.
— KOKIDEN[1] (eldest daughter).
— OBOROZUKIYO (sixth daughter), wife of Suzaku, who is Emperor for a time, but soon retires.

A FORMER EMPEROR.
— PRINCE HYOBUKYO.
  — MURASAKI (Genji's second wife).
— FUJITSUBO.
  — RYOZEN (supposed to be the old Emperor's child; really Genji's). Becomes Emperor in Suzaku's stead.

[1] Whom in this volume I call Oborozuki for short.

The Tale of Genji: Part Two

THE SACRED TREE

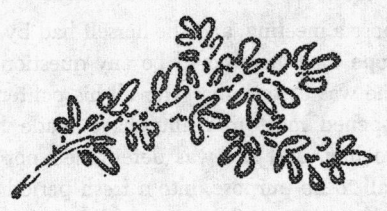

Chapter I

THE SACRED TREE

As the time for her daughter's departure came near,
Lady Rokujo fell into utter despair. It had at first been
generally supposed that the death of the lady at the
Great Hall would put an end to all her troubles and
the attendants who waited upon her at the Palace-in-
the-Fields were agog with excitement. But their expectations remained unfulfilled. Not a word came from
Genji, and this unprecedented treatment on his part finally convinced her that something[1] had indeed happened which it was impossible for him to forgive. She
strove to cast out all thought of him from her heart so
that when the time came she might set out upon her
journey without misgiving or regret. For a parent to accompany her daughter on such an occasion was in the
highest degree unusual; but in this case the Virgin's extreme youth was a convenient excuse, and Rokujo put
it about that as the child still needed surveillance she had
decided to quit the temporal world in her daughter's
company. Even after all that had happened the prospect
of parting with her for ever was extremely painful to
Genji, and as the day drew near he again began to send
her letters full of tenderness and solicitude. But he did

[1] Rokujo was still uncertain whether it was her jealousy that
had killed Yugao.

not propose a meeting, and she herself had by now given up all hope that there could be any question of such a thing. She was certain that (for all his politeness) what had happened must in reality have made her utterly odious to him, and she was determined not to plunge herself, all to no purpose, into a fresh period of conflict and agitation. From time to time she made short visits to her palace, but so secretly that Genji did not hear of it. The Palace-in-the-Fields was not a place where he could see her without inconvenient restrictions and formalities. He fully intended to see her, but put off the visit from day to day till at last months had elapsed since she left the city. Then the ex-Emperor's health began to decline. He had no definitely serious or alarming symptoms, but constantly complained of feeling that there was something wrong with him. Genji's thoughts were therefore a great deal occupied with his father's condition; but he did not want Rokujo to leave with the impression that he had lost all feeling for her, nor did he wish those who knew of their friendship to think that he had treated her heartlessly, and despite all difficulties he set out one day for the Palace-in-the-Fields. It was the seventh of the ninth month and the departure of the Virgin for Ise was bound to take place within the next few days. It may be imagined that Rokujo and her maids were in no condition to receive visits, but he wrote again and again begging her to see him even if it were only at the moment of her departure, and at last, despite the fluster into which her whole household was plunged, and feeling all the while that she was acting very imprudently, she could no longer fight against her longing once more to see him and sent word secretly that, if he came, she would contrive to speak to him for a moment from behind her screen-of-state. As he made his way through the open country that stretched out endlessly on every side, his heart was strangely stirred. The au-

tumn flowers were fading; along the reeds by the river
the shrill voices of many insects blended with the mourn-
ful fluting of the wind in the pines. Scarcely distinguishable from these somewhere in the distance rose and fell
a faint, enticing sound of human music. He had with
him only a handful of outriders, and his attendants were
by his orders dressed so as to attract as little notice as
possible. They noted that this lack of show contrasted
strangely with the elaborate pains which their master
had bestowed upon his own equipment, and as they
looked with admiration at the fine figure he cut, the
more romantically disposed among them were thrilled at
the thought that it had befallen them to accompany him
upon a journey, every circumstance of which was calculated to stir to the depth such sensitive hearts as theirs.
So delighted was Genji with the scene before him that
he continually asked himself why it was that he had deferred this visit for so long; and he regretted that while
Rokujo was at the Palace-in-the-Fields he had not made
a constant practice of visiting her. They came at last to
a group of very temporary-looking wooden huts surrounded by a flimsy brushwood fence. The archways,[2]
built of unstripped wood, stood out black and solemn
against the sky. Within the enclosure a number of priests
were walking up and down with a preoccupied air. There
was something portentous in their manner of addressing
one another and in their way of loudly clearing their
throats before they spoke. In the Hill of Offering there
was a dim flicker of firelight, but elsewhere no single
sign of life. So this was the place where he had left one
who was from the start in great distress of mind, to shift
for herself week after week, month after month! Suddenly he realized with a terrible force all that she must
have suffered. He hurried to the place where she had
told him he would find her (a room in the northern

[2] Torii.

outbuilding) and sent in a long message contrasting his
present quiet and serious existence with his now discarded frivolities. She in return replied with a message,
but did not suggest that they should meet. This angered
him. 'You do not seem to realize,' he said, 'that such
excursions as this are now no part of my ordinary existence and can only be arranged with the greatest difficulty. I had hoped that instead of keeping me beyond
the pale, you would hasten to relieve all the anxiety that
I have had concerning you in the long months since we
met.' To this appeal were added the protests of her
waiting-ladies who were scandalized at the idea of
Prince Genji being left waiting outside the house. At first
she pleaded the impossibility of receiving a guest in surroundings so cramped and wretched, her duty towards
her daughter at this critical hour, the undesirability of
such an interview just on the eve of her permanent departure. But though the prospect of facing him filled her
with unspeakable depression, she had not the heart to
treat him unkindly, and at last, looking very grave, with
sighs and hesitation at every step she came forward to
meet him. 'I presume that here one is allowed no further
than the verandah,' he said, and mounting the narrow
bamboo platform that surrounded the building he took
his seat there. An evening moon had risen and as she
saw him moving in its gentle light she knew that all this
while she had not been wrong; he was indeed more
lovely, more enticing than anyone in the world beside.
He began trying to explain why it was that for so many
months on end he had not been able to visit her; but he
soon got into a tangle, and feeling suddenly embarrassed he plucked a spray from the Sacred Tree[3] which
grew outside her room and handing it to her through
her blinds-of-state he said: 'Take this evergreen bough

[3] The *sakaki*, a species of evergreen oak, is planted at
Shinto shrines.

in token that my love can never change. Were it not so, why should I have set foot within the boundaries of this hallowed plot? You use me very ill.' But she answered with the verse: 'Thought you perchance that the Holy Tree from whose boughs you plucked a spray was as "the cedar by the gate"?'[4] To this he replied: 'Well knew I what priestess dwelt in this shrine, and for her sake came to pluck this offering of fragrant leaves.'

Though the position was not likely to be a very comfortable one, he now thrust his head under the reed blinds and sat with his legs dangling over the wooden framework of the bamboo platform. During all the years when he could see her as often and as intimately as he chose and she on her side withheld nothing from him, he had gone on serenely assuming that it would be always so, and never once in all that time had he felt so deeply moved as at this moment. Suddenly he realized with astonishment that though after that unhappy incident he had imagined it to be impossible for them to meet and had so avoided all risk of his former affection being roused to new life, yet from the first moment of this strange confrontation he had immediately found himself feeling towards her precisely as he had before their estrangement. Violently agitated he began to cast his mind rapidly over the long years of their friendship. Now all this was over. It was too horrible. He burst into tears. She had determined not to let him see what she was suffering, but now she could restrain herself no longer and he was soon passionately entreating her not to go down to Ise after all. The moon had set, but the starlit sky was calm and lovely. Pausing often to gaze up into the night he began at last to speak to her of what had lain so heavily on his heart. But no sooner was it

---

[4] In allusion to the old song, 'My home is at the foot of Miwa Hill. If you like me, come some day to visit me. You will know the house by the cedar which grows at the gate.'

openly mentioned between them than all the pent-up bitterness of so many weeks was suddenly released and vanished utterly away. Little by little, in preparation for her final departure, she had at last accustomed herself to think of him almost with indifference. Now in a moment all this was undone, and when she heard Genji himself entreating her to abandon the journey her heart beat violently, and the wildest thoughts agitated her brain. The garden which surrounded her apartments was laid out in so enchanting a manner that the troops of young courtiers, who in the early days of the retreat had sought in vain to press their attentions upon her, used, even when she had sent them about their business, to linger there regretfully; and on this marvellous night the place seemed consciously to be deploying all its charm. In the hours which followed, no secret was withheld on her side or on his; but what passed between them I shall not attempt to tell.

At last the night ended in such a dawn as seemed to have been fashioned for their especial delight. 'Sad is any parting at the red of dawn; but never since the world began, gleamed day so tragically in the autumn sky,' and as he recited these verses, aghast to leave her, he stood hesitating and laid her hand tenderly in his.

A cold wind was blowing. The pine-crickets in neighbouring trees were whispering in harsh despairing tones, as though they knew well enough what was toward. Their dismal voices would have struck a chill to the heart of any casual passer-by, and it may well be imagined what cheer they gave to lovers already at the height of distraction and anguish. She recited the verse, 'Sad enough already is this autumn parting; add not your dismal song, O pine-crickets of the moor.' He knew that it was his neglect that had forced this parting upon them. But now it was too late to make amends. Full of useless regrets, while the grey light of morning spread over the sky, he journeyed back disconsolately to the town, through meadows deep in dew. As she watched him go she could no longer restrain herself, and at the thought that she had lost him for ever broke into a fit of reckless weeping. Her gentlewomen, who on the evening before caught a fleeting glimpse of him in the moonlight, enjoyed next morning the excitement of detecting in their mistress's room a lingering fragrance of the princely scent which he had carried.[5] It may well be imagined that they at any rate were far from condemning the crime to which she had been accessory. 'It would have to be a marvellous journey indeed that I was going to take, before I could bring myself to part from such a one as this young prince!' So one of the ladies exclaimed; and at the thought that they had seen him for the last time all were on the verge of tears.

His letter, which arrived during the day, was so full and affectionate that had it been within her power she might have attempted to alter her plans. But matters had gone too far for that and it was useless to think of it. Nor were his feelings towards her (she was convinced) of a sort to warrant such a step. Much of what he had said was inspired simply by pity for her. But the mere fact that he took the trouble to say such things—that he thought it worth while to comfort her—showed that he still retained something of his old feeling, and the thought that even upon such remnants of affection as this she must now soon turn her back for ever, filled her mind with the most painful longings and regrets. He sent her many costumes and all else of which she could possibly have need upon the journey, with suitable presents to all her ladies. But to these handsome and costly gifts she gave hardly a thought. Indeed as the hour of her departure drew near she sank into a state of utter collapse. It was as though she had never till that moment

[5] Princes used rich scents forbidden to commoners.

fully realized the desolation and misery into which an intrigue, undertaken originally in a reckless and frivolous spirit, had at last plunged her. Meanwhile the Virgin, who had to the last been far from certain that her mother really meant to accompany her, was delighted that all was now fixed beyond power of recall. The unusual decision of the mother to accompany her daughter was much discussed in the world at large. Some scented a scandal; a few were touched by so rare an exhibition of family attachment. It is indeed in many ways more comfortable to belong to that section of society whose actions are not publicly canvassed and discussed. A lady in Rokujo's conspicuous position finds her every movement subjected to an embarrassing scrutiny.

On the sixteenth day of the seventh month the Virgin was purified in the Katsura River. The ceremony was performed with more than ordinary splendour, and her escort for the journey to Ise was chosen not from among the Chamberlains and Counsellors, but from noblemen of the highest rank and reputation. This was done in compliment to the old ex-Emperor who showed a particular interest in the Virgin, his favourite brother's child. At the moment of her departure from the Palace-in-the-Fields Rokujo was handed a letter. It was from Genji and was couched in all those tender terms that had once been current between them. Remembering the sacred errand upon which she was bound he tied the letter to a streamer of white bark-cloth.[6] 'Such love as ours,' he wrote, 'not even the God of Thunder whose footsteps shake the fields of Heaven . . .'[7] and added the verse: 'O all ye Gods of the Kingdom, Rulers of the Many Isles, to your judgment will I hearken; must needs this parting

---

[6] Used in making offerings to Shinto gods.
[7] An allusion to the poem (*Kokinshu* 701), 'Can even the God of Thunder whose footfall echoes in the sky put those asunder whom love has joined?'

sever a love insatiable as ours?'[8] Though the letter arrived just when the procession was forming and all was bustle and confusion, an answer came. It was not from Rokujo but from the Virgin herself, and had been dictated by her to her aunt who was acting as Lady Intendant: 'Call not upon the Gods of Heaven to sit in judgment upon this case, lest first they charge you with fickleness and pitiless deceit.' He longed to witness the presentation of the Virgin and her mother at the Palace,[9] but he had a feeling that since it was to avoid him that Rokujo was leaving the City, it would be embarrassing for both of them if he took part in the ceremonies of farewell, and overcoming his desire to see her once more, he stayed in his own palace sunk in idle thoughts. The reply of the Virgin showed a quite astonishing precocity, and he smiled as he read it through again. The girl had begun to interest him. No doubt she was precocious in charm as well as intelligence, and since it was his foible invariably to set his heart upon possessing, even at the cost of endless difficulties, whatever custom and circumstance seemed to have placed beyond his utmost reach, he now began thinking what a misfortune it was that he had in earlier days never once availed himself of his position in the house to make her acquaintance, which would indeed at any time have been perfectly easy. But after all, life is full of uncertainties; perhaps one day some unforeseen circumstance would bring her into his life once more.

The fame of Lady Rokujo brought many spectators to view the procession and the streets were thronged with coaches. The Palace Gates were entered at the hour of the monkey.[10] Lady Rokujo, sitting in the sacred pal-

[8] In reality an appeal to the Virgin (representative of the Gods) to dissuade her mother from accompanying her.

[9] Before departing for Ise the Virgin was presented to the Emperor and formally invested.

[10] 4 P.M.

anquin by her daughter's side, remembered how her father, the late Minister of State, had brought her years ago to these same gates, fondly imagining that he would make her the greatest lady in the land.[11] Thus to revisit the Palace now that so many changes had come both to her life and to the Court, filled her with immeasurable depression. At sixteen she had been married, at twenty she had been left a widow and now at thirty again she had set foot within the Ninefold Palisade. She murmured to herself the lines: 'Though on this sacred day 'twere profanation to recall a time gone by, yet in my inmost heart a tinge of sadness lurks.'

The Virgin was now fourteen. She was extremely handsome and her appearance at the presentation-ceremony, decked in the full robes of her office, made a profound impression. The Emperor, when he came to setting the Comb of Parting in her hair, was deeply moved and it was observed that he shed tears.

Outside the Hall of the Eight Departments a number of gala-coaches were drawn up to witness the departure of the Virgin from the Palace. The windows of those coaches were hung with an exquisitely contrived display of coloured scarves and cloaks, and among the courtiers who were to go down to Ise there were many who thought with an especial pang of one who in his honour had added some gay touch of her own to the magnificence of this unprecedented show. It was already dark when the procession left the Palace. When after traversing the Second Wood they turned into the Doi Highway the travellers passed close by Genji's palace. Deeply moved, he sent the following poem tied to a spray of the Holy Tree—'Though today you cast me off and lightly set upon your way, yet surely when at last you

[11] Prince Zembo, her father, was at that time Heir Apparent.

ferry the Eighty Rapids of Suzuka Stream[12] your sleeve
will not be dry.' When this message was brought to her
it was already quite dark. This and the noisy bustle of
her journey prevented her from answering till the next
day. When her reply came it was sent back from beyond
the Barrier: 'Whether at the Eighty Rapids of Suzuka
Stream my sleeve be wet or no, all men will have forgotten me long ere I come to Ise's Land.' It was hastily
written, yet with all the grace and distinction that
habitually marked her hand; but his pleasure in it was
marred by the strange bitterness of her tone. A heavy
mist had risen, and gazing at the dimly-veiled sem-
blances that were belatedly unfolding in the dawn he
whispered to himself the lines: 'O mist, I long to follow
with my eyes the road that she passed; hide not from
me in these autumn days the slopes of Meeting Hill.'[13]
That night he did not go to the western wing,[14]
but lay sleepless till dawn, brooding disconsolately upon
a turn of affairs for which, as he well knew, he alone
was responsible. What *she* suffered, as day by day
she travelled on through unknown lands, may well be
guessed.

By the tenth month the ex-Emperor's condition had
become very grave indeed. Throughout the country
much concern was felt. The young Emperor was in great
distress and hastened to pay him a visit-of-state. Weak
though he was the sick man first gave minute instructions as to the upbringing of the Heir Apparent and then
passed on to a discussion of Genji's future. 'I desire you,'
he said, 'still to look upon him as your guardian and to
seek his advice in all matters, whether small or great;
as indeed I have accustomed you to do during my life-

[12] A river in the Province of Ise.
[13] 'Osaka' means Hill of Meeting; a gentle slope on the road
from Kyoto to Otsu.
[14] I.e. to Murasaki.

time. In the handling of public business he shows a competence beyond his years. There is no doubt that his natural vocation is to administer the affairs of a people rather than to lead the secluded life of a Royal Prince, and when I attached him to a clan devoid of Royal Blood it was that he might the better keep watch for us over the public affairs of our kingdom. I therefore entreat you never to act contrary to his advice.' He gave many other parting instructions to his successor, but such matters are not for a woman's pen and I feel I must apologize for having said even so much as this.

The young Emperor, deeply moved, repeatedly signified that he would obey all these instructions in every particular. It gave his father great comfort and pleasure to note that he was already growing up into a fine handsome young fellow. But after a short while Court affairs necessitated the Emperor's immediate presence, and his father, who longed to keep him by his side, was in the end more distressed than comforted by this brief visit. The Heir Apparent was to have come at the same time as the Emperor; but it was thought that this arrangement would be too tiring and the little boy[15] was brought on another day. He was big for his age and very pretty. The old man looked fondly at him and the child, unconscious of the purpose for which he had been summoned, stood watching him with laughter in his face. Fujitsubo, who sat near by, was weeping bitterly; and, suddenly catching sight of her, the ex-Emperor for a while lost his composure. To this little prince also he gave a variety of instructions; but it was evident that he was too young to understand what was being said, and remembering the uncertainties of his future the ex-Emperor gazed at the child with pity and distress. In his final instructions to Genji concerning the management of

---

[15] Genji's son by Fujitsubo; supposed to be the Emperor's child. He was now four years old.

public affairs he recurred again and again to the question of the Heir Apparent and the importance of giving him due protection and advice. It was now late at night and the Heir Apparent was taken off to bed. A vast number of courtiers followed in his train, so that his visit created almost as much bustle and confusion as that of the Emperor himself. But this visit had seemed to the sick man only too short and it was with great distress that he watched the procession depart. The Empress Mother, Lady Kokiden, had also intended to come; but hearing that Fujitsubo was at his side she felt somewhat disinclined, and while she was trying to decide whether to go or not, His Majesty passed quietly and painlessly away.

The ex-Emperor's death caused profound consternation in many quarters. Though it was some while since he resigned the Throne, he had continued to control the policy of the government just as in former days. The present Emperor was a mere child; his grandfather, the Minister of the Right, was known to be a man of hasty temper and treacherous disposition. Courtiers and noblemen alike regarded with the greatest apprehension a government subjected to his arbitrary power. But among them all none had better reason than Fujitsubo and Prince Genji to dread the coming reign. It was indeed natural that this prince should take a foremost part in the ceremonies of mourning which were performed by the family on each seventh day, and in the Filial Masses for the dead man's soul; but his piety was generally noted and admired. Despite the unbecoming dress which custom required, his beauty made everywhere a deep impression; and this, combined with his evident distress, procured him a great share of sympathy.

He had lost in one year his wife and in the next his father. The scenes of affliction through which he had passed weighed heavily upon his spirits and for a while

deprived him of all zest for life. He thought much of
retiring from the world, and would have done so had he
not been restrained by many earthly ties. During the
forty-nine days of mourning the ladies of the late ex-
Emperor's household remained together in his apartments. But at the expiration of this period they retired
to their respective homes. It was the twentieth day
of the twelfth month. The dull sky marked (thought
Fujitsubo) not only the gloom of the departing year, but
the end of all fair prospects. She knew with what feelings Kokiden regarded her and was aware that her existence at a Court dominated by this woman's arbitrary
power could not be otherwise than unhappy. Above all
it was impossible for her to go on living in a place where,
having for so many years enjoyed the old Emperor's
company, she found his image continually appearing to
her mind. The departure of all his former ladies-in-
waiting and ladies-of-the-household rendered her situation unendurable and she determined to move to her
mansion in the Third Ward. Her brother Prince Hyobukyo came to fetch her away. Snow was falling, blown
by a fierce wind. The old Emperor's quarters, now
rapidly becoming denuded of their inhabitants, wore a
desolate air. Genji happened to be there when Hyobukyo
arrived and they fell to talking of old times. The great
pine-tree in front of the Palace was weighed down with
snow and its lower boughs were withered. Seeing this,
Hyobukyo recited the verses: 'Because the great pine-
tree is withered that once with wide-spread branches
sheltered us from the storm, lo! we the underboughs
droop earthward in these last moments of the year.' No
very wonderful poem, but at that moment it moved
Genji deeply, and noticing that the lake was frozen all
over he in his turn recited the poem: 'Now like a mirror
shines the frozen surface of the lake. Alas that it reflects
not the form and face we knew so well!' Such was the

thought that came to him at the moment, and he gave it utterance well knowing that the prince would think it forced and crude. Omyobu, Fujitsubo's gentlewoman, now interposed with the verse: 'The year draws in; even the water of the rock-hewn well is sealed with ice, and faded from those waters is the face that once I saw.' Many other poems were exchanged; but I have other things to tell.

Fujitsubo's return to her mansion was carried out with no less ceremony than on former occasions, but to her mind the transit seemed this time a distressing affair and more like a journey to some strange place than a home-coming; and as she approached the house her thoughts travelled back over all the months and years that had passed since this place had been her real home.

The New Year brought with it none of the usual novelties and excitements. Genji, in very dismal humour, shut himself up in his room. At the time when the new appointments were being made, during the old Emperor's reign and to an equal extent even after his retirement, Genji's doors had always been thronged with suitors. But this year the line of horses and carriages waiting outside his palace was thin indeed, and the bags[16] of courtiers were no longer to be seen at all.

When he looked about him and saw his reception halls frequented only by his personal retainers, who looked as though time were hanging heavily on their hands, the thought that this was but a pretaste of the dreariness and insignificance with which his whole life would henceforth be tinged reduced him to a state of great depression.

In the second month Oborozukiyo was made chief Lady of the Bedchamber, the former occupant of this office having at the ex-Emperor's death become a nun.

[16] In which they packed the costumes they wore while on duty at the palace.

Her birth and education, together with her unusual charm both of person and disposition, combined to make her much sought after even at a Court where such qualities were to be found in remarkable profusion. Her sister Lady Kokiden was now seldom at Court, and on the rare occasion when she needed a room she lodged in the Umetsubo, resigning her old apartments to the Lady of the Bedchamber. No longer was Oborozukiyo buried away in the inconvenient Tokwaden; she had space and light and a vast number of ladies in her employ, while all about her was in the gayest and newest style. But she could not forget a certain brief and unexpected adventure[17] which had once befallen her, and was very unhappy. A desultory correspondence was still carried on between them with the greatest caution and secrecy.

He knew well enough how fatal would now be the consequences of discovery; but this, as has often been noted, so far from discouraging him served only to increase his interest in such an affair.

During the late Emperor's lifetime Kokiden had been obliged to behave with a certain restraint. Now she was free to revenge herself with the ferocity of a long-curbed malice upon those who had hitherto been sheltered from her spite. Genji found himself thwarted at every turn. He had expected these intrigues, but having for so long enjoyed a favoured and protected existence he was at a loss how to cope with them.

The Minister of the Left felt that his influence was gone and no longer presented himself at Court. Kokiden had never forgiven him for marrying the late princess his daughter to Genji instead of giving her, as had originally been intended, to her son the present Emperor. Moreover there had always been a certain amount of ill-feeling between the families of the two Ministers. Dur-

[17] Her relations with Genji. See Part I, p. 203. She had now become the Emperor's mistress.

ing the late Emperor's reign the Minister of the Left had managed things pretty much as he chose, and it was but natural that he now had no desire to take part in the triumph of his rival. Genji continued to visit him as before and was assiduous in his attention to Aoi's maids-of-honour, as also in providing for the education of the little prince her son. This delighted the old Minister and he continued to treat his son-in-law with the same affectionate deference as in old days.

The high position to which Genji had been raised two years ago had entailed much tiresome business and made considerable inroads upon his leisure. He found himself in consequence obliged to discontinue many of the intimacies in which he had been previously engaged. Of his lighter distractions he was now thoroughly ashamed and was glad to abandon them; so that for a while his life became altogether quiet, regular and exemplary. The announcement of his marriage with Murasaki was very well received by the world at large. Shonagon and her companions naturally attributed their little mistress's success to the prayers of her pious grandmother the late nun, and in secret conclave congratulated themselves on the turn which events had taken. Her father Prince Hyobukyo asked for nothing better than such a match. But his wife, who had not managed to do half as well for her own children on whom she doted, was extremely jealous of her step-child's triumph, and this marriage continued to be a very sore point with her. Indeed, Murasaki's career had been more like that of some step-child in fiction[18] than of a real young person.

The Vestal Virgin of Kamo, third daughter of the late Emperor by Lady Kokiden, was now in mourning and had to resign her charge. Her successor was the Princess

[18] The neglected step-child who in the end triumphs over her pampered rivals is a favourite theme in Japanese stories. Cf. the *Sumiyoshi Monogatari* and the *Ochikubo*.

Asagao.[19] It had not very often happened that a collateral descendant of the Emperor was chosen for this post; but on this occasion no other princess of suitable age and lineage was available. Genji's admiration for this lady had not, in all the years that had passed since he first courted her, in any degree abated, and it was painful to him to learn that she was now to embark upon so different a way of life. She still sent him an occasional message and he had never ceased to write to her. He had known her as a Lady of the Court. Now he must try to picture her to himself as a priestess. This he could not manage to do, and his repeated failure to evoke any image which corresponded to her as she now was bitterly tormented him.

The young Emperor punctiliously obeyed his father's last injunctions and treated Genji with great consideration. But he was still very young, and being somewhat weak and yielding in character he was easily influenced by those about him. Again and again, under pressure from Kokiden or the Minister of the Right, he allowed public measures to be taken of which he did not really in the least approve. Meanwhile Kokiden's sister the Lady Oborozukiyo, though her new position rendered the carrying on of a secret intrigue in the highest degree difficult and perilous, was becoming more and more unhappy, and at last found a means of informing Genji of her unaltered attachment. He would have been glad enough if she had felt otherwise; but after what had passed between them he could not disregard such a message. Accordingly he waited till the Court was immersed in the Celebration at the Five Altars[20] and went secretly to her apartments. The encounter was brief and dream-

---

[19] See Part I, pp. 46 and 213.

[20] A ritual in honour of the Five Mysterious Buddhas of the Tantric Sect, to wit: Gosanze, Gundari, Dai-itoku, Kongo-yasha and Fudo.

like as on that first occasion, on the night of the Flower-feast.[21] Her maid Chunagon smuggled him in by the little side door which had before caught his attention. There happened to be a good many people about at the time, and it was with great trepidation that this lady conducted him through the exposed and frequented ante-chambers which led to her mistress's apartments. To look upon Prince Genji was a ceaseless delight even to those who daily served him. It can be imagined then what rapture his visit brought to one who had waited so long for his return. Nor was Genji on his side by any means indifferent to her charms. She was at the height of her youth and good-looks; lively, graceful, confiding. Indeed, save for a certain light-heartedness and inconsequence, there was nothing in her which he would wish to change. Suddenly he heard people stirring in the corridor outside and for a moment thought that it must already be morning. He soon realized however that these were not the people of the house, but members of the Imperial Guard come to report themselves. No doubt some officer of the Guard was known to be spending the night in this part of the Palace; but for a moment Genji had the wild idea that some malicious person had revealed to the soldiers of the Guard the unexpected presence of their Commander.[22] He was amused at his mistake, but at the same time horrified at the realization of the risks which he was running. Outside in the corridor they could still hear the soldiers tramping up and down looking for their officer and calling out as they went, 'First hour of the Tiger Watch, first hour of the

21 See Part I, pp. 201 seq.
22 Genji was Commander of the Imperial Guard. The soldiers of the Guard had to report at 4 A.M. to the senior officer of the Guard who happened on that night to be in the Palace. They had really come to report to some subordinate officer who happened to be lodging close by.

Tiger Watch!'[23] Then Oborozukiyo whispered the
verse: 'Though the watch-man of the night cries out
"Enough!" yet seems it from your tears and mine we
are not of his mind.'[24] Her plaintive tone touched his
heart and he answered with the verse: 'Must we, because they say the time is spent, in tears relinquish what
our own hearts' reluctance bids us still enjoy?' So saying
he left her. Though daylight had not yet come and the
setting moon was heavily veiled in mist, he felt very uneasy. And in fact, despite his disguise, his bearing and
figure were so notable that he was at once recognized by
a brother of Lady Jokyoden[25] who happened, at the
moment when Genji passed unsuspecting on his way, to
have just left Fujitsubo's old quarters and was now
standing in the shadow of a trellis-gate. This gentleman was vastly amused and did not fail to make good
use of the episode in his conversation.

So great were the risks he had run that for some time
afterwards Genji found himself wishing Fujitsubo's prudence and reserve were more commonly practised, and
at such times he almost applauded her unkindness. At
any rate it saved him from these nerve-racking experiences. But such moods did not last long. With the Lady
of the Bedchamber his deeper feelings were not involved,
whereas he was drawn towards Fujitsubo as though by
some secret power, and except at rare moments her coldness caused him nothing but torment and despair.

This princess, though she no longer felt at ease in the
Palace and could not bring herself to visit it, was distressed that she was now unable to see her son. It was
very awkward that there was no one to advise her about

[23] I.e. 4 A.M. They had to go on calling the hour till their
officer replied 'So be it' to show that he had heard them.
[24] There is a play of words on *aku* 'enough' and *aku* 'dawn';
in the next poem between *aku* 'enough' and *aku* 'open.'
[25] Wife of the young Emperor Suzaku.

the child except Prince Genji, who unfortunately still persisted in regarding her with the same strange adoration. She was in a continual panic lest he should take advantage of her dependence upon him. True the Emperor had died without betraying the least suspicion concerning the child's parentage. But she shuddered to think of the predicament in which this deception had involved her. Any renewal of their relationship, quite apart from the effect it might have upon her own fortunes, would react disastrously upon her son. So heavily did this matter weigh upon her that when she was supposed to be at her prayers she did nothing but turn over in her mind, a hundred times this way and that, how best she might persuade him to feel differently towards her.

Yet despite all her precautions he managed one night to enter the house and get very near indeed to the room where she was sitting. Not a soul in the house had conspired with him or expected his coming. He seemed to have risen mysteriously up among them like a figure in a dream. He sent her many passionate messages, such as I cannot here transcribe, but she would not let him come to her. At last, worn out by his persistency, she began to feel so faint that Omyobu, Myobu no Ben and the rest of her favourite waiting-women took fright and were soon busily employed in attending to her. Meanwhile Genji, in a frenzy of irritation and disappointment, scarce knew how he came to be in her ante-chamber nor thought how he was going to retire from it. So completely had he lost all sense of real things that though broad daylight was come he did not stir from where he stood. The news of her indisposition quickly spread through the house. There was a sound of footsteps, and Genji, still but half conscious, groped his way into a large lumber-room or clothes-cupboard that happened to be near by. An embarrassed lady-in-waiting hastily stowed away a cloak and other effects which she saw lying about.

Fujitsubo herself remained in much distress both of body and mind throughout the night. As she was feeling very giddy, her brothers, who had now arrived upon the scene, sent out for a priest. All this Genji heard from his hiding-place with great grief and alarm. The day was far advanced when she began at last to mend. She had not of course the least idea that he was still in the house and her ladies feared that if they were to tell her of his presence the news might cause a recurrence of last night's attack. At last she dragged herself from her bed to the chair in which she generally sat, and her brothers, thinking that the worst was now over, withdrew and she was left alone. Even her intimate and personal attendants had retired from her daïs and could be heard moving away to and fro behind the screens at the other end of the room. The sole preoccupation of Omyobu and the few other ladies who shared the secret of Genji's presence was now how best to get him out of the house. They were certain that if he stayed where he was the same scene would be repeated that night, with the same unhappy effects, and they were whispering together in a tone of great concern when Genji, first cautiously pushing the door a little ajar and then gently slipping out, darted from his hiding-place to the shelter of one of the screens which surrounded her daïs. From this point of vantage he was able at last to gaze upon her to his heart's content, and as he did so tears of joy and wonder filled his eyes. 'I am wretched, wretched,' she was murmuring; 'but soon my misery will end, soon all will be over. . . .' She was looking out towards the centre of the room and he caught a profile view of her face which he found inexpressibly charming. Presently Omyobu came with fruit for her breakfast. Though the cover of the fruit-box was of rare and beautiful workmanship she did not so much as glance at it, but sat rigidly staring in front of her, like one for whom life has lost all interest and meaning.

How beautiful she was! And, now that it was possible to compare them on equal terms, how like in every minutest detail of pose and expression to the girl at home! Particularly in the carriage of her head and the way her hair grew there was the same singular charm. For years Murasaki had served to keep Lady Fujitsubo, to some extent at any rate, out of his thoughts. But now that he saw how astonishingly the one resembled the other he fancied that all the while Murasaki had but served as a substitute or eidolon of the lady who denied him her love. Both had the same pride, the same reticence. For a moment he wondered whether, if they were side by side, he should be able to tell them apart. How absurd! Probably indeed, he said to himself, the whole idea of their resemblance was a mere fancy; Fujitsubo had for so many years filled all his thoughts. It was natural that such an idea should come to him. Unable to contain himself any longer, he slipped out of his hiding-place and gently crept between her curtains-of-state, till he was near enough to touch the train of her cloak. By the royal scent which he carried she knew at once that it was he, and overcome by astonishment and terror she fell face downwards upon her couch. 'Can you not bear to set eyes upon me?' he cried, and in despair clutched at the skirt of her cloak. She in panic slipped the cloak from her shoulders and would have fled, leaving it in his hands; but by ill luck her hair caught in the buckle and she was held fast. With horror she realized that a fate too strong for her was planning to put her at his mercy. He for his part suddenly lost all dignity and self-restraint. Sobbing violently he poured out to her, scarce knowing what he said, the whole tale of his passion and despair. She was horrified; both the visit and the outburst seemed to her unpardonable, and she did not even reply. At last, hard-pressed, she pleaded illness and promised to see him some other time. But he would not be put off and continued to pour out his tale of love. In the midst of all this talk that so much displeased her and to which she paid no heed at all, there came some phrase which caught her attention and for some reason touched her; and though she was still determined that what had happened on that one unhappy occasion should never, never be repeated, she began to answer him kindly. Thus by skilful parryings and evasions she kept him talking till this night too was safely over. By her gentleness she had shamed him into submission and he now said: 'There cannot surely be any harm in my coming occasionally to see you in this way. It would be a great relief to me if I could do so.' This and much else he said, now in a far less desperate mood. Even in quite commonplace people such situations produce strange flights of tenderness and fancy. How much the more then in such lovers as Genji and the queen!

But it was now broad daylight. Omyobu and her daughter arrived and soon took possession of their mistress. Genji, retiring from the room, sent her many tender messages. But now she sat staring vacantly in front of her as though she were but half alive. Exasperated by her martyred attitude, he cried out at last: 'Answer me, answer me! I cannot live without you. And yet, what use to die? For I know that in every life to come I am doomed to suffer the torment of this same heinous passion.' Still, to the alarm of those who waited upon her, she sat staring fixedly in front of her. He recited the verse: 'If indeed the foeman fate that parts us works not for today alone, then must I spend Eternity in woe.' When she heard him saying that the bonds of her love would hold him back from Paradise, she began to weep and answered with the verse: 'If to all time this bond debars you from felicity, not hostile fate but your own heart you should with bitterness condemn.' The words were spoken with a tenderness that was infinitely precious to him; yet he knew that a prolongation of the interview could not but be painful to both of them, and he rushed from the room.

He felt that he made himself odious to her. He would never be able to face her again, and contrary to custom he wrote no morning letter. For a long while he paid no visit either to the Emperor or to the Heir Apparent, but lay in his room brooding upon Fujitsubo's unkindness. Misery and longing brought him at last to so pitiable a plight that it was as though with agonizing pain his inmost soul were dissolving within him. Often there ran in his head the lines: 'Soon upon causeways of resounding stone my footsteps shall beat out their song!'[26] And indeed the world again seemed to him so cheerless that his decision would soon have been taken had he not remembered that there was one over whose happiness he was pledged to watch. So exquisite, so trustful a creature he could not abandon, and the project was soon put aside.

Fujitsubo too reflected upon what had taken place with great uneasiness of mind. She had now learnt how he had concealed himself for a whole day in her house without giving her the slightest intimation of his presence. This fact Omyobu and the rest had not, in their indignation at his plight, managed to restrain themselves from revealing to her. Such conduct she could not tolerate. Yet she well knew that if she showed her displeasure Genji would feel a disinclination towards the Heir Apparent, and this she was above all things anxious to avoid. In a fit of despair he might even take some step which could not be rectified, and that thought, despite the torment of his importunity, filled her even now with

26 I.e. in a monastery.

horror. If such an occurrence as that of last night were
often to be repeated it was certain that both their repu-
tations would soon be irrecoverably destroyed. She felt
that it would in a way disarm the censures of the world
if she were to give up the rank of Empress, the bestowal
of which had been received with such caustic comments
by Lady Kokiden. She remembered with what intention
and with what explicit injunctions this title had been
granted her by the late Emperor. But she felt herself no
longer bound by his instructions; for since his death the
whole position at Court had utterly changed. She had
no fear of suffering the fate of Lady Chi,[27] but she had
every reason to suppose that her position as Empress
would henceforth be both ludicrous and humiliating.
She felt no inclination to struggle against ridicule and
opposition. Soon her mind was made up. She must renounce the world. But first she must visit her son. She
could not bear that he should never again see her as
he had known her in days of old. She drove to the Palace
without public escort. On many occasions when she had
travelled in even less state than this, Genji had attended her and arranged every detail of her progress.
This time he pleaded sickness and was not present.
Previously he had been in the habit of sending constantly to enquire after her health. The fact that he had
discontinued this practice was cited by the sympathetic
Omyobu as a proof that he must be now plunged in the
utmost misery.

The little prince[28] had grown into a handsome boy.
His mother's visit surprised and delighted him and he
was soon telling her all his secrets. She looked at him

---

[27] Who, after the death of her lover, the Chinese Emperor
Kao Tsu, was tortured and mutilated (c. 200 B.C.) by his
wife.
[28] Genji's child by Fujitsubo: supposed by the world to be
the late Emperor's son.

sadly. The step that she contemplated seemed unendurably hard to take. Yet a glance at the Palace reminded her how great were the changes and upheavals that had taken place, how insecure had now become her own position at the Court. The Lady Kokiden still showed the same unrelenting hostility, finding at every turn some means to inconvenience or humiliate her. Her high rank, so far from protecting her, now imperilled both herself and her son. For a long while she hesitated, torn by many conflicting feelings. At last she succeeded in saying to the child: 'What would you think if I were to go away for a long while and, when at last I came back to see you, were to look quite different, almost as though it were another person?' She watched his face while she spoke. 'What would happen to you?' he said, very much interested. 'Would you become like old Lady Shikibu? Why do you want to be like that?' and he laughed. It was very difficult to tell him. She began again: 'Shikibu is ugly because she is so old. That is not what I mean. I shall have even less hair than Shikibu and I shall wear a black dress, like the chaplain whom you have seen coming to say prayers here in the evenings; but it will be a long while before they let me come here to see you.' He saw that she was crying and at once said very decidedly: 'If you do not come for a long while, I shall miss you terribly.' He too began to cry, and ashamed of his tears, turned his head away. As he did so his long hair fell rippling across his check. The eyes, the brow—all was as though a cast had been taken from the face she knew so well. He had not yet lost his baby-teeth. One or two of them were a little decayed, their blackness amid a row of white giving to his smile a peculiar piquancy and charm. As she watched him standing there in his half-girlish beauty and suddenly realized how like he was to his father, she became more than ever unhappy. But if the resemblance was painful to her and seemed to her at that moment almost to spoil his beauty, it was only because she dreaded the gossip to which this likeness would give rise.

Genji too was longing to see his son, but while Princess Fujitsubo was at Court he was resolved to keep away. Perhaps this would make her realize how completely he had been frustrated by her harshness; for she would certainly be expecting to meet him in the young prince's apartments.

He was in very ill humour and the time hung heavily on his hands. It was now autumn and it seemed a pity not to be in the country. He decided to spend a little while at the Temple in the Cloudy Woods.[29] Here in the cell of his mother's elder brother, a master of the Vinaya,[30] he spent several days reading the sacred texts and practising various austerities. During this time much happened both to move and delight him. The maple leaves in the surrounding forests were just turning and he remembered Sojo's song written in the same place: 'Proud autumn fields. . . .' In a little while he had almost forgotten that this quiet place was not his home. He gathered about him a number of doctors famous for their understanding of the Holy Law and made them dispute in his presence. Yet even in the midst of scenes such as these, calculated to impress him in the highest degree with the futility of all earthly desires, one figure from the fleeting world of men still rose up importunately before him and haunted every prayer. One day at dawn by the light of a sinking moon the priests of the temple were making the morning offering of fresh leaves and flowers before an image that stood near by. He could hear the clink of the silver flower-trays as they scattered chrysanthemum and maple leaves of many hues around the Buddha's feet. It seemed to him then that the life

[29] The Unrinin, near Kyoto.
[30] Books on monastic discipline, and morality in general.

these people led was worth while, not merely as a means to salvation but for its own pleasantness and beauty. Again and again he marvelled that he could have for so long endured his own aimless existence. His uncle, the Vinaya-master, had an extremely impressive voice and when he came to the passage, 'None shall be cast out, but take unto him all living things that call upon his name,' Genji envied him the assurance with which he uttered the Buddha's promise. Why should not he too avail himself of this promise, why should not he too lead this sanctified existence? Suddenly he remembered Murasaki and his home. What must she be thinking of him? It was many days since he had seen her, and he hastened to repair this neglect: 'I came here as an experiment,' he wrote, 'that I might decide whether it would not be better for me to withdraw for ever from the world. Since I have been here it has been gradually becoming clearer to me that my present way of life can bring me nothing but misery; and today I heard something read out loud which made a deep impression upon me and convinced me that I ought not any longer to delay. . . .' The letter was written on sandalwood paper of Michinoku, informally but with great elegance. With it he sent the poem: 'Because I left you in a home deep-girt with dewy sedge, with troubled mind I hear the wild winds blow from every side.' This he said and much else beside. She cried when she read it. Her answer was written on a white slip: 'First, when the wild wind blows, flutters the dewy web that hangs upon the wilting sedge-row in the fields.' He smiled to himself with pleasure as he read it, noting how swiftly her hand had improved. He had written her so many letters that her writing had grown to be very like his, save that to his style she had added some touches of girlish delicacy and grace. In this as in all else she at least had not disappointed him.

It occurred to him that Kamo was not so very far off

and he thought he would send a message to the Vestal Virgin.[31] To Chujo her maid he sent the letter: 'That here among strangers in deep affliction I languish unconsoled, your mistress cannot know.' To this he added a long tale of his present woes and to the Virgin herself addressed the poem: 'Goddess Immaculate, the memory of other days has made me bold to hang this token at thy shrine!' And to this, quoting an old song, he added the words: 'Would that like a ring upon the hand I might turn Time around till "then" was "now."' He wrote on light green paper, and with the letter was a twig of the Sacred Tree festooned with fluttering tassels of white as befitted the holy place to which it was addressed. In answer the maid Chujo wrote: 'There is so little here to break the sameness of the long empty days that sometimes an idle memory of the past will for a moment visit the Virgin's heavenly thoughts. Of you she has spoken now and again, but only to say that now all thought of you is profitless.' The gentlewoman's letter was long and written with great care. On a small strip tied to a white ritual tassel the Virgin herself had written the poem: 'Full well you know that in those other days no secret was between us for you to hang as ritual-token at your heart.' It was not written with much pains, but there was an easy flow in the cursive passages which delighted his eye and he realized that the Court had lost one who would in time have grown to be a woman of no ordinary accomplishments.

He shuddered. How pitiless is God! Suddenly he remembered that only last autumn the melancholy gateway of the Palace-in-the-Fields had filled him with just such an indignation and dismay. Why should these Powers be suffered to pursue their hideous exactions?

That strange trait of perversity, so often noted, was indeed at work again under the most absurd circum-

[31] Princess Asagao.

stances. For in all the years when Asagao was within reach he had not made one serious effort to win her, but had contented himself with vague protestations and appeals. But now that she was utterly unattainable he suddenly imagined that he had never really cared for anyone else! Believing him to be the victim of an inconsolable passion, the Virgin had not the heart to leave his letters unanswered, and a correspondence of a rather strange and unreal kind was for some while carried on between them.

Before he left the Temple in the Cloudy Woods he read the whole of the Sixty Chapters,[32] consulting his uncle on many obscure points. The delight of the priests, down to the humblest servitor, may well be imagined. It seemed as though the Lord Amida must hold their poor country temple in especial favour, or he would not have vouchsafed that such a radiance should shine among them.

But soon Genji began to grow restless. His mind strayed constantly to mundane affairs, and though he dreaded the return, there was one whom it was not in his heart any longer to neglect. Before his departure he ordered a grand chanting of the Scripture to be held and gave suitable presents to all the resident priests both high and low, and even to the peasants of the surrounding country. Then, after many other rituals and benefactions, he drove away. The country people from far and near crowded round the gates to see him go, uncouth figures strangely gnarled and bent. His carriage was draped with black and he himself was still dressed in the drab unbecoming robes of mourning. Yet even the momentary glimpse of him that they caught as he entered his carriage sufficed to convince them that a prince of no ordinary beauty had been dwelling near to them and many were moved to tears.

[32] The canonical book of the Tendai Sect.

It seemed to him when he was back in his palace that Murasaki had in these last months become far less childish. She spoke very seriously of the changes at Court and showed great concern for his future. That in these last weeks his affections had been much occupied elsewhere could hardly have escaped her notice. He remembered with a pang that in the last poem she had sent him there was some reference to 'the wilting sedge-row,' and full of remorse he treated her with more than ordinary kindness. He had brought her a branch of autumn leaves from the country temple where he had been staying. Together they compared it with the trees in his palace garden, and found when they set them side by side that the country leaves were dyed to a yet deeper red. There was one who was at all times paramount in his thoughts, and the sight of these leaves, tinged with so strong a hue that they eclipsed whatever colours were set beside them, reminded him that to her alone he had given no token of his return. The desire to have news of her so tormented him that at last he wrote a letter to Omyobu announcing that he had left the temple: 'I heard with surprise and joy of your Lady's visit to the Court. I longed for news both of her and of the young prince; but though I was uneasy on their account, I could not interrupt my appointed course of penance and study. Thus many days have passed since last I gave you any news. Here are some sprays of autumn leaf. Bid your Lady look at them when she feels so disposed, lest unregarded they should waste their beauty "like silken stuffs spread out by night."'

They were huge, leaf-laden boughs, and when she looked closer, Fujitsubo saw that the usual tiny strip of paper, such as he always used in writing to her, was tied to one of them. Her gentlewomen were watching her, and as she examined the offering she felt herself blushing. So he was still in the same deplorable state of mind!

Surely he must realize that it was very embarrassing for her to receive offerings of this kind from one who was known to be her admirer! Wishing that he would show more regard for her feelings and reputation she bade a servant put the boughs in a vase and stand it against one of the pillows on the verandah, as far out of the way as possible.

In her reply she confined herself to matters of business upon which she needed his advice. Her cold and impersonal tone deeply wounded him. But as it was his usual practice to assist her in every difficulty, he felt that his absence on the day of her departure from Court would give rise to unwelcome speculations, and hearing that the day had been fixed he hastened to the Palace. He went first to the apartments of the young Emperor and finding him at leisure settled down to a long conversation. In person His Majesty much resembled the late Emperor, but he was of a quicker and livelier disposition. He was very easy to get on with and they were soon exchanging recollections of their late father. The Emperor had heard that Genji was still on intimate terms with his aunt the Princess Oborozuki, and had on his own account observed many signs of such an attachment. If the affair had begun since the princess's arrival at Court he would have felt bound to take cognizance of it. But he knew that the friendship between them was of very old standing and felt that under these circumstances there was no great impropriety in it.

They discussed all manner of affairs together, including their Chinese studies, and the Emperor consulted him about the interpretation of various difficult passages. They then repeated to one another such poems of gallantry as they had lately addressed to ladies of the Court, and it was in the course of this conversation that the Emperor mentioned his admiration of the Lady Rokujo's daughter and his distress on the occasion of her departure for Ise. This emboldened Genji, and soon he was telling the Emperor about his own visit to the Palace-in-the-Fields and all the sad circumstances attending it. The waning moon had begun at last to rise. 'It is at such moments as this,' said the Emperor sadly, 'that one longs for music.'[33]

Genji now took his leave, explaining that he must wait upon the ex-Empress before she retired again to her own home. 'You will remember,' he said, 'that the late Emperor our father committed the Heir Apparent to my guardianship and protection. There happens unfortunately to be no one else to watch over his interests, and as I am very uneasy concerning his future I am obliged to take counsel fairly frequently with his mother.' 'Our father certainly asked me to retain him as Heir Apparent,' replied the Emperor, 'and I have always tried to help him in any way I could. But there is really nothing much that I can do for him. I hear he has made astonishing progress with his handwriting and is in every way satisfactory. I am afraid he is more likely to be a credit to me than I a help to him.' 'He does indeed seem to be in most ways very forward and intelligent,' said Genji, 'but his character is still quite unformed.' And after some further description of the child's attainments he proceeded to the Heir Apparent's apartments.

There was a certain To no Ben, a son of Kokiden's elder brother To Dainagon. Being young, good-looking and popular he had grown somewhat out of hand. This young man was now on his way to the rooms of his sister Princess Reikeiden. For a moment Genji's servants who were preceding him to the Heir Apparent's rooms blocked his path and forced him to stand waiting till they had passed. In a low voice, but quite distinctly enough for Genji to hear every word, the young courtier

[33] The Court was still in mourning and music was not allowed.

chanted the lines, 'When a white rainbow crossed the sun the Crown Prince[34] trembled.' Genji flushed, but it was obviously best to let the matter pass.

That Kokiden should have succeeded in infecting her whole clan with her venomous hostility towards him was both vexatious and alarming. Genji was indeed much disquieted; but he contrived on all such occasions to conceal his discomfiture.

In arriving at Fujitsubo's rooms he sent in a message to explain that he had been detained in the Presence. It was a moonlit night of unusual beauty. It was at such times as this that the old Emperor would call for music. Fujitsubo remembered those dazzling midnight parties. Here were the old courtyards, the old gardens and rooms, and yet this was not the Palace after all! Through Omyobu her maid she sent to him the poem: 'Though now dark exhalations hide from sight the Palace of the Ninefold Wall, yet goes my heart to the bright moon[35] that far above the cloud-bank dwells.' She did not in this message give any hint that she wished to see him; yet her tone was not unkind, and forgetting all his rancour he wrote with tears in his eyes: 'Though lovely still as in past years the moonbeams of this night, for me in vain their beauty, since now in shadows of unkindness they are wrapped.'

She was to leave the Palace at dawn and was much preoccupied with the young prince her son. In her anxiety for his future she overwhelmed him with warnings and instructions. The child understood but little of what she was saying, and seeing that his attention had wandered, she felt more than ever that he was of no age

[34] The Crown Prince sent an assassin to murder the King of Ch'in; whereupon the above phenomenon was observed and the Crown Prince felt convinced that the plot would fail. The young courtier vaguely hints that Genji is meditating treason.
[35] I.e. the late Emperor.

to shift for himself. He usually went to bed very early, but on this occasion he had asked to sit up till his mother started. It was evident that he was very much upset by her departure, but he was very brave about it, and this made her feel more than ever remorseful at leaving him.

Genji could not banish from his mind the thought of To no Ben's insolent behaviour. It spoilt all his enjoyment in life and for a long while he wrote to no one, not even to Oborozuki. The autumn rains set in and still no word came from him. She began to wonder what could be amiss, and at last sent him the poem: 'While leaf by leaf autumn has stripped the trees, all this long windy while have I in sadness waited for the news that did not come.' Doubtless it had cost her some trouble to communicate with him in secret; moreover the poem itself was not at all displeasing. Genji detained the messenger, and going to his desk opened the drawer where he kept his Chinese writing-paper and chose the prettiest piece he could find. Mending his pen with the greatest care, he indited a note so elegant even in its outside appearance that on its arrival there was quite a stir among the ladies who were at her side. Who could be the sender of such a missive? Significant glances were exchanged. 'I have for some while, for reasons about which it would be useless to speak, been in the last depths of depression.' So he wrote and to this he added the poem: 'Why, think you, fell the rains of autumn yet faster than of yore? It was my tears that swelled them, my tears because we could not meet.' He told her too that if the path of their friendship were but clear, he should soon forget the rain and his depression and all that was amiss in the world. He took much pains with this letter. There were several other people who had written to complain of his neglect, but though he sent them all encouraging replies there were some of them about whom he did not feel very strongly one way or the other.

On the anniversary of the Emperor's death, in addition to the usual ceremonies, he caused the Service of the Eight Recitals[36] to be celebrated with particular magnificence. The day of national mourning was the first of the eleventh month. A heavy snow was falling. He sent to Fujitsubo the poem: 'Though once again the time of his departure has come back, not yet dare hope we for the day when we shall meet.'[37] It happened that on that day she felt in utter despair, seeing no hope of happiness on any side. She answered: 'Though sad to have outlived him for so long, yet in this day's return found I some peace; it was as though the world again were in his rule.'

It was not written with very great display of penmanship, but there was (or Genji fancied that there was) a peculiar distinction and refinement in the writing. It was not quite in the fashion of the moment; but that did not matter, for she had a style that was completely of her own invention.

But this, he remembered, was the day of the great masses for his father's soul. He must put Fujitsubo out of his thoughts; and wet through by the perpetual downpour of rainy snow, he played his part in the elaborate rituals and processions.

The Service of the Eight Recitals was to be celebrated in Fujitsubo's house on the tenth of the twelfth month and the four succeeding days. She was at great pains to render the ceremony as impressive as possible. The tents to be used on each of the five days were wound on rods of ivory; they were backed with thin silk and laid in cases of woven bamboo. All was ordered with a splendour such as had seldom been seen before. But un-

[36] Of the Hokkekyo.
[37] Ostensibly the poem refers to the late Emperor, but it has a hidden reference to the meeting of Fujitsubo and Genji. There is a pun on *yuki*, 'snow,' and *yuki*, 'go.'

der her management even the most trivial daily arrangements became invested with a singular beauty and completeness. It did not therefore surprise Genji that the Recitals were carried out with unequalled impressiveness and dignity. The adornments of the Buddha, the coverings of the flower-altars, all were of a beauty that made him dream he was indeed a dweller in Amida's Land of Bliss.

The first day's Recital was dedicated to the memory of her father;[38] the next was on behalf of her mother, the deceased Empress; the third day was in memory of her husband, the late ex-Emperor. It is on this day that the fifth book is read; despite the disapproval of Kokiden and her flatterers, the ceremony was attended by the greater part of those about the Court. The readers of this third day had been chosen with especial care, and when they came to the passage: 'Then he gathered sticks for firewood and plucked wild berries and the fruit of the mountains and trees,' the words that all had heard so many times before took on a strange significance. It fell to the lot of the dead man's sons to officiate at the altar, circling it with gold and silver dishes held aloft in their hands, and these dishes piled high with offerings of many kinds. This rite was performed by Genji with a grace and deftness that was not equalled by any of his companions. You will say that I have noted this superiority many times before; that is true, and I can only plead in excuse that people were actually struck by it afresh each time they saw him.

The last day's Recital was on behalf of her own salvation. To the astonishment of all present it was announced that she herself wished to take this opportunity of abandoning the world, and had desired the clergy to intimate her renunciation to the Lord Buddha. It may

[38] Of whom we are vaguely told that he was 'a former Emperor.'

well be imagined with what consternation both Prince Hyobukyo her brother and Genji himself received this utterly unexpected announcement. It was made in the middle of the service, and Hyobukyo, without waiting for the Recital to end, left his seat and went at once to her side. But all his pleading was in vain. At the end of the service she sent for the Head of the Tendai Sect[39] and told him that she was ready to receive the Rules forthwith. Her uncle the High Priest of Yogawa thereupon ascended the daïs and shaved her head. A murmur of horror ran through the hall; there was a sound of sobbing. There is something strangely moving in the spectacle of such a renunciation, even when some decrepit old woman decides at last that it is time to take her vows. But here a lady in the prime of her beauty, who till now had given the world no inkling of her intention, was suddenly casting herself away. Her brother found himself weeping with the rest; and even strangers who had come merely for the sake of the service felt, under the spell of the reader's solemn voice and of this sudden declaration, that a personal calamity had befallen them. The sons of the late Emperor who remembered her proud bearing at their father's Court were particularly distressed, and all of them intimated their regret at the step which she had taken. Only Genji stood rooted to the spot in speechless horror and dismay. At last he realized that his behaviour must be attracting attention, and when all the princes had left her he made his way to her daïs.

Most of the people had cleared off and only a few ladies-in-waiting, all of them on the verge of tears, sat here and there in small disconsolate groups. An unclouded moon heightened the sparkling radiance of the fresh snow which lay around the house. Old memories crowded to his mind and for a moment he feared that

[39] The bishop of the Enryakuji on Mount Hie.

he would break down. But at last controlling himself he said very quietly, 'What made you suddenly decide to do this?' 'I have been meaning to for a long while, but so many things were happening and I had not time to think about it quietly. . . .' He was standing outside her curtains-of-state. This answer was not spoken directly to him, but was brought by Omyobu, her maid. Within the curtains he knew that her favourites were gathered round her. He could hear a faint, reiterated rustling, as though a company of silent mourners were swaying in inconsolable grief. How well he understood their utter despair! From the hanging incense-burner behind her curtains-of-state there rose a heavy perfume of *kurobo*,[40] carried through the room by the fierce snow-wind which had blown since dusk; and with it mingled a faint remnant of the holy incense which the priests had that day been burning in the house. Add to this the princely scent which Genji wore and you may well imagine that the night air was fragrant as the winds of Paradise.

A messenger came from the Heir Apparent's household. There rose before her mind the memory of the child's pretty speeches and ways, that last morning in the Palace. It was more than she could bear, and lest she should break down altogether she left the message unanswered. Seeing the messenger go away empty-handed, Genji wrote a few words on her behalf. It was now time for him to take his leave; but both he and she were in a state of agitation which they could barely control, and he dared not utter the thoughts that were at that moment passing through his mind. Through Omyobu he sent her this poem: 'Though fain I too would seek that stainless tract whither the moon has climbed, yet how unguided in the darkness should those small feet not go

---

[40] An incense made of sandalwood, cloves, etc.

astray?'[41] He spoke of his regret at the step she had taken, but only in formal terms, for he knew that she was not alone. Of the tumultuous thoughts which surged through his brain there was not one to which he could at such a time give vent. And answer came: 'Though now upon life and all its sorrow I have looked my last, yet are there certain earthly things I shall not soon forget. . . .' 'The stain of the world clings fast to me. . . .' This and much else was in the answer; but he guessed that a great part of it had been supplied by those who were about her.

There was no more to be done, and heavy at heart he left the house. At the Nijo-in he lay alone upon his bed, never once closing his eyes. He was now firmly convinced that if it were not for his duty to Fujitsubo's son he would certainly retire from the world. The late Emperor had hoped that by investing Lady Fujitsubo with definite public rank he would assure the boy's future. But now, by becoming a nun, she had upset all his calculations; for it was almost certain that she would not continue to hold her present position in the State. Were Genji also now to desert the child, what would become of him? These were the thoughts that still perplexed him when morning came. He remembered that Fujitsubo would now have to provide herself with such articles as appertain to a nun's life. In this matter at least he could assist her, and he hastened to send to her palace before the end of the year a suitable provision of rosaries, prayer-desks and the like. He heard that Omyobu also had renounced the world that she might keep her mistress company, and to this gentlewoman he sent a mes-

---

[41] I should like to become a priest, but I must stay and look after the child. There is an allusion to the famous poem on the death of a child: 'Because in Death's dark land he will not know the way, I will make offerings to the Guardian of Souls that on his shoulders he may carry him.'

sage of affectionate condolence. In this letter he touched
on many incidents of their common past, and a correspondence ensued, of such length that it would not be
possible to record it. As was natural on so affecting an
occasion many poems were exchanged between them,
and as these were of considerable merit I regret that they
must be omitted.

Now that Fujitsubo had definitely embraced the religious life she felt that there was less impropriety in her
receiving him, and on several occasions she no longer
conversed through an intermediary, but actually admitted him to her presence. His feelings towards her
were absolutely unchanged, but now that there could
be no question of intimacy between them he could face
her with some degree of tranquillity.

The close of that year ended the period of Court
mourning, and the New Year was celebrated at the Palace with the usual festivities, including the Imperial
Banquet and the Dance Songs.[42] But of these things no
echo reached Fujitsubo's house. Day after day was spent
in prayers, penances and meditations on the life to come,
and he who had been at once her comfort and despair
no longer found any place in her thoughts. She continued to use the old palace-chapel for her daily observances; but for the celebration of more elaborate rites
she built a new chapel in front of the west wing, but at
some distance from the house.

He visited her on New Year's Day. Nowhere was there
a sign of renewal or rejoicing. The house was very quiet
and seemed almost deserted. Here and there stood a few
of her most devoted retainers, looking (or was it only his
fancy?) very downcast and depressed. Of the usual
New Year offerings from the Palace only the white

[42] Performed by girls on the 16th day and by young men
on the 14th and 15th days of the first month.

horse[43] had this year arrived. The gentlewomen of the house could not but remember how at this season in former years princes and courtiers had thronged these halls. Now they drove straight past, making one and all for the great palace in the next Ward.[44]

This was under the circumstances perfectly natural and Fujitsubo had fully expected it. Yet when it happened she became very depressed. But now the arrival of one whom she would not have exchanged for a thousand visitors put all this chagrin out of her head.

So great were the changes that had taken place since he was last in her room that for a while he could do nothing but stare about him in bewilderment.

The canopy of her daïs and the hangings of her screen-of-state were now of dark blue; here and there behind the curtains he caught a glimpse of light grey and jasmine-coloured sleeves. The effect was not displeasing and he would gladly have studied it more closely.

The ice on the lake was just beginning to break up. The willows on the banks showed a faint tinge of green; they at least remembered that a new season had begun. These and other portents of the approaching spring he watched till it grew dark. From behind the curtains Fujitsubo gazed at him as he sat singing softly to himself the song: 'Happy the fisher-folk[45] that dwell . . .'; she thought that in all the world there could be no one so beautiful.

She remained all the while behind her curtains, but a great part of the room was taken up by images and altars, so that she was obliged to let him sit very near

[43] Twenty-one white horses were offered to the Emperor on the 7th day, and afterwards distributed by him among members of his family.

[44] The residence of the Minister of the Right, Kokiden's father.

[45] *Ama*, 'fishermen,' also means 'nun.'

the daïs and he did not feel wholly cut off from her.

A number of elderly nuns were installed at her side, and fearing lest in their presence his parting words might betray too great an emotion he stole in silence from the room. 'What a fine gentleman he has grown up to be!' they exclaimed after Genji's departure. 'One might have thought that it would have spoiled him always having things his own way as he did in his father's time, and being first in everything. How little can he then have guessed that he would ever come to know the world's ingratitude! But you can see that he bears his troubles manfully, though there is a graver look in his face now than there was in the old days. Poor gentleman, it makes one's heart bleed to see him so sad!' So the old ladies whispered together, shaking their heads and calling blessings upon him, while to Fujitsubo herself came many painful recollections.

It was the time when the yearly distribution of honours took place. Fujitsubo's kinsmen and retainers were entirely passed over. This was quite natural and she did not resent it; but she noticed that even the usual bounties were withheld, and promotions which had always been taken as a matter of course were in many cases not granted. There was a great deal of disappointment and annoyance. Moreover on the ground that she would shortly have to give up her official rank and would not then be able to maintain so large an establishment,[46] many other changes and readjustments were made.

All this she had expected. It was indeed the inevitable consequence of her retirement from secular life; but when she saw her former pensioners and retainers going about with dismal faces and in many instances left without proper support, she was very much upset. But above all her thoughts were centred on one persistent desire;

[46] The State grant allowed to an ex-Empress was sufficient to maintain 2,000 dependants.

that, even though she herself should come to utter ruin, the Heir Apparent might in due course come peacefully to the Throne, and it was to this end that she caused perpetual services to be celebrated in the chapel attached to her house.

To what secret peril was the young prince's life exposed? Those who were called upon to officiate at these incessant litanies could themselves form no conjecture. But her own prayers were more explicit. Again and again she called upon the Buddha to save the young prince from the ruin which would immediately overtake him should the true story of his birth be known; and she prayed with all her heart that, if retribution must needs come, it might fall upon herself rather than upon the child. These prayers had at least the effect of bringing her to a calmer state of mind. Genji, for his part, regarded them as by no means superfluous.

His own servants and retainers had in the recent distribution of honours fared little better than hers and were in very ill humour. Thoroughly discontented with the march of public affairs both they and their master henceforward appeared but seldom at Court. About this time the Minister of the Left decided to send in his resignation. The changes in his home as well as the decline of his own political influence had recently told very much upon his spirit and he no longer felt equal to his charge. The Emperor remembered the unbounded confidence which his father had placed in this Minister's sagacity, and how in his last hours the old Emperor had said that to dispense with such a man's counsel must needs endanger the security of the Throne. He was therefore very reluctant to give this resignation effect and for a while attempted to ignore it. But the Minister stuck to his point and, though his retirement had not been formally accepted, no longer appeared at Court.

Henceforward the whole government of the country

fell into the hands of a single family, that of Kokiden's
father, the Minister of the Right. The powerful influence
of the retired Minister had indeed been the last check
upon the complete dominance of this ascendant faction,
and his withdrawal from public affairs was regarded
with grave apprehension both by the young Emperor
himself and by all right-thinking people.

The late Minister's sons, who had hitherto enjoyed a
consideration in the world somewhat beyond that to
which their own abilities would have entitled them, were
mortified to discover that they could no longer have everything their own way. The most crestfallen of them all
was To no Chujo, who through his connection[47] with
the family which was now dominant, might have been
expected to fare rather better than the rest. Unfortunately he was still on very bad terms with his wife, and
his neglect of her had deeply offended the Minister, who
no longer received Chujo as a son-in-law. No doubt as a
punishment for his misdemeanour, his name had been
altogether omitted from the list of New Year honours
and promotions. Such things however did not much interest him and he was not nearly so disappointed as the
Minister had hoped. He could indeed hardly expect to
enjoy much influence when even Genji's fortunes were
so obviously on the decline, and leaving public business
to look after itself he would go off to Genji's palace,
where the two of them spent the time in the study of
music and letters. Often they would remind one another
of the many absurd exploits in which they had once been
rivals; and even in their present quiet pursuits the old
rivalry continued. Genji was much occupied with the
readings of Holy Scripture which are appointed for
spring and autumn, and with the performance of various

[47] His wife was the fourth daughter of the Minister of the
Right.

other annual observances.[48] He also gathered round
him a number of scholars who seemed, no doubt owing
to the present state of public affairs, to be out of employment, and put them to writing Chinese poems and
essays. He also spent many hours in playing literary
games such as rhyme-covering and the like. He soon became so interested in these trivial pursuits that for a
month on end he never once set foot in the Palace. This
incivility, together with his enthusiasm for what were
considered frivolous and undignified occupations, was
commented upon very unfavourably in many quarters.

The summer rains had set in, and one day when a
steady downpour made other amusements impossible
Chujo arrived at the palace with a great pile of books.
Genji too opened his library, and after exploring several
cases which had not been unlocked for a long time he
produced some very remarkable collections of ancient
Chinese poetry. There happened to be with him that day
several friends who, though they were not scholars by
profession, had a very considerable knowledge of such
matters. From among these gentlemen and the learned
doctors who were present Genji picked sides, and rang-
ing them to left and right of the room instituted a grand
competition with very handsome prizes. In the course
of the rhyme-covering contests they came across some
most unusual and puzzling rhyme-words, and even well-
known scholars were occasionally at a loss. More than
once Genji was able to come to their rescue. They were
astonished at his knowledge. How, they wondered, did
he find time to pick up so many accomplishments? There
seemed to be no art or pastime in which he did not show
the same marvellous proficiency. The 'right' won easily
and it fell to Chujo's lot to provide the winners with a
feast. This took place on the following day. It was not

[48] Such as Buddha's birthday, Maya's birthday, Buddha's
Nirvana day, etc.

an elaborate affair, but consisted of a collation served in elegant luncheon boxes.

Various prizes were also given and when this was over the doctors of literature were again called upon to divert the company with essays. The rose-trees at the foot of the steps were in full bloom and coming as they did in a somewhat dull season, when the brightness of spring is over and the riot of autumn colours has not yet begun, these flowers gave Genji an especial pleasure.

Chujo's son, a little boy of eight or nine who had only that year been introduced at Court, was present that day. He sang well and could play the *sho*. Genji was very fond of him and they used often to practise together. He was Chujo's second son by his wife, the sister of Kokiden, and as grandson of the all-powerful Minister of the Right he was treated by everyone at Court with great deference. But he was also not only handsome but extremely intelligent, and in the present company his performance received so much encouragement that he was soon singing that rather noisy song the *Ballad of Takasago*, which he got through with great credit and applause. As a reward for this song Genji laid his own cloak on the boy's shoulders, and as he sat flushed with the excitement of the party and wearing only an un-lined shirt of thin gauze that showed the delicate texture of his skin beneath, the old doctors of literature stared at him with delight and amazement from the distant part of the room where they had respectfully taken up their stand; and many of them shed tears of wonder and de-light. At the close of the stanza: 'May I be there where lilies bloom,' Chujo picked up the wine-bowl and handed it to Genji, reciting as he did so the poem: 'Not the first rose, that but this morning opened on the tree, with thy fair face would I compare.' Laughing, Genji took the cup and whispered the poem: 'Their time they knew not, the rose-buds that today unclosed. For all their fragrance

and their freshness the summer rains have washed away.'
Then Chujo, who had become somewhat excited, ac-
cused Genji of toying with the wine-bowl and forced
him to drink what he considered a proper draught.

Much else happened before the banquet closed. But
to describe in detail all that was said and done on an
occasion such as this would, I think, be very unfair to
the persons concerned. I will therefore observe Tsura-
yuki's warning and refrain from tiring you with any further particulars. Suffice it to say that the company made
a great many poems both in Chinese and Japanese, all
of them containing flattering references to their host, and
Genji soon began to feel in very good humour with himself. He could not help thinking of the passage in Chinese
history where the Duke of Chou boasts that he is 'the
son of King Wen and the brother of King Wu.' These
were very good names and fitted his case exactly. 'Son
of King Wen, brother of King Wu.' Suddenly, as he
murmured these words, he remembered that the Chinese
duke had added 'and uncle of King Ch'eng.' But here he
was on difficult ground; something seemed to have gone
wrong with the parallel. The 'King Ch'eng'[49] of his case,
though something more than a nephew, was still a very
long way from being a king!

Prince Sochi no Miya[50] frequently joined these gath-
erings, and as he was not only a man of taste and fashion
but also an excellent performer on various instruments,
his presence added greatly to the pleasure of the company.

About this time Princess Oborozuki left the Court for
a while and went to stay at her father's house. She had
for some time been suffering from slight attacks of
malaria and it was thought that she could be treated for

[49] The Heir Apparent, Genji's son by Fujitsubo, supposed
to be the old Emperor's child.
[50] One of Genji's stepbrothers.

this illness more conveniently at her home than amid the
bustle of the Court. Priests were summoned and their
incantations were at once effective. Among the many
people who wrote to congratulate her upon her recovery
Genji was naturally one, and as both of them happened
for the moment to have a good deal of time on their
hands, a correspondence ensued which led in the end to
his paying her a somewhat reluctant visit. This was followed by others and he was soon seeing her every night.
She was well made, tending even to plumpness, so that
the slight pallor and thinness which had ensued from her
recent indisposition only enhanced her charm. It happened that at the time Kokiden was also staying in the
house. This made Genji's visits particularly imprudent,
but it was just this added risk which attracted him and
induced him to repeat them. It was not of course long
before several inmates of the house became aware that
something of this kind was going on, but they were too
frightened of Kokiden to say anything to her about it,
nor had the Minister of the Right any suspicion whatever.

One night when Genji was with her a violent storm
suddenly came on. The rain fell in such torrential floods
as to be quite alarming and just after midnight tremendous crashes of thunder began. Soon the whole place
was astir. The young princes and Kokiden's gentle-
men-in-attendance seemed to be wandering all over the
house, while the ladies-in-waiting, terrified by the thunderstorm, were clinging to one another hysterically in
the passage just outside. There were people everywhere
and Genji began to wonder how he was ever going to
escape.

It was now broad daylight. Oborozuki's maids had
entered the room and seemed to be crowding round the
great curtained bed. Genji was appalled by the situation.
Among these ladies there were two who knew the secret,

but they quite lost their heads in this emergency and were unable to be of any use. The thunderstorm was over and the rain was now less violent. The Minister was now up and about. He first paid his elder daughter a visit, and then, just at a moment when the rain was falling rather heavily, stepped lightly and briskly into Oborozuki's room. The rain was making such a noise that they did not hear him and it was not till a hand was thrust through the bed-curtains that they realized what had happened. 'We have had a very bad thunderstorm,' he said, pulling the curtain slightly aside as he spoke. 'I thought of you in the night and had half a mind to come round and see how you were getting on, but somehow or other I didn't. Your brothers were on duty at the Palace last night. Just fancy . . .' So he went on, speaking in an excited inconsequent manner which, even in his present quandary, Genji could not help contrasting with the gravity and good sense of that other Minister, Aoi's father, and he smiled to himself. Really if he had so much to say he had better come right inside and have done with it. Oborozuki, determined to screen her lover if she could, now crept to the edge of the bed and issued cautiously from between the curtains. Her face was so flushed and she looked so very ill at ease that her father was quite alarmed. 'What have you been doing?' he said. 'You are not looking at all well. I am afraid we stopped the treatment too soon. These attacks are very troublesome to get rid of. . . .' As he spoke his eye suddenly fell upon a man's pale violet-coloured belt that had got mixed up with her clothes, and at the same time he noticed a piece of paper with writing upon it lying near the bed. How did these things come to be in his daughter's room? 'Whose is this?' he asked, pointing at the paper. 'I think you had better give it to me; it may be something important. I shall probably know the writing.' She looked where he was point-

ing. Yes, there was Genji's paper lying conspicuously
upon the floor. Were there no means of heading her father away from it? She could think of none and did not
attempt to answer his question. It was evident that she
was acutely embarrassed, and even though she was his
own child he ought to have remembered that she was
now a lady of some consequence, whose feelings, however reprehensible might be her conduct, he was bound
in some measure to respect. Unfortunately there was not
in his nature a particle either of moderation or restraint.
He stooped to pick up the paper, and as he did so, without the slightest hesitation or compunction he opened
the bed-curtains and peered right in. There full length
upon the bed and apparently quite at his ease lolled a
charming young man, who when the curtain stirred
merely rolled quietly over and hid his face in the pillows.
Enraged, astonished as the Minister was, even he had
not quite the courage to press the discovery home. Blind
with fury he thrust the paper into his pocket and rushed
out of the room.

Genji was indeed extremely concerned about the consequences of this incident, coming as it did in the wake
of so many other indiscretions. But his first care was to
comfort his companion, which he did as best he could.

Self-restraint had never been a characteristic of the
lady's father and now that he was getting old he found
it more than ever impossible to keep anything to himself.
It was therefore only to be expected that without considering the consequences or turning the matter over in
his mind for a single moment, he went and told the
whole story to his daughter Kokiden.

'Well, there it is,' he wound up, 'and you will not be
surprised to hear that the handwriting was that of no
less a person than Prince Genji! Of course I know quite
well that this affair has been going on for a long time.
A good deal of licence is allowed to people in his posi-

tion and unfortunately I was weak-minded enough to let the matter pass. Then came the death of his wife, and it seemed certain that he would now legitimize his relations with your sister. Instead of doing so he suddenly abandoned her in the most heartless and disgraceful fashion. I was very uneasy about what had happened, but there was nothing to do except to make the best of a bad business, and I sent her to Court, fully trusting that His Majesty would not regard this one escapade as a fatal objection. Unfortunately he looked upon her as still more or less betrothed to Genji and left her severely alone. One would have thought she had suffered enough already! It is really disgusting, after what has happened, that he should have the face to start the thing all over again. You may say that a young man is bound to have his fling; but this Prince Genji goes a great deal too far. I hear that he has been behaving very badly with the Vestal Virgin of Kamo, carrying on a secret correspondence with her, and according to some people going a good deal further than that. If he has no respect for her holy calling he might at least realize that this kind of thing does his own reputation no good. How anyone holding an important and responsible position in the State can bring himself to behave in this way I simply cannot imagine. . . .' Kokiden had always detested Genji and she now burst out angrily: 'They call him their Emperor, but from the very beginning they have gone out of their way to heap every sort of indignity upon him. Even before he came to the Throne they had already begun to treat him abominably. Remember how the Minister of the Left behaved about the marriage of his cherished only daughter! He insisted forsooth in giving her to this wretched Prince Genji instead of to my son, though my boy was older and had already been proclaimed Heir Apparent, while Genji did not count as

a member of the royal family at all and was so young
that the wedding took place on the same day as his
Initiation! We too, you may remember, were planning
to give my sister to Genji when we were outwitted by
this hasty wedding, of which till the last minute no one
was given the slightest intimation. Everyone was indeed
astonished that we should allow ourselves to be tricked
in this unscrupulous fashion. We should all much have
preferred to see her married to this young man, but
when that fell through there was nothing for it but to
do the best we could for her at Court. It is really extraordinary that after all the painful experiences she has
had with this wretch she should still imagine she can
make a permanent conquest of him. I have no doubt he
is treating the Vestal Virgin in just the same way; and
his behaviour in this matter, as indeed in many others,
is causing His Majesty the greatest anxiety; which is not
to be wondered at, seeing that the heir to the Throne is
entirely in this Prince Genji's hands.'

She went on in this strain for so long and with so
much rancour that her father, who never remained angry for more than a short time, soon began to sympa-
thize with Genji rather than with her and was sorry that
he had mentioned the matter at all. 'I think that for the
present,' he said, 'you had better not speak of this to
anyone, not even to His Majesty your son. Prince Genji's
conduct is certainly outrageous; but you are very fond
of your sister and you cannot denounce him without getting her too into trouble. Leave the matter to me. I intend to speak to her very seriously, and if this has no
effect, then we shall have done our best and she must
take the consequences.' But it was too late to mend matters; she was indeed only further exasperated by his attempt to conciliate her. That Genji should have been
carrying on this intrigue in her own house, and that too

at a time when he knew she was in residence, showed an impudent contempt for her authority which deeply wounded her, and all that she now thought of was how best she might use this discovery to his undoing.

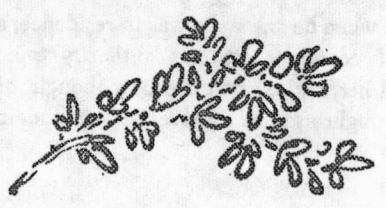

Chapter II

THE VILLAGE OF
FALLING FLOWERS

The outlook was very black. Not only were his private affairs in a state of grievous entanglement, but also his position at Court was being made every day more difficult. So despondent did he become that he had serious thoughts of giving everything up and quitting the Capital. But this was by no means easy now that so many persons were dependent upon him. For example there was Lady Reikeiden, a lady of his father's Court. She had no children to look after her and had, since the old Emperor's death, been living in very bad circumstances. But for Genji's assistance she would never have pulled through. With her lived a sister much younger than herself with whom he had once had a fugitive affair when both of them were living at the Palace. He never forgot anyone to whom he had stood, even for the briefest period, in such a relation as this. Their friendship had never been resumed; but he had reason to suppose that on her side the attachment was still as strong as ever. During the period of emotional tumult through which he had just passed he had many times brooded upon his relations with this lady. At last he felt that he could neglect her no longer, and the rains of the fifth month having given place to an enchanting spell of fine warm weather, he set out for her sister's house. He went without any outriders and took care that there should be nothing to distinguish his coach from that of an ordinary individual. As he was nearing the Middle River he noticed a small house standing amid clumps of trees. There came from it the sound of someone playing the zithern; a well-made instrument, so it seemed, and tuned to the eastern mode.[1] It was being excellently played. The house was quite near the highway and Genji, alighting for a moment from the carriage, stood near the gate to listen. Peeping inside he saw a great laurel-tree quavering in the wind. It reminded him of that Kamo festival long ago, when the dancers had nodded their garlands of laurel and sun-flower.[2] Something about the place interested him, seemed even to be vaguely familiar. Suddenly he remembered that this was a house which he had once visited a long while before. His heart beat fast. . . . But it had all happened too long ago. He felt shy of announcing himself. All the same, it seemed a pity to pass the house without a word, and for a while he stood hesitating. Just when he was about to drive away, a cuckoo flew by. Somehow its note seemed to be an invitation to him to stay, and turning his chariot he composed the following poem, which he gave into Koremitsu's hands: 'Hark to the cuckoo's song! Who could not but revisit the hedge-row of this house where once he sung before?' There seemed to be several people sitting together in a room on the left. This must be the lady's own apartment. Several of the voices Koremitsu thought he could remember having heard before. He made a slight noise to attract attention and delivered the poem. He could hear it being discussed within by a number of young women who seemed somewhat puzzled by

[1] I.e. as a *wagon* or Japanese zithern, not in the Chinese style.
[2] See Part I, p. 214.

it. Presently a reply was brought: 'That to my garden Cuckoo has returned, his song proclaims. But how, pray, should I see him, caged behind the summer rain?' Koremitsu made sure that they were only pretending not to know who their visitor was. The lady indeed, though she hid her feelings from the rest, was very loath to send Koremitsu away with this hollow message. But so long a time had elapsed since her adventure with Genji that she may very well have had good reasons for doing so. Suddenly, as he drove away, there came into his mind a picture of this lady dancing with four others at the Palace. Yes, that was who she was. She had been one of the Gosechi dancers one winter long ago. How much he had admired her! And for a moment he felt about her exactly as he had felt before. It was this strange capacity of his for re-creating in its full intensity an emotion suspended for months or even years and overlaid by a thousand intervening distractions, that gained for him, faithless though he was, so large a number of persistent admirers.

At last he arrived at Lady Reikeiden's house. Noting that it wore an aspect fully as cheerless and deserted as he had feared, he hastened at once to the elder lady's room. They talked much of old times and the night was soon far advanced. It was the twentieth day and the moon had now risen, but so tall were the surrounding trees that the garden still looked dark and gloomy as before. The lady herself sat in a room pervaded by the fragrance of orange-trees. She was no longer young, but still preserved much dignity and charm. Though she had never been singled out as a particular favourite with the late Emperor, they had been on very familiar terms and she was able to entertain Genji with many intimate recollections of his father's life and habits. Indeed so vivid a picture of those old days soon rose before his mind that the tears came into his eyes. A cuckoo was suddenly

heard in the garden outside, perhaps the very same that
had sung when he was waiting at the gate of the little
house; its note at any rate seemed strangely similar.
Had it followed him? Pleased with this idea he sang
softly to himself the old song, 'Knows the cuckoo when
he sings?' Presently he handed to her this poem: ' "It is
the scent of orange-trees that draws the cuckoo to the
Village of Falling Flowers." I knew you would remind
me of many things that I would not gladly forget; that is
why I made my way straight to your room. Though life
at Court gives me much both to think of and to feel,
there are often times when I should like to have about
me people who would talk of the past, and now that the
world has given its allegiance to new powers such people
are hard to find. But if I, amid the bustle of the town,
feel this deprivation, how much the more must you in
your long hours of tedious inactivity!'

His prospects had indeed changed very much for the
worse since she had first known him, and he certainly
seemed to feel those changes deeply. But if her heart
went out to him it was perhaps rather because of his
youth and beauty than because she regarded his position in the world as calling for any particular commisera-
tion. She answered him with the poem: 'To these wild
gardens and abandoned halls only the scent of orange-
trees could draw the traveller's steps!' She said no more
and he took his leave. Yes, despite the fact that greater
beauties had overshadowed her at his father's Court,
this lady had a singular charm and distinction of her
own.

Her sister was living in the western wing. He did not
hide from her that he was only calling upon her on his
way from Lady Reikeiden's rooms. But in her delight at
his sudden arrival and her surprise at seeing him under
circumstances so different she forgot to take offence either at his having visited her sister first or having taken

so long in making up his mind to come at all. The time that they spent together was in every way successful and agreeable, and she can scarcely have thought that he did not care for her.

It was often thus with those whom he met only in this casual way. Being women of character and position they had no false pride and saw that it was worth while to take what they could get. Thus without any ill will on either side concerning the future or the past they would enjoy the pleasure of each other's company, and so part. However, if by chance anyone resented this kind of treatment and cooled towards him, Genji was never in the least surprised; for though, as far as feelings went, perfectly constant himself, he had long ago learnt that such constancy was very unusual. The lady in the little house by the road-side was clearly an example of the latter class; she had resented the infrequence of his visits and no longer felt disposed to receive him.

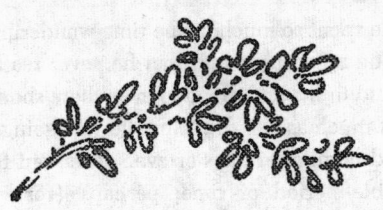

Chapter III

EXILE AT SUMA

The intrigue against him was becoming every day more formidable. It was evident that he could not in any case go on living much longer where he was, and by a voluntary withdrawal he might well get off more lightly than if he merely allowed events to take their course.

There was Suma. It might not be such a bad place to choose. There had indeed once been some houses there; but it was now a long way to the nearest village and the coast wore a very deserted aspect. Apart from a few fishermen's huts there was not anywhere a sign of life. This did not matter, for a thickly populated, noisy place was not at all what he wanted; but even Suma was a terribly long way from the Capital, and the prospect of being separated from all those whose society he liked best was not at all inviting. His life hitherto had been one long series of disasters. As for the future, it did not bear thinking of! Clearly the world held in store for him nothing but disappointment and vexation. But no sooner had he proved to himself convincingly that he was glad to leave the Capital than he began to recollect a thousand reasons for remaining in it. Above all, he could not imagine what would become of Murasaki if he were to leave her. Even when for one reason or another he was obliged to pass a few days away from his palace, he spent so much of the time wondering how she was getting on without him that he never really enjoyed himself and in the end dreaded even these short absences almost as much as she did. Now he was going away not for a fixed number of days or even years, but for a huge, incalculable period of time; perhaps (for who knew what might not happen either to him or her?) for ever. The thought that he might never see her again was unendurable and he began to devise a scheme for hiding her in his retinue and secretly taking her with him. He soon saw however that this was quite impracticable. First there was the difficult sea-journey; and then, at Suma, the total lack of amusements and society. The waves and winds of that desolate shore would make poor companions for one used to the gaieties of a fashionable house. It would moreover be utterly impossible in such a place to make adequate provision for the comfort of a fastidious and delicately-nurtured lady. Her presence would soon involve him in all sorts of difficulties and anxieties. She herself felt that she would rather face every danger, every hardship, than be left behind at the Nijo-in, and that he should doubt her courage wounded her deeply.

The ladies at the 'Village of Falling Flowers,' though in any case they saw him but seldom, were dismayed at the news of his departure, not for personal reasons only, but also because they had come to depend in numerous ways on his patronage and support. Many others whose acquaintance with him was very slight, were, though they would not have confessed it, shattered at the prospect of his disappearance from the Court. The abbess[1] herself feared that if she showed him any open mark of sympathy at this turn in his fortunes she would give new life to rumours which had already been used against him

---

[1] Fujitsubo.

by his enemies. But from the time when his decision was
first announced she contrived to send him constant secret
messages. He could not help reflecting with some bitterness that she might sometimes have shown an equal concern while it was still possible for her to console him in
more concrete ways. But it seemed to be fated that
throughout all this long relationship each, however well
disposed, should only cause torment to the other. He left
the City about the twentieth day of the third month.
The date of his departure had not been previously dis-
closed and he left his palace very quietly, accompanied
only by some seven or eight intimate retainers. He did
not even send formal letters of farewell but only hasty
and secret messages to a few of those whom he loved
best, telling them in such words as came to him at the
moment what pain it cost him to leave them. Those notes
were written under the stress of deep emotion and would
doubtless interest the reader; but though some of them
were read to me at the time, I was myself in so distracted
a state of mind that I cannot accurately recall them. Two
or three days before his departure he paid a secret visit
to Aoi's father. He came in a rattan-coach such as
women use, and heavily disguised. When they saw that
it was indeed Prince Genji who had stepped out of this
humble equipage the people at the Great Hall could
hardly believe that this was not some strange dream.
Aoi's old room wore a dismal and deserted air; but the
nurses of his little boy and such of Aoi's servants as were
still in the house soon heard the news of his unexpected
arrival and came bustling from the women's quarters to
gaze at him and pay him their respects. Even the new
young servants who had not seen him before and had
no reason to take his affairs particularly to heart were
deeply moved at this farewell visit, which brought home
to them so vividly the evanescence of human grandeurs.
The little prince recognized him and at once ran up to

him in the prettiest and most confiding way. This delighted Genji; taking the child on his knee he played with it so charmingly that the ladies could hardly contain their emotion. Presently the old Minister arrived: 'I have often meant,' he said, 'during these last months when you have been living so much at home, to come round and talk over with you various small matters connected with the past; but first I was ill and for a long time could not attend to my duties, and then at last my resignation was definitely accepted. Now I am merely a private person, and I have been afraid that if I came to see you it would be said that it must be to promote some personal intrigue that I was bestirring my aged bones. As far as I am concerned I am out of it all, and have really nothing to be afraid of. But these new people are very suspicious and one cannot be too careful. . . . I am distressed beyond measure that you should be obliged to take the course which you are now contemplating; I would gladly not have lived to witness such a day. These are bad times, and I fully expected to see a great deal of mischief done to the country. But I confess I did not foresee that you would find yourself in such a situation as this, and I am heart-broken about it, utterly heart-broken. . . .' 'We are told,' answered Genji, 'that everything which happens to us in this life is the result of our conduct in some previous existence. If this is to be taken literally I suppose I must now accept the fact that in a previous incarnation I must have misbehaved myself in some way. It is clear, at any rate, that I am in bad odour at Court; though, seeing that they have not thought it necessary to deprive me of my various offices and titles, they cannot have very much against me. But when the Government has shown that it mistrusts a man, he is generally considered much to blame if he continues to flaunt himself at Court as though nothing were amiss. I could cite many instances in the history both of our own and other countries. But distant banishment, the penalty which I hear is contemplated in my case, has never been decreed except as the penalty of scandalous and open misdemeanour. My conscience is of course perfectly clear; but I see that it would be very dangerous to sit down and await events. I have therefore decided to withdraw from the Capital, lest some worse humiliation should befall me.' He gave the Minister many further details of his proposed flight. The old man replied with a multitude of reminiscences, particularly of the late Emperor, with anecdotes illustrating his opinions and policies. Each time that Genji tried to go his father-in-law gripped his sleeve and began a new story. He was indeed himself deeply moved by these stories of old days, as also by the pretty behaviour of his little son, who while they were talking of policies and grave affairs constantly ran up to one or the other with his absurd, confiding prattle. The Minister continued: 'Though the loss of my dear daughter is a sorrow from which to my dying day I shall not recover, I find myself now quite thankful that she did not live to see these dreadful days. Poor girl, she would have suffered terribly. What a nightmare it all is! More than anything else I am distressed that my grandson here should be left with us elderly people and that for months or even years to come you will be quite cut off from him.

'As you say, exile has hitherto been reserved as a punishment for particularly grave offences. There have indeed been many cases both here and in China of innocent persons being condemned to banishment, but always in consequence of some false charge being made against them. But against you a threat of exile seems to have been made without any cause being alleged. I cannot understand it. . . .'

To no Chujo now joined them and wine was served. It was very late, but Genji showed no signs of going, and presently all the gentlewomen of the household collected round him and made him tell them stories. There was one among them, Chunagon by name, who, though she never spoke of it, had always cared for Genji far more deeply than did any of her companions. She now sat sad and thoughtful waiting to say something to him but unable to think of anything to say. He noticed this and was very sorry for her. When all the rest had gone to their rooms he kept her by him and talked to her for a long while. It may perhaps have been for her sake that he stayed so long. Dawn was beginning to come into the sky and the moon, which had not long risen, darted its light among the blossoms of the garden trees, now just beyond their prime. In the courtyard leafy branches cast delicate half-shadows upon the floor, and thin wreaths of cloud sank through the air till they met the first flicker of the white grass-mists which, scarcely perceptible, now quivered in the growing light.

He hung over the balustrade outside the corner room and for a while gazed in silence at this scene, which transcended even the beauty of an autumn night. Chunagon, that she might watch him go, had opened the main door and stood holding it back. 'I shall return,' Genji said, 'and we shall surely meet again. Though indeed, when I think about it, I can find no reason to suppose that I shall ever be recalled. Oh, why did I not make haste to know you in better days, when it would have been so easy for us to meet?' She wept but made no answer.

Presently Aoi's mother sent a message by Saisho, the little prince's nurse: 'There are many things that I want to talk over with you, but my mind is nowadays so clouded and confused that I hesitate to send for you. It is kind of you to have paid us so long a visit and I would ask you to come to me; but I fear that to talk with you would remind me too much of all that is now so changed. However, pray do not leave the house till your poor little son is awake.' He answered with the poem: 'To a shore I go where the tapering smoke of salt-kilns shall remind me of the smoke that loitered by her pyre.' He wrote no letter to go with the poem, but turning to the nurse he said: 'It is sad at all times to leave one's friends at dawn. How much the more for one such as I, who goes never to return!' 'Indeed,' she answered, ' "farewell" is a monster among words, and never yet sounded kindly in any ear. But seldom can this word have had so sinister an import as to all of us on this unhappy morning.'

Touched by her concern at his departure he felt that he must give her what she evidently expected—some further message for her mistress, and he wrote: 'There is much that I should like to say, but after all you will have little difficulty in imagining for yourself the perplexity and despair into which my present situation has plunged me. I should indeed dearly like to see the little prince before I go. But I fear that the sight of him might weaken my resolution to forsake the fleeting world, and therefore I must force myself to leave this house without further delay.'

The whole household was now awake and everyone was on the watch to see him start. The moon shone red at the edge of the sky, and in its strange light he looked so lovely, yet so sad and thoughtful, that the hearts of wolves and tigers, nay of very demons, would have melted at the sight of him. It may be imagined then with what feelings those gentlewomen watched him drive away, many of whom had known and loved him since he was a child. But I had forgotten to say that Aoi's mother replied with the poem: 'Seek not another sky, but if you love her,[2] stay beneath these clouds with which her soul is blent.' When he reached his own palace he found that none of the gentlewomen there had

[2] The dead Aoi, Genji's first wife.

slept a wink. They were sitting a few here, a few there, in frightened groups, looking as though they would never lift their heads again. Those officers of his household and personal retainers who had been chosen to go with him to Suma were busy preparing for their departure or saying good-bye to their friends, so that the retainers' hall was absolutely deserted; nor had the gentlewomen whom he was leaving behind dared to present themselves on the occasion of his departure, for they knew that any demonstration of good will towards an enemy of those in power would be remembered against them by the Government. So that instead of his doors being thronged, as once they had been, by a continual multitude of horsemen and carriages, he found them that morning utterly deserted and realized with bitterness how frail is the fabric of worldly power. Already his great guest-tables, pushed against the wall, were looking tarnished and dusty; the guest-mats were rolled up and stowed away in corners. If the house looked like this now, what sort of spectacle he wondered would it present when he had been absent for a few months?

On reaching the western wing he found the partition door still open. Murasaki had sat there watching till dawn. Some of the little boys who waited upon her were sleeping on the verandah. Hearing him coming they now shook themselves and rose with a clatter. It was a pleasant sight to see them pattering about in their little pages' costumes; but now he watched them with a pang at his heart, for he could not help remembering that while he was away they would grow up into men and in the end have to seek service elsewhere. And indeed during those days he looked with interest and regret on many things which had never engaged his attention before. 'I am so sorry about last night,' he said. 'One thing happened after another, and by the time I was free to come back it would not have been worth while. You must have thought it horrid of me. Now that there is so little time left, I hate to be away from you at all. But my departure from the Court naturally involves me in many painful duties, and it would be quite impossible for me to remain shut up here all the time. There are other people, some of whom I may very likely never see again, who would think it unkind of me if I did not even bid them good-bye. . . .' 'It is your going away that matters,' she answered; 'nothing else is of any consequence now. . . .' She said no more, but sat staring before her in an attitude of the profoundest despair. And indeed, as Genji realized, she had every possible reason to dread his departure. Her father Prince Hyobukyo had never put himself out for her, and since Genji's disgrace he stopped writing and no longer even enquired about her. She was ashamed of his worldly caution and dreaded lest others should notice it. For her part she was resolved that, since he showed no interest in her, she would be the last to remind him of her existence. Someone told her that her stepmother[3] went about saying: 'This is what comes of trying to get on too quickly in the world. Look how she has been punished! All her relatives expire and now her lover takes flight!' She was deeply distressed and felt that she could not ever communicate with her stepmother again. There was indeed no one to whom she could turn for help, and her position was likely to be in every way unhappy and difficult. 'I promise,' said Genji to comfort her, 'that if my exile seems likely to last for a considerable time, I will send for you to join me, even if I can offer you nothing better to live in than a hole in the rocks. But it would be considered most improper for me to take you with me now. People who are disapproved of by the Government are expected to creep about miserably in the dark, and if they try to

[3] Hyobukyo's wife. Murasaki was his illegitimate daughter.

make themselves happy and comfortable it is considered
very wicked. I have not of course done anything wrong,
but my misfortune must certainly be due to some sin in
a previous life, and I am sure that if I did anything so
unusual as to take my lady into exile with me, fate
would find some yet more cruel way to punish me for
the presumption.'

He then lay down and slept till noon. Later in the
day his half-brother Prince Sochi no Miya and To no
Chujo called and offered to help him dress. He reminded
them that he had resigned his rank and they brought
him a cloak of plain silk without any crest or badge. This
costume had an informal air which became him better
than they had expected. When he went to the mirror
that his servants might do his hair he could not help
noticing how thin his face had lately grown, and he
said, 'What a fright I look! Can I really be such a skele-
ton as this? It is indeed a bad business if I am.' Murasaki,
her eyes full of tears, came and peeped at the mirror.
To distract her he recited the poem: 'Though I wander
in strange lands and far away, in this mirror let me leave
my image, that it may never quit your side.' 'That, yes,
even so little as that, would comfort me, if indeed this
mirror might hold the image of your distant face.' So she
answered, and without another word sank into a seat
behind the roof-pillar, that her tears might not be seen.
His heart went out to her, and he felt at this moment
that among all the women he had known she was indeed the most adorable.

His stepbrother now fell to reminding him of scenes
in their common childhood, and it was already growing
dark when he left Genji's room. The lady at the 'Village
of Falling Flowers' had written to him constantly since
she heard the news of his approaching departure. He
knew that she had many reasons for dreading his absence and it seemed unfeeling not to pay her one more

visit before he left. But if he spent another evening away from his palace Murasaki would be very disappointed, and he therefore did not start till late in the night. He went first to the room of Princess Reikeiden, who was flattered and delighted beyond measure that hers should be the only house to which he paid the honour of a farewell visit. But what passed between them was not of sufficient interest to be recorded. He remembered that it was only through his help and protection that she had managed to overcome the difficulties and anxieties of the last few years. Now matters would go from bad to worse. In the house nothing stirred. The moon had risen and now shimmered faintly through the clouds. The lake in front of the building was large and wild, and dense thickets of mountain-trees surrounded it. He was just thinking that there could hardly in all the world be a lovelier, stranger place, when he remembered the rocky shore of Suma—a thousand times more forbidding, more inaccessible!

The younger sister had quite made up her mind that Genji was going to leave the house without visiting her, and she was all the more surprised and delighted when at last, more lovely than ever by moonlight and in the grave simplicity of his exile's dress, he stole into her room. At once she crept towards the window and they stood together gazing at the moonlight. They talked for a while, and found to their astonishment that it was nearly day. 'How short the night has been,' said Genji. 'Yet even such a hasty meeting as this may never be ours again. Why did I not know you better in all those years when it would have been so easy to meet? Never have such misfortunes befallen an innocent man before, nor ever will they again. I go from torment to torment. Listen . . .' and he was beginning to recount to her the disasters and miscalculations of the past when the cock crowed, and fearing detection he hastened away.

The moon was like last night, just on the point of setting; it seemed to him a symbol of his own declining fortunes. Shining through the dark purple of her dress the moonlight had indeed, as in the old poem, 'the leaden look of those who weep,' and she recited the poem: 'Though to the moonlight my sleeve but narrow lodging can afford, yet might it dwell there for ever and for ever, this radiance[4] of which my eyes can never tire.' He saw that she was deeply moved by this parting and in pity sought to comfort her with the poem: 'In its long journeying the moon at last shall meet a clearer sky; then heed not if for a while its light be dimmed.' 'It is foolish,' he added, 'to spoil the present with tears for sorrows that are still to come,' and with that he hurried away, that he might be out of the house while it was still dark.

At home he had a great many things to arrange before his departure. First of all he had to give instructions concerning the upkeep of his palace to the few faithful retainers who had taken the risk of remaining in his service. When these had at last all been assigned their functions, difficulties arose about some of the attendants who were to have gone with him into exile, and a fresh choice had to be made. Then there was the business of deciding how much luggage he should take with him to his mountain fastness. Some things were obviously indispensable; but even when he cut down his equipment to the barest possible necessities there were still all kinds of odds and ends, such as writing-materials, poems, Chinese books, which all had to be fitted into the right sort of boxes. And then there was his zithern; he could not leave that behind. But he took no large objects of furniture nor any of his more elaborate costumes, having resigned himself to the prospect of a completely bucolic existence. Finally he had to explain to Murasaki

[4] Genji.

all the arrangements he had made about the servants who were to stay behind, and a hundred other matters. Into her charge too he put all the documents concerning his various estates and grazing-lands in different parts of the country. His granaries and storehouses he put into the keeping of the nurse Shonagon whose vigilance and reliability he had often noted, giving her the help of one or two trusted household officers. And here again there were numerous arrangements to be made.

With the gentlewomen of his palace he had never been on intimate terms. But he kept them in a good humour by sending for them occasionally to talk with him, and he now summoned them all, saying to them: 'I am afraid it will be rather dull here while I am away. But if any of you care to stay in my service on the chance that I may one day return to the Court, which if I live long enough is indeed certain to happen sooner or later —please consider yourselves at the disposition of the Lady in the western wing.' So saying he sent for all the other servants, high and low, and distributed suitable keepsakes among them.

No one was forgotten; to the nurse of Aoi's little son and even to the servants at the 'Village of Falling Flowers' he sent tokens of his appreciation, chosen, you may be sure, with the greatest taste and care.

To Oborozuki, despite a certain reluctance, he wrote at last: 'That after what happened between us you should have ceased to communicate with me was both natural and prudent. But I would now have you know that the unparalleled ferocity of my enemies has at last driven me from the Court. "The rising torrent of your reproachful tears has carried me at last to the flood-mark of exile and disgrace." I cannot forget that this folly alone was the instrument of my undoing.' There was some danger that the letter might fall into wrong hands before it reached its destination, and for that reason he made it brief and vague.

The lady was heart-stricken, and though she strove to hide her tears, they flowed in a torrent that her sleeve was not broad enough to dam. She sent him the poem: 'Long ere I reach the tide of your return shall I, poor scum upon the river of tears, be vanished out of sight.' She was weeping violently when she wrote it, and there were many blotches and mistakes, but her writing was at all times elegant and pleasing. He would very much have liked to see her once more before his departure, and he many times thought of arranging it. But she was too intimately connected with just those people who had been chiefly responsible for his undoing, and somewhat regretfully he put the idea aside.

On the evening of the day before his departure he went to worship at his father's tomb on the Northern Hills. As the moon did not rise till after midnight he found himself with time on his hands, and went first to visit the Abbess Fujitsubo. She allowed him to stand close up to her curtain, and on this occasion spoke to him with her own mouth. She naturally had many questions to talk over concerning the future of her son, which was now more than ever uncertain. But apart from this, two people who had once lived on such terms as this prince and princess, could not now fail to have much to say to one another of a far more intimate and tender character. He thought her every bit as charming and graceful as in old days, and this made him allude with bitterness to her heartless treatment of him. But he remembered in time that her present state made any such complaints in the highest degree unseemly and inappropriate. He was allowing his feelings to get out of hand, and withdrawing for a while into his own thoughts, he said at last: 'This punishment has come upon me quite unexpectedly, and when I try to account for it, one possible explanation of a most alarming character presents itself to my mind. I am not thinking of the danger to myself should a certain fact be known, but of the disastrous consequences of such a disclosure upon the career of the young prince, your son. . . .' The same possibility had of course occurred to her. Her heart beat wildly, but she did not answer. The many painful scenes in which he had recently taken part had broken his spirit and he now wept unrestrainedly. 'I am going to the Royal Tombs,' he said at last. 'Have you any message?' She answered with the poem: 'He that was, is not; and he that is, now hides from the afflictions of the world. What increase but of tears did my renunciation bring?'

At last the moon rose, and he set out. Only five or six attendants were with him, men of low rank, but all of them deeply attached to him. Genji himself rode on horseback like the rest. This was quite natural on such an occasion, but his companions could not help contrasting this melancholy cavalcade with the splendours of his retinue in former days. Among them the most downcast was Ukon,[5] who had formed part of his special escort on the occasion of the Kamo festival a few years ago. This gentleman had since that time seen himself repeatedly passed over at the annual distribution of honours, and finally his name disappeared altogether from the lists. Being without employment he had been obliged to go into service, and was now acting as Genji's groom. As they rode along Ukon's eye lighted on the Lower Shrine of Kamo which lay quite near their road, and remembering that wonderful day of the festival he leapt from his horse and holding Genji's bridle he recited the verse: 'Well I remember how, crowned with golden flowers, we rode together on that glorious day! Little,

[5] See Part I, pp. 214 seq.

alas, they heed their worshippers, the churlish gods that in the Shrine of Kamo dwell.'

Genji well knew what was passing through the man's mind. He remembered with indignation and pity how Ukon had been the gayest, the most resplendent figure among those who had ridden with him on that day. Genji too alighted from his horse and turning his face towards the Shrine repeated this parting poem: 'Thou who art called the Righter of Wrongs, to Thee I leave it to clear the name that stays behind me, now that I am driven from the fleeting haunts of men.' Ukon was a very impressionable youth, and this small episode thrilled and delighted him beyond measure.

At last they reached the Tombs. Genji's mind was full of long-forgotten images. He saw his father seated on the throne in the days of his prime, the pattern of a kindly yet magnificent king. Who could then have guessed that death would in an instant deface all memory of that good and glorious reign? Who could have foreseen that the wise policies which, with tears in his eyes, he had time and again commended to those about him, would in an instant be reversed, and even his dying wishes contemptuously cast aside? The path to the Royal Tombs was already overgrown with tall thick grass, so that in pressing his way along it he became soaked with dew. The moon was hidden behind clouds, dank woods closed about him on either hand, such woods as give one the feeling one will never return through them alive. When at last he knelt at the tomb, his father's face appeared so vividly before him that he turned cold with fear. Then murmuring the verse: 'How comes it that thy vanished image looms before me, though the bright moon, symbol of thy high fortunes, is hidden from my sight?' he set out towards the town, for it was now broad daylight. On his return he sent a message to the Heir Apparent. Omyobu had taken charge of the child since Fujitsubo's

retirement and it was through her that Genji now addressed his son: 'I leave the City today. That I have
been unable to visit you once more is the greatest of my
many vexations. You indeed know better than I can tell
what thoughts are mine in this extremity, and I beg you
to commend me to your little master in such terms as
you deem best.' With this letter he enclosed a spray of
withered cherry-blossoms to which was tied the poem:
'When again shall I see the flowers of the City blossom-
ing in Spring, I whom fortune has cast out upon the
barren mountains of the shore?' This she passed on to the
boy who, young though he was, quite well understood
the import of the message, and when Omyobu added,
'It is hard at present to say when he will return . . . !'
the young prince said sadly, 'Even when he stays away
for a little while I miss him very much, and now that
he is going a long way off I do not know how I shall get
on. . . . Please say this to him for me.'

She was touched by the simplicity of his message.
Omyobu often called to mind all the misery which in
past days had grown out of her mistress's disastrous attachment. Scene after scene rose before her. How happy
they might both have been, if only . . . And then she
would remember that she and she alone had been the
promoter of their ruin. She had pleaded for Genji, arranged those fatal meetings! And a bitter remorse filled
her soul. She now sent the following reply: 'His Highness
dictated no formal answer. When I informed him of
your departure, his distress was very evident. . . .' This
and more she wrote, somewhat incoherently, for her
thoughts were in great confusion. With the letter was
the poem: 'Though sad it is to mark how swift the flowers fall, yet to the City Spring will come again and with
it, who can tell. . . .' 'Oh, if that time were come!' she
added, and spent the hours which followed in recounting
such moving tales of Genji's wisdom and kindness that

everyone in the Palace was soon dissolved in tears. If these people who but seldom caught sight of him were distressed at the prospect of his departure, it may be imagined what were the feelings of those whose duties brought them constantly into his presence. At the Nijo-in everyone down to the mere scullery-maids and outdoor servants, who could never hope to exchange a single word with him and had thought themselves very lucky if they obtained an occasional glance or smile, had always been in despair when it was known that he would be absent from the Palace even for a few days. Nor was his downfall by any means welcome in the country at large. Since his seventh year he had enjoyed the privilege of running in and out of the old Emperor's rooms just as he felt inclined. Everything he asked for had been granted without question, and there were few who had not at one time or another found themselves beholden to his boundless good-nature and generosity. Even among the great nobles and Ministers of the Crown there were some who owed their first promotion to Genji's good offices; and countless persons of less importance knew quite well that they owed everything to him. But such was their dread of the present Government, with its ruthless methods of persecution and suppression, that not one of them now came near him. Expressions of regret were everywhere heard; but it was only in the secrecy of their own hearts that these sympathizers dared blame the Government for happenings which they universally deplored. After all, what was the good of risking their own positions by showing to the exiled prince civilities which could be of no real use to him? There was some sense in this, but on Genji their prudence made a most painful and dispiriting impression. He suddenly felt the world was inhabited by a set of mean and despicable creatures, none of whom were worth putting oneself out for in any way at all.

He spent the whole of that day quietly with Murasaki at his palace. He was to start soon after midnight. She hardly knew him as he stood before her dressed in his queer travelling clothes. 'The moon has risen,' he said at last. 'Come out to the door and see me start. I know that at the last minute I shall think of all kinds of things I meant to say to you today. Even when I am only going away for a few nights, there are always so many things to remember. . . .' He raised the curtain-of-state behind which she was sitting and drew her with him towards the portico. She was weeping bitterly. Her feet would not obey her and she stumbled haltingly at his side. The moonlight fell straight upon her face. He looked down at her tenderly. The thought came to him that he might die at Suma. Who would look after her? What would become of her? He was indeed no less heart-broken than she; but he knew that if he gave way to his feelings her misery would only be increased and he recited the verse: 'We who so long have sworn that death alone should part us, must suffer life for once to cancel all our vows.' He tried to speak lightly, but when she answered: 'Could my death pay to hold you back, how gladly would I purchase a single moment of delay,' he knew that she was not speaking idly. It was terrible to leave her, but he knew that by daylight it would be harder still, and he fled from the house. All the way down to the river her image haunted him and it was with a heart full to bursting that he went aboard the ship. It was a season when the days are long, and meeting with a favourable wind they found themselves at Suma between three and four o'clock in the afternoon.[6]

[6] The distance is about 60 miles. It could, says Moto-ori, in no circumstances have been covered in one day. He therefore concludes that the travellers spent a night at Naniwa (the modern Osaka) on the way. A much more probable solution is that Murasaki was herself rather vague about the time which such a journey would take.

It was indeed a trifling journey, but to Genji, who had never crossed the sea before, the experience was somewhat alarming, though his fears were mingled with wonder and delight. As they came in sight of that wild and lonely headland where stands the Hall of Oye[7] marked by its solitary pine, he recited the verse: 'A life more outcast shall be mine among these hills than all those exiles led whose sufferings the books of Kara[8] have rehearsed.' He watched the waves lapping up over the sands and then creeping back again. It put him in mind of the ancient song: 'Oh would that like the tides I went but to return!' Those who were with him knew the song well enough, but never before had it moved them as now when Genji murmured to himself the long-familiar words. Looking back he saw that the mountains behind them were already melting into the hazy distance, and it seemed to him that he had indeed travelled the classical 'three thousand leagues' of which the Chinese poets so often speak. The monotonous dripping of the oars now became almost unendurable. 'Now is my home hid from me by the mist-clad hills, and even the sky above me seems not the lovely cloudland that I knew.' So he sang, being for the moment utterly downcast and dispirited.

His new home was quite close to the place where in ancient days Ariwara no Yukihira[9] once lived in exile, 'trailing his water-buckets along the lonely shore.' At this point the sea bends back, forming a shallow inlet, encompassed by desolate hills.

He proceeded to inspect the hut which had been prepared for his reception. Never had he seen such a place

[7] Near Naniwa. It was here that the returning Vestals of Ise lodged on their way back to the Capital.

[8] China.

[9] For the story of his exile, see the Nō play *Matsukaze* in my *Nō Plays of Japan*, p. 268.

before. Even the hedge was built in quite a different way from what he was used to; and the hut itself, with its thatched roof and wide-spreading gables covered with wattled bullrushes, semeed to him the most extraordinary place to live in. But he could not help admiring the ingenuity with which it was constructed, and he knew that if he had come there under different circumstances the prospect of staying in such a cottage would have fascinated and delighted him. How, in the old days, he had longed for such an experience!

Many repairs and alterations were necessary, and Genji sent at once for the bailiffs of some of his estates which lay in the neighbourhood. They and their workmen, directed by the faithful Yoshikiyo, soon carried out Genji's plans, and the place began to assume a much more habitable air. The pond was dredged and deepened, plantations were laid out. Soon he settled down to his new life in a way that he would never have dreamed to be possible. The governor of the province had formerly been attached to his household, and though he did not dare to give him a public welcome, he made it clear in private that his sympathies were on Genji's side. Thus even in this remote spot he was not entirely deprived of society; but there was no one with whom he was really intimate and such conversation as he could get was of the most superficial and uninteresting kind. He felt almost as isolated as if he had been cast up on a desert island, and the prospect of spending months, nay years, buried away amid these uncivilized surroundings still appalled him. He was just beginning to reconcile himself a little to his rustic employments when the summer rains set in. During this tedious period of inactivity he thought much of his friends at the Capital. Often he called to mind the picture of Murasaki's misery in those last hours, of the Heir Apparent's infant beauty or the heedless antics of Aoi's little son.

He determined to send a courier to the City, and began writing letters to everybody. While he wrote to the Lady of his palace and again while he wrote to Fujitsubo in her cloister he wept so bitterly that the letters had many times to be put aside. To Oborozuki he dared not write direct, but as he had sometimes done before enclosed a message to her in a letter to Lady Chunagon, with the acrostic poem: 'That I, though cast like weed upon the barren margin of the sea, am unrepentant still, how should they guess—these fisherfolk that tend their salt-kilns on the shore?' To the retired Minister and to Nurse Saisho he sent many instructions concerning the upbring-ing of the child. It may well be imagined that the ar-rival of his post-bag in the City set many hearts a-flutter.

The condition of Murasaki after his departure had gravely alarmed her attendants. She lay for many days utterly overcome by the shock of his departure. Every effort to cheer her was in vain. The sight or mention of things which she connected with him, a zithern which he had once played, the perfume of a dress which he had left behind, threw her at once into a new paroxysm of grief. She behaved indeed for all the world as though he were not merely exiled but already in his grave. At last Shonagon, becoming seriously alarmed, sent for her uncle the priest and begged his aid. The liturgy of inter-cession which he conducted had for its aim both the recovery of Lady Murasaki from her present prostration and the early recall of Genji himself. For a while she was somewhat calmer and began to go about the house again. She spent much time at her devotions, praying fervently that he might soon return and live with her as before. She sent him sleeping-clothes and many other comforts which she feared he might not otherwise be able to secure. Among the garments which she packed were a cloak and breeches of plain homespun. She folded them with a sigh, remembering his Court apparel with its figured silks and glittering badges. And there was his mirror! He had left it behind as in his poem he had jestingly promised to do; but his image he had taken with him, and much good was a mirror that reflected another face than his! The places where he used to walk, the pine-wood pillar against which he used to lean—on these she could still never look without a bitter pang. Her situation might well have dismayed even a woman long inured to the world; for an inexperienced girl the sudden departure of one who had taken the place of both father and mother, to whom she had confided everything, to whom she had looked on every occasion for comfort and advice, was a blow from which it could hardly be expected that she would quickly recover. Deep down in her heart there was the haunting fear that he might die before his recall. But apart from this dread (which did not bear thinking of), there was the possibility that gradually, at such a distance as this, his affection for her would cease. True, she could write to him, and had his absence been fixed at a few weeks or months she would have had no great anxiety. But as it was, year might follow year without the slightest change in his prospects, and when he found that this was so who knew what might not come . . . ?

The Lady Abbess too was at this time in great distress. The sin of the Heir Apparent's birth was a constant weight upon her heart. She felt that she had up to the present escaped more lightly than her *karma* in any degree warranted and that a day of disastrous reckoning might still be at hand. For years she had been so terrified lest her secret should become known that she had treated Genji with exaggerated indifference, convinced that if by any sign or look she betrayed her partiality for him their attachment would at once become common knowledge at Court. She called to mind countless occasions when, longing for his sympathy and love, she had turned coldly away. The result of all her precautions did indeed seem to be that, in a world where everything that anyone knows sooner or later gets repeated, this particular secret had, so far as she could judge by the demeanour of those with whom she came in contact, remained absolutely undivulged. But the effort had cost her very dear, and she now remembered with pity and remorse the harshness which this successful policy had involved. Her answer to the letter which he sent from Suma was long and tender; she sought indeed to explain and expiate her seeming heartlessness in former days.

An answer also came from Oborozuki: 'Not even to fishers that on the shore of Suma their faggots burn must we reveal the smouldering ashes of our love.' 'More I have no heart to write,' she added in the margin of this poem, which was on a tiny strip of paper discreetly hidden between the pages of a note from Lady Chunagon. In her own letter this lady gave a most melancholy account of her mistress's condition. All these tales of woe made the arrival of Genji's return post-bag a somewhat depressing event.

Murasaki's letter was full of the tenderest allusions and messages. With it was the poem: 'Look at the sleeves of the fisherfolk who trail salt-water tubs along the shore: you will not find them wetter than mine were on the night you put out to sea.' The clothes and other odds and ends which she sent him were all of the most delicate make and colour. She had evidently taken immense trouble, and he reflected that she could now have little indeed to employ her. No doubt she had in her loneliness deliberately prolonged this task. Day and night her image floated before him and at last, unable to endure any longer the idea of her remaining by herself in that dull lonely palace, he began to make fresh plans for bringing her out to join him. But after further reflection he changed his mind. Such a step would at once bring down upon him the full retribution of his offences, and putting the idea out of his head he took to prayer and fasting, in the hope that Buddha would have pity on him and bring his exile to a speedy end. He was also somewhat distressed at being separated from Aoi's son. But here the case was different from that of older people. There was every probability that he would eventually see the child again, and meanwhile he had the comfort of knowing that it was in excellent hands.

But stay! There has been so much to tell that one important matter had quite escaped me. I ought to have told you that before his departure he sent a message to Ise with a letter informing Lady Rokujo of the place at which she must in future address him. An envoy now arrived at Suma with her reply. It was long and intimate. Both the handwriting and mode of expression showed just that extraordinary distinction and fineness of breeding which he had always admired in her. 'I find it impossible,' she wrote, 'to conceive of you in such a place as that at which you bid me to address you. Surely this must be some long, fantastic dream! I cannot but believe that I shall soon hear of you as again at the Capital; alas, even so it will be far longer before *my* fault is expiated and we can meet face to face. "Forget not those who for salvation dredge their misery by Ise's shore, while you with fisherfolk drag dripping buckets to the kiln."' This and much more was written, not as it seemed at one time, but bit by bit as fresh waves of feeling prompted her. There were altogether four or five large sheets of white Chinese paper, and there were many passages which in the handling of the ink were quite masterly. This woman, whom he once so passionately admired, had, after the fatal outcome of her jealousy, become utterly distasteful to him. He knew well enough that she was not to blame for what had occurred and that his own feelings towards her were utterly unreasonable, and now that he was himself suffering the penalty of exile he felt more than ever ashamed of having driven her away by his sudden coldness. Her present letter moved him so deeply that he detained the messenger for several days, questioning him upon every detail of the life at Ise. The man was a young courtier of good family and was enchanted at the opportunity of living in the company of this famous prince at such close quarters as the limited accommodation of the cottage made necessary. In his reply Genji said: 'Had I known that I was to be driven from the Court, I might have done well to join you in your journey. "Were I but in the little boat that the men of Ise push along the wave-tops of the shore, some converse would at least be mine." . . . Now, alas, there is less prospect even than before that we shall ever meet again. . . .'

He had now acquitted himself of all his epistolary duties, and no one had any right to complain. Meanwhile a letter arrived from the lady in the 'Village of Falling Flowers,' or rather a journal in which she had from time to time noted down her impressions since his departure. The manner in which she recorded her despondency at his absence was both entertaining and original. The letter was a great distraction and aroused in him a quite new interest in this lady. It had come to his ears that the summer rains had done considerable damage to the foundations of her house and he sent word to his people at the Capital to get materials from such of his farms as were nearest to the ladies' home and do whatever was necessary in the way of repairs.

The Emperor still showed no signs of summoning Princess Oborozuki to his side. Her father imagined that she felt her position and, since she was his favourite daughter, was most anxious to get matters put right. He spoke about it to Kokiden, begging her to use all her influence, and indeed went so far as to mention his daughter's disappointment to the Emperor himself. It was hoped that he might be prevailed upon to install her, if not as a regular mistress, at any rate in some dignified capacity in his immediate entourage. The Emperor had hitherto neglected her solely because of her supposed attachment in another direction. When at last, yielding to the persuasion of her relatives, he summoned her to him, she was as a matter of fact more than ever absorbed in her unlucky passion. She moved into the Inner Palace during the seventh month. As it was known that the Emperor had previously been very much in love with her, no surprise was felt when he began immediately to treat her as a full lady-in-waiting. From the first he showered upon her a multitude both of endearments and reproaches. He was by no means distasteful to her either in person or character, but a thousand recollections crowded to her mind and continuously held her back. He did not fail to notice this, and once when they were at music together he said to her suddenly: 'I know why you are unhappy. It is because that man has gone away. Well, you are not the only one who misses him; my whole Court seems to be plunged in the darkest gloom. I see what it is; I ought never to have let him go. The old Emperor on his death-bed warned me of all this, but I took no notice, and now I shall suffer for it.' He had become quite tearful. She made no comment, and after a while he continued: 'I get very little pleasure out of my life. I am fast realizing that there is no point in any of the things I do. I have the feeling that I shall probably not be with you much longer. . . . I know quite well that you will not be much upset; certainly much less than you were recently. That poet was a fool who prayed that he might know what happened to his mistress after he was gone. He cannot have cared much about her, or he would certainly rather not have known.' He really seemed to set such store by her affection and spoke in so bitter and despondent a tone that she could bear it no longer and burst into tears. 'It is no good your crying like that,' he said peevishly, 'I know well enough that your tears are not in any way connected with me.' For a while he was silent. Then he began again: 'It is so depressing not to have had any children. Of course I shall keep Lady Fujitsubo's son as my Heir Apparent, since the old Emperor desired it. But there is sure to be a great deal of opposition, and it is very inconvenient. . . .'

In reality, the government of the country was not in his hands at all; at every turn he saw his own wishes being violated and a quite contrary policy pursued by men who knew how to take advantage of his inexperience and weakness of character. All this he deplored but was powerless to alter.

At Suma autumn had set in with a vengeance. The little house stood some way back from the sea; but when in sudden gusts the wind came 'blowing through the gap' (the very wind of Yukihira's poem[10]) it seemed as though the waves were at Genji's door. Night after night he lay listening to that melancholy sound and wondering whether in all the world there could be any place where the sadness of autumn was more overwhelming. The few attendants who shared the house with him had all gone to rest. Only Genji lay awake, propped high on his pillow, listening to the storm-winds which burst upon the house from every side. Louder and louder came the noise of the waves, till it seemed to him they must have mounted the fore-shore and be surging round the very bed on which he lay. Then he would take up his zithern and strike a few notes. But his tune echoed so forlornly through the house that he had not the heart to continue and, putting the zithern aside, he sang to himself the song:

[10] See *No Plays of Japan*, p. 268.

'The wind that waked you,
Came in from where my Lady lies,
Waves of the shore, whose sighs
Echo my sobbing?'

At this his followers awoke with a start and listened to
his singing with wonder and delight. But the words filled
them with an unendurable sadness, and there were some
whose lips trembled while they rose and dressed.

What (Genji asked himself) must they think of him?
For his sake they had given up their homes, parents,
brothers, friends from whom they had never been absent
for a day; abandoned everything in life which they had
held dear. The thought that these unfortunate gentlemen should be involved in the consequences of his indis-
cretion was very painful to him. He knew that his own
moodiness and ill humour had greatly contributed to
their depression. Next day he tried to cheer them with
jokes and amusing stories; and to make the time pass
less tediously he set them to work to join strips of
variegated paper into a long roll and did some writing
practice, while on a piece of very fine Chinese silk he
made a number of rough ink sketches which when
pasted on to a screen looked very well indeed. Here
before his eyes were all those hills and shores of which
he had so often dreamed since the day long ago when
they had been shown to him from a far-off height.[11]
He now made good use of his opportunities and soon
got together a collection of views which admirably illustrated the scenery of this beautiful coast-line. So delighted were his companions that they were anxious he
should send for Chiyeda and Tsunenori[12] and make
them use his sketches as models for proper-coloured

[11] See Part I, pp. 108 seq.
[12] Tsunenori was a famous painter, c. 950 A.D. So presumably was Chiyeda. Some people say Chiyeda was a name
used by Tsunenori.

paintings. His new affability soon made them forget all
their troubles, and the four or five retainers who habitually served him felt that the discomforts of exile were
quite outweighed by the pleasure of waiting upon such
a master.

The flowers which had been planted in front of the
cottage were blooming with a wild profusion of colour.
One particularly calm and delightful evening Genji came
out on to the verandah which looked towards the bay.
He was dressed in a soft coat of fine white silk with
breeches of aster-colour. A cloak of some dark material
hung loosely over his shoulders. After reciting the formula of submission ('Such a one, being a disciple of the
Buddha Sakyamuni, does obeisance to him and craves
that in the moonlit shelter of the Tree of Knowledge he
may seek refuge from the clouds of sorrow and death')
he began in a low voice to read a passage from the
Scriptures. The sunset, the light from the sea, the tower-
ing hills cast so strange a radiance upon him as he
stood reading from the book, that to those who watched
he seemed like some visitant from another world. Out
beyond the bay a line of boats was passing, the fishermen singing as they rowed. So far off were these boats
that they looked like a convoy of small birds afloat upon
the high seas. With the sound of oars was subtly blended
the crying of wild-geese, each wanderer's lament swiftly
matched by the voice of his close-following mate. How
different his lot to theirs! And Genji raised his sleeve to
brush away the tears that had begun to flow. As he
did so the whiteness of his hand flashed against the
black wooden beads of his rosary. Here indeed, thought
those who were with him, was beauty enough to console them for the absence of the women whom they had
left behind.

Among his followers was that same Ukon who had
gone with him to the old Emperor's tomb. Ukon's father

had become governor of Hitachi and was anxious that he should join him in his province. He had chosen instead to go with Genji to Suma. The decision cost him a bitter struggle, but from Genji he hid all this, and appeared to be quite eager for the journey. This man, pointing to the wild-geese above, now recited the poem: 'Like flocks that unafraid explore the shifting highways of the air, I have no fear but that my leader should outwing me in the empty sky.'

About this time the Secretary to the Viceroy came back to Court. As he was travelling with his wife, daughters and a very large staff of attendants he preferred to make the whole journey by water. They were proceeding in a leisurely fashion along the coast and had intended to stop at Suma which was said to be the most beautiful bay of all, when they heard that Genji was living there. The giddy young persons in the boat were immediately in the wildest state of excitement, though their father showed no signs of putting them ashore. If the other sisters, who did not know Genji, were in a flutter, it may be imagined what a commotion was going on in the breast of Lady Gosechi.[13] She could indeed hardly restrain herself from cutting the tow-cord, and when the boat put in so near the shore that a faint sound of string-music could be heard floating down from Genji's cottage, the beauty of the shore, the proximity of so interesting a personage and the interrupted strains of the tune combined to make a powerful impression upon the imaginations of these young people, and the tears came into their eyes. The Secretary sent the following letter ashore: 'I had hoped that after my long absence it would be from your lips that I should first hear all the gossip of the Capital. I now learn to my intense surprise and, if you will allow me to say so, to my deep regret, that you are at present living in retirement in

[13] See above, p. 58.

this remote place. As we are a large and mixed party, I must excuse myself from troubling you, but I hope to have the pleasure of your society upon some other occasion.' This letter was brought by his son the governor of Echizen, a nobleman who had been one of Genji's equerries and had been treated by him with particular kindness. He was distressed at his former master's ill fortune and did not wish to seem ungrateful; but he knew that there were persons in his father's train who had their eye upon him and would, if he lingered in Genji's company, denounce him to the authorities. He therefore handed in the letter and at once hurried away. 'You are the first of my friends to visit me since I left the Capital,' said Genji. 'I cannot sufficiently thank you for sparing me so much of your time. . . .' His reply to the Viceroy's letter was couched in much the same terms. The young governor returned in very low spirits, and his account of what he had seen and heard provoked loud expressions of sympathy not only from the ladies of the party but also from the Viceroy himself. Lady Gosechi contrived to send a short message on her own account, together with the poem: 'Little you guessed that at the sound of your distant lute one hand was near indeed to severing the tow-cord of the boat.' 'Do not think me forward if under these strange circumstances I have ventured once more to address you,' she added. He smiled as he read the letter. She seemed to have become very demure. 'Had you in truth been minded to visit me, what easier than to cut the cable that drags you past this shore?' So he wrote and again: 'You are a little taken aback, I think, to find me "among the fishers at their toil." ' So much did he long for some distraction that he would indeed have been delighted if she had found courage to come ashore; nor is this strange when we remember how not far away from this same place a mighty exile[14] found solace in the company of an ostler.

In the Capital Genji's absence was still universally deplored. His stepbrothers and some of the noblemen with whom he was most intimate had in the early days of his exile sent sometimes to enquire about him and had composed elegies in his honour, to which he had replied. This soon reached Kokiden's ears. She was furious at this proof of his continued popularity: 'It is unheard of,' she burst out angrily, 'that a man condemned of offences against the Government of his country should be allowed to live as he pleases and even share in the literary pastimes of the Court. There he sits (by the way I hear he has got a very pretty house!) railing all day at the Government, and no doubt experimenting on loyal servants of the Crown for all the world like that man in the history book who declared that a stag was a horse.'[15] Henceforward Genji received no letters from Court.

The lady at the Nijō-in remained inconsolable. The servants in the eastern wing had at first been somewhat reluctant to transfer their services to her; but after a while her charming manners and amiable disposition completely won their hearts, and none of them showed any signs of seeking service elsewhere. Their employment had given them opportunity of observing, albeit at a distance, most of the great ladies of the Court. They were soon willing to allow that in beauty of character Murasaki far excelled them all, and they well understood why Genji had singled her out to be his pupil.

[14] The great statesman Sugawara no Michizane, 845–903.
[15] Chao Kao was plotting to overthrow the Second Emperor (3rd cent. B.C.). He brought His Majesty a stag, telling him it was a horse. The Emperor laughed, but some of the courtiers were so much afraid of Chao Kao that they sided with him and insisted that it was indeed a horse. Then Kao knew that they feared him more than the Emperor and definitely decided to revolt.

He, meanwhile, longed more and more to have her with him. But apart from the fact that the roughness of life at Suma would be utterly unsuited to her, he knew that his sending for her would be regarded as an impudent challenge to those who had achieved his downfall.

They were within easy distance of Akashi, and Yoshikiyo naturally thought of the strange lady whom he had once courted there, daughter of the eccentric recluse[16] who had made his home near the bay. He wrote to her several times, but received no reply. Finally a note came not from her but from her father, saying that he had something to tell Yoshikiyo and would be glad if he could find time to call. It was quite clear what this meant. The old man merely wanted to tell him that his suit was unwelcome. Yoshikiyo saw no point in going to the house on purpose to be snubbed, and left the letter unanswered. As a rule provincial governors seem to think that there are no reputable families in the land except those of other provincial governors, and it would never occur to them to marry their daughters into any other class. But this ex-governor was a man who not only had ideas of his own but clung to them with passionate obstinacy. For years past, the sons of provincial officials had been courting his daughter, and one and all he had sent them about their business. His own notion of a husband was very different. Then came Genji's arrival at Suma. So soon as he heard of it, the ex-governor said to his wife: 'I hear that Lady Kiritsubo's boy, Prince Hikaru Genji, has got into some sort of trouble with the authorities and has come to live at Suma. I confess I am delighted to hear it. What a splendid opportunity for our girl. . . .'

'You must be mad!' broke in the mother. 'I have been told by people at Court, that he already keeps several

16 See Part I, p. 110.

ladies of the highest rank as his mistresses; and not content with that, it appears that he has now got into trouble about some lady in the Imperial Household. I cannot imagine why you suppose that a coxcomb of this kind is likely to take any interest in a simple, country girl. . . .' 'You know nothing whatever about it,' interrupted the father testily. 'I have very good reasons for thinking as I do, and I must trouble you to fall in with my plans. I intend to invite Prince Genji over here at the earliest possible opportunity.' He now spoke in a gentler tone, but it was evident that he meant to have his own way, and to his wife's consternation he began to make the most lavish preparations for Genji's entertainment. 'I cannot imagine,' she said, 'why you are so set upon marrying our daughter to this man. However exalted his position may once have been, that does not alter the fact that he has now been expelled from the City as a criminal. Even if by any chance he did take a fancy to her, the idea of accepting such a person as our son-in-law is one which you cannot surely entertain even as a joke. . . .' 'What is all this about criminals?' he growled. 'Surely you know that some of the most distinguished men in history both here and in China have been forced at one time or another to retire from Court. There is nothing disgraceful about it. Just consider for a moment who this prince is. His mother was the daughter of my own uncle, the late Inspector of Provinces, who having made a name for himself by his public services was able to obtain for her a position in the Imperial Palace. Here she at once became the idol of our beloved Monarch, and although the very exceptional favour with which she was treated aroused a good deal of jealousy and in the end brought about her undoing, her career cannot be considered unsuccessful, since she became the mother of His Majesty's most cherished son. In short, the family with which his august father was not ashamed to ally himself is surely good enough for this young prince, and though our daughter is a country-bred girl, I do not think you will find he turns up his nose at her. . . .'

The young woman in question was not remarkably handsome, but she had considerable distinction and charm. Indeed many of the greatest ladies at Court had, so far as good looks went, far less to boast of. She was painfully conscious of her own deficiencies and had made up her mind that no one of good position would ever take any notice of her. Men of her own rank in life she knew that she had no opportunity of meeting. Sooner or later her parents would die, and then she would either become a nun or else drown herself in the sea; she was not sure which. Her father brought her up with extreme strictness, and her only outings were pilgrimages to the Shrine of Sumiyoshi, whither he brought her regularly twice a year, secretly hoping that the God would be moved to assist his ambitious designs.

The New Year had begun. The days were growing longer and already there was a faint show of blossom on the cherry-trees which Genji had planted in his garden at Suma. The weather was delightful, and sitting idly in the sunshine he recalled a thousand incidents that were linked in his mind with former springs. The twentieth day of the second month! It was just a year ago that he left the Capital. All those painful scenes of farewell came back vividly to his mind, bringing with them a new access of longing. The cherry-trees of the Southern Hall must now be in full bloom. He remembered the wonderful Flower Feast of six years ago, saw his father's face, the elegant figure of the young Crown Prince; and verses from the poems which he had himself made on that occasion floated back into his mind.

All this while To no Chujo had been living at the Great Hall, with very little indeed to amuse him. He had been put down again into the Fourth Rank and was very much discouraged. It was essential to his prospects that he should not come under any further suspicion, but he was an affectionate creature and finding himself longing more and more for Genji's society, he determined, even at the cost of offending the Government, to set out at once for Suma. The complete unexpectedness of his visit made it all the more cheering and delightful. He was soon admiring Genji's rustic house, which seemed to him the most extraordinary place to be living in. He thought it more like some legendary hermit's hut in a Chinese book than a real cottage. Indeed the whole place might have come straight out of a picture, with its hedge of wattled bamboo, the steps of unhewn stone, the stout pine-wood pillars and general air of improvisation. Chujo was enchanted by the strangeness of it all. Genji was dressed in peasant style with a grey hunting-cloak and outer breeches over a suit of russet-brown. The way in which he played up to this rustic costume struck Chujo as highly absurd and at the same time delighted him. The furniture was all of the simplest kind and even Genji's seat was not divided off in any way from the rest of the room. Near it lay boards for the games of go and *sugoroku,* and chessmen, with other such gear as is met with in country houses. The meals, which were necessarily of a somewhat makeshift character, seemed to Chujo positively exciting. One day some fishermen arrived with cockles to sell. Genji sent for them and inspected their catch. He questioned them about their trade and learned something of the life led year in and year out by those whose homes were on this shore. It was a story of painful unremitting toil, and though they told it in a jargon which he could only half understand, he realized with compassion that their feelings were, after all, very much like his own. He made them handsome presents from his wardrobe and they felt that these shells had indeed been life-giving.[17]

The stable was quite close by and in full view of the cottage. It amused Chujo to watch the labourers fetching rice-husks from a queer building which seemed to be a sort of store-house or granary and using them as provender for the horses; and he would sing the ballad: 'Sweet is the shade . . .'[18]

He had of course a great deal to tell to his friend, and it was sometimes with laughter, sometimes with tears that they went step by step over all that had happened in the long months of their separation. There were many stories of Aoi's little son, happily still too young to understand what was going on in the world around him, of the old Minister, who now was sunk into a state of unremitting melancholy, and of a thousand other happenings at the Great Hall and Court, which could not possibly be recounted in full and would lose all interest if told incompletely. Neither of them had any inclination to sleep, and at dawn they were still exchanging Chinese odes.

Though Chujo had said that he no longer cared what the authorities thought of him, he was reluctant to aggravate his offence by lingering on this forbidden shore, and he now announced that he must start for home again immediately. This was a terrible blow to Genji who knew that so short a visit would leave him even more wretched than before. Wine was brought and as they drank the farewell cup they murmured in unison the words of Po Chü-i's parting poem:

[17] There is here a play on words. The other meaning is: 'That life was indeed worth living.'
[18] 'Sweet is the shade, the lapping waters cool, and good the pasture for our weary steeds. By the well of Asuka, here let us stay.' See Part I, p. 36.

'Chin on hand by the candle we lay at dawn
Chanting songs of sadness, till the tears had splashed
Our cup of new-made wine. . . .'

Chujo had brought with him some delightful presents from the Capital. With many apologies Genji offered him in return a black colt, saying as he did so: 'I fear that it may be embarrassing for you to receive even so poor a gift as this from one in my position. But I beg of you to accept it as a symbol of my longing to return, for in the *Old Poem* it is written:

'"The Tartar horse neighs into the northern wind;
The bird of Yüeh nests on the southern bough."'

It was in fact a magnificent horse and could hardly have been matched in all the kingdom. Among the presents brought by Chujo was a celebrated flute which had long been in his possession, and many other small but beautiful objects such as could easily be secreted and would serve as tokens of his affection without exciting troublesome comment.

The morning was well advanced before Chujo set out. He could hardly believe that the long-dreamed-of meeting was already over and looked back again and again to where his friend was standing. The sight of Genji gazing after him as the boat drew away made it more difficult than ever to endure so speedy a parting, and he cried out, 'When, when shall we meet again? I cannot think that they will let you go on much longer. . . .' At which Genji answered him with the poem: 'O crane, who travellest at will even to the very margin of the Land on High, look well upon me, whether in intent I be not cloudless as this new day of Spring.'[19] 'Sometimes for a while I have hope,' he added; 'but of those

---

[19] I.e. You have access to the Emperor, put in a word on my behalf.

who before have been in my case even the most grave
and virtuous have seldom managed to repair their fortunes. I fear I shall not see the precincts of the Capital
again.' 'Hapless in cloudland shall your crane's solitary
voice re-echo till with his lost friend, wing to wing again,
he can renew his flight.' This was the poem that Chujo
now recited as his boat left the shore.

The third month was now beginning and someone who
was supposed to be well up in these matters reminded
Genji that one in his circumstances would do well to
perform the ceremony of Purification on the coming
Festival Day.[20] He loved exploring the coast and readily
consented. It happened that a certain itinerant magician
was then touring the province of Harima with no other
apparatus than the crude back scene[21] before which he
performed his incantations. Genji now sent for him and
bade him perform the ceremony of Purification. Part of
the ritual consisted in the loading of a little boat with a
number of doll-like figures and letting it float out to sea.
While he watched this, Genji recited the poem: 'How
like these puppets am I too cast out to dwell amid the
unportioned fallows of the mighty sea.' . . . These verses
he recited standing out in the open with nothing but
the wind and sky around him, and the magician, pausing to watch him, thought that he had never in his life
encountered a creature of such beauty. Till now there
had not been the least ripple on the face of the sea.
Genji, wondering what would in the end become of him,
began to review the whole course of his past life and
the chances of better fortune in the future. He gazed
on the quiet aspects of both sky and sea. 'The Gods at
least, the myriad Gods look kindly on my fate, knowing
that sinful though I be, no penalty have I deserved such

[20] The third day of the third month.
[21] *Zesho*, a screen or in some cases curtain with a pine-tree
painted on it; used as a background to sacred performances.

as I suffer in this desolate place.' As he recited these words, the wind suddenly rose; the sky grew dark and without waiting to finish the ceremony everyone began hastily preparing to make for home. Just when they had decided to return as quickly as possible, a squall of rain commenced, beginning so unexpectedly that there was no time even to put up umbrellas. The wind was now blowing with unparalleled violence and things which the calmness of the morning had tempted them to leave carelessly lying about the shore were soon scattered in every direction. The sea too was rapidly advancing and they were obliged to run for their lives. Looking back they saw that the whole surface of the bay was now covered with a blanket of gleaming white foam. Soon the thunder was rolling and great flashes of lightning fell across the sky. It was all they could do to make their way home. The peasants had never witnessed such a gale before. 'It blows pretty stormy sometimes,' they said; 'but you can generally see it coming up a long while before.' Of such a storm as this, coming on without a moment's warning, they could make nothing at all. Still the thunder crashed, and the rain fell with such violence that each shaft struck deep into the earth. It seemed indeed as though the end of the world were come. Some of Genji's servants became very restless and uneasy; but he himself settled quietly in his chair and read out loud from the Scriptures. Towards evening the thunder became less violent, but the wind remained very high all night. It was soon apparent that if the wind did not change, the waves would carry away their house. Sudden high tides had often before done great damage on the coast, but it was agreed that such a sea as this had never been seen before. Towards dawn everyone went off to get a little rest. Genji too began to doze a little. There appeared to him in his dream a vague and shadowy figure who said: 'I have come from the Palace

to fetch you. Why do you not follow me?' He tried to
obey the command, but suddenly awoke. He realized
that the 'Palace' of his dream did not mean, as he had
at first supposed, the Palace of the Emperor, but rather
the dwelling of the Sea God. The whole import of the
dream was that the Dragon King[22] had taken a fancy
to him and wished to detain him yet longer on the shore
of his domains. He became very depressed and from
this time onwards took a dislike to the particular part of
the coast in which he had chosen to reside.

[22] Sovereign of the Ocean.

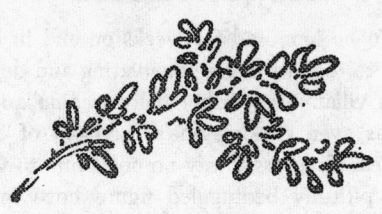

Chapter IV

AKASHI

The bad weather continued; day after day nothing but rain, wind and repeated thunderstorms, bringing with them countless troubles and inconveniences. So depressing was the past to look back upon and so little hope did the future hold out for him that, try as he might, Genji could no longer keep up even the appearance of cheerfulness. His prospects were indeed dark. It was just possible that he might some day be permitted to return to the Capital. But with the dominant faction at Court still working against him he would be subject to unendurable slights and vexations. He thought more than once of withdrawing from the coast and seeking shelter at some point well back among the inland hills. But he knew that if he did so it would be said he had been scared away by a few days of foul weather. The smallest actions of people in his position are recorded, and he did not care to figure in the history books as the prince who ran away from a storm. Night after night he had the same dream of a messenger summoning him to the realms below the sea. It seemed as though the Dragon of the Ocean had indeed set his heart upon him.

Day followed day without the least break showing in the sky. It was now a long time since he had heard any news from the Capital, and he was becoming very

anxious. To be immured for weeks on end in his small
house was to the last degree enervating and depressing;
but in this villainous weather there was no question of
so much as even sticking one's head out of doors for
two minutes. Needless to say no one came to visit him.
At last a pitifully bedraggled figure hove into view,
fighting its way through the storm. A messenger from
the Nijo-in. So he announced himself; but the journey
had reduced him to such a plight that Genji would
scarce have known that this tattered, dripping mass was
a human being at all. He was indeed a common peasant,
such a one as in old days would have been unceremoni-
ously bundled out of Genji's path. Now Genji found
himself (not without some surprise at the degree of con-
descension to which his misfortunes had brought him)
welcoming the fellow as an equal, and commiserating
with him upon his plight.

In her letter Murasaki said: 'In these odious days
when never for a single instant has the least gleam or
break pierced our sodden sky, the clouds have seemed
to shut you off from me and I know not behind which
part of this dark curtain to look for you. "How fiercely
must the tempests be blowing on your shore, when even
here my sleeves are drenched with ceaseless spray!"'

The letter was full of sad and tender messages. He
had no sooner opened it than a darkness spread before
his eyes and tears fell in floods, 'belike to swell the
margin of the sea.'

He learnt from the messenger that at Kyoto too the
storm had raged with such violence and persistency that
it had been proclaimed a national Visitation, and it was
said that the great Service of Intercession[1] had been

_____
[1] Instituted in China in the 6th century. It centred round
the reading of the *Jen Wang Ching* (Nanjio No. 17) in
which Buddha instructs the great kings of the earth how to
preserve their countries from calamity.

held in the Palace. So great were the floods that the officers of the Court were unable to reach the Inner City, and all business was at a standstill. He told his story confusedly and in a broken jargon that was very hard to follow. But what matter? Such as it was, his news came from Kyoto, from the City, and that in itself was enough to make Genji catch eagerly at every word. He had the messenger brought to his own room and was soon plying him with questions. It seemed that the same continuous downpour had gone on day after day without a moment's break, varied only by occasional hurricanes of wind. Thunder they had not had, nor the alarming hailstorms which along the coast were of such violence that the hailstones had penetrated far down into the earth. Such horror came into the man's face as he recalled the scenes through which he had passed, and so lamentable was his present condition that even those who had taken the storm somewhat lightly now began to feel seriously alarmed. It seemed indeed as though a continuance of the present deluge must speedily wash the world away; but worse was to come, for next day, from dawn onwards, an even more violent wind raged, causing a tremendous flood-tide along all the shore. Soon the breakers were crashing with a din so stupendous that you would have thought the rocks, nay the very hills, could not long resist them. Suddenly a blaze of lightning, inexpressibly fierce and dazzling, rushed earthward. They realized that something must have been struck, and there was now no longer anyone who even pretended to take the situation lightly. Each of Genji's servants was wondering in his heart what he had done to deserve at the hand of Fate so hideous an experience. Here, it seemed, they were all to die; never again to meet mother or father, far from the pitying faces of wife, of children, or of friends. Genji himself had no desire to end his existence on this inhospitable shore, but he managed to control his feelings and did his best to introduce some order among his followers. This proved to be by no means easy. At last he set them to offering up prayer-strips and ribbons to the God of Sumiyoshi and himself called upon the God to save from calamity a shore that was so near his own Holy Abode and, if indeed he were a Present Deity, to prove it now by his aid. So he prayed, with many other vows and supplications. And his servants, as they heard him, forgot for a while the peril that threatened their own lives, and could think only of the calamity which would befall their country should such a prince be lost amid the waters of this deserted shore. Then one, who was of greater courage than the rest and had now somewhat regained the use of his faculties and better feelings, began to call upon the God to take his life and welcome, so be it Genji were saved. And after this, all began in chorus to invoke both Buddhas and Gods of their own land; and presently one said: 'Though nurtured in a palace of princes and inured from infancy to softness and delights, our master has not hidden his face from common men; for in every corner of the Eight Islands his patience and kindness are known. How many that were downcast and obscure has he not helped upward to greatness? Tell us now, Heaven, tell us, Earth, of what crime has he been guilty, that he should be cast away, a victim to the winds and seas? Guiltless he has been punished, has been robbed of rank and office, has been torn from home and country, nor has been suffered to be at peace either by day or night. . . .' Genji himself prayed again to the gods, saying: 'With such sights and sounds about us we cannot but wonder whether the end of our days is come. Do ye now, O Powers, put an end to this grievous visitation, whether it be the fruit of *karma* or the punishment of present crimes; lest we should doubt if Gods and Buddhas can indeed make manifest their will.' Then turning

in the direction of the Sumiyoshi Shrine he uttered many
further prayers to that God, to the Dragon King of the
Ocean and to a thousand and one other Gods and Spirits.
Suddenly, however, while he was in the midst of these
prayers, there was a louder thunderclap than ever, and
at the same time lightning struck a pent-house which
actually adjoined Genji's room. Flames shot up and that
part of the building was soon in ashes. His men were now
without exception in such a state of panic that they
could do nothing. Finally Genji got them to move his
things into a sort of shed at the back of the house, which
had sometimes been used as a kitchen. Here, huddled
with all his followers and grooms, he spent the rest of the
day, wearied by their ceaseless lamentations, which indeed bid fair to out-din the thunder. The sky was still
black as ink when night fell. However, the wind began
to subside and presently the rain grew a little less heavy;
and at last an occasional star began to twinkle. The
thought of their master spending the night in so strange
and undignified a situation was very perturbing to his
attendants and they began trying to make his proper
bedroom habitable again. This, however, did not prove
to be feasible, for although a great part of it had not
been actually touched by the fire, 'the Storm God in his
boisterous passage' had left a terrible havoc behind him
and the room was strewn with the tattered wreckage of
furniture, screens and bedding. It was agreed that nothing could be done till next day.

Genji said his prayers and began to consider the situation. It was indeed sufficiently alarming. So high had
the tide risen that, now the moon was up, the line of the
incoming waves was plainly visible from his house, and
standing at the open wicker door he watched the fierce
breakers plunge and recoil. Such conditions of storm and
tide had not occurred in recent times and no one was
prepared to say how far matters were likely to go. This

being the only gentleman's house in the neighbourhood many of the fishing people and peasants who lived along the shore had now collected in front of it. Their queer, clipped dialect and the rustic topics of their conversation were alike very strange to him; but he would not suffer them to be driven out of earshot. 'If this wind does not go down,' one of them was saying, 'we shall have the sea right on top of us before the tide turns. God's help alone can save us.' It may be imagined that these predictions were far from disposing the townsmen towards a quiet night's rest. A brisk sea wind was again driving onward the swollen tide, and though he tried to reassure his men Genji was himself in considerable anxiety; when suddenly and quite unexpectedly he fell into a doze and dreamed that his father, looking exactly as in the old days when he was on the throne, stood beside the crazy bed which had been improvised for him in this disordered place. 'How comes it that you are sleeping in such a place as this?' the vision asked, and taking his hand made as though to drag him from the bed. And again, 'Put your trust in the God of Sumiyoshi. Leave this place, take to your ship and He will show you where to go.' What joy it was to hear that voice once more! 'Father,' Genji answered, 'since your protection was taken from me nothing but sorrow and ill-fortune have befallen me, and now I am fully expecting to perish miserably upon this forsaken shore.' 'It is not to be thought of,' answered the Emperor. 'Your offence was not so great that you must needs be driven to such a place as this. Unfortunately I myself am at present expiating a few small offences (such as it is indeed impossible to avoid; for the Judges of the Dead have not managed to prove that during my whole reign I did serious harm to anyone). However, for the present this expiation keeps me very busy, and I have not been able to keep an eye upon what is happening here. But your late misfortunes have been such as I could not bear to think of, and though it cost me great labour, I have made my way through the depths of ocean and up again on to the shore, that I might be with you in your suffering. Yet this time I must not stay longer, but will go straight to the Palace and tell these things to him who is now Ruler there.' So he spoke, and turned to fly away. 'Let me go with you. Do not leave me!' cried Genji in his dream. But looking up he found that there was no one there at all. The full-faced moon stared down at him, cold and undreamlike; a cloud trailed across the sky, shaped to the dim semblance of a figure in flight.

It was many years since he had dreamed of his father, though in his waking hours he had never ceased to mourn for him and long for his company. This sudden vision which, though so brief, had all the vividness of a real encounter, brought him great comfort. The thought that at the hour of his greatest despair, nay when death itself seemed close at hand, his father's spirit had hastened through the air to succour him, made him almost glad that Fate had brought him to the extremity which had moved his father's compassion. So full was he of new hope and comfort that in his exultation he utterly forgot the perils that encompassed him, and lay trying to recall stray fragments of his father's dream-speech which had faded from his waking mind. Thinking that the dream might be repeated, he tried to sleep again; but this time all his efforts were in vain, and at daylight he was still awake.

Next morning there landed at a point in the bay opposite to Genji's house a little boat with two or three persons aboard her. It proved on enquiry that they had come from the Bay of Akashi and that the boat belonged to the ex-governor of the province, now turned lay-priest. The messenger explained that his master was himself aboard and desired to have a word in private with

the Genshonagon[2] Yoshikiyo, if he were at present to be
found at Suma. Yoshikiyo thought this very peculiar.
The ex-governor was perfectly well aware of all that
went on in the district; but though he had been acquainted with Yoshikiyo for years, he had not during
all the while they had been at Suma paid the slightest
attention to him. It seemed indeed (thought Yoshikiyo)
as if he were definitely in the old man's bad books. And
now, in the middle of an atrocious storm, he took it
into his head to pay a call. It was all very queer. But
Genji, who saw in this new happening a possible fulfilment of his dream, said at once, 'You had better go,'
and Yoshikiyo accordingly accompanied the messenger
back to the boat. How they had ever managed to launch
it at all, under the conditions which must have prevailed
at the time they left Akashi, was a complete mystery
to him. 'On the first day of this month,' the old man
began, 'I had a most singular and interesting dream.
What it portended seemed to me at the time very improbable; but part of the dream was that if I wished
to see the promise fulfilled, I must get ready a boat and
on the thirteenth day, so soon as there was the slightest
lull in the storm, make straight for this coast. As this
injunction was several times repeated I had the boat
manned and at the appointed time waited for a chance
of getting to sea. There was a fearful gale blowing; rain
was falling in torrents and a thunderstorm was in progress. It certainly did not seem a very good moment to
start. But there are many instances in foreign history of
people saving a whole country from peril by obeying an
apparently senseless dream. I feared that if I delayed
my departure beyond the day which had been named

[2] A Court title. Yoshikiyo was son of the governor of
Harima and had courted the Lady of Akashi. See Part I, p.
110.

my journey would be of no service to anyone. And so,
determined that you should know of the divine indica-
tion which had been vouchsafed to me, I launched my
boat. What was my surprise to discover that we had a
quite moderate wind blowing nicely in our wake! We
had this wind behind us all the way, and I cannot but regard the whole affair as a clear instance of divine in-
tervention. It is possible that on your side too there has
been some warning or message which fits into the revela-
tions which I have received. I am very sorry to disturb
His Highness; but I should be obliged if you would tell
him of what has passed.' Yoshikiyo accordingly went
back to Genji and told him the whole story. The matter
needed some consideration. Here was a chance which
it would not be wise to let pass. Both actual events, such
as the destruction of his bedroom, and a general rest-
lessness induced by his own singular dream, with its
warning to quit this place, inclined him to make use of
the ex-governor's visit. No doubt that if he retired to
Akashi his move would become the subject of a great
many scurrilous jokes;[3] but on the other hand he would
look even more foolish if it turned out that he had not
availed himself of a genuine warning from the Gods.
And this must be a very dangerous thing to do; for even
human beings are extremely annoyed if one disregards
their advice. His situation could hardly be worse than it
was already. The old governor was many years his
senior; was even, as things went now, his superior in
rank, and was certainly viewed by the authorities in a
very different light from that in which Genji was regarded. In fact it would be most unwise not to take
advantage of his visitor's evident friendliness and desire
to be connected with him. To go to Akashi would be to

[3] It would be said that he was running after the Lady of
Akashi, the old recluse's daughter.

beat a retreat. But a wise man[4] of ancient times has told
us that 'to retreat is no disgrace.' And then there was
his own dream, in which his father had begged him to
leave this place. He had made up his mind about it. He
would ask if he might go back with them to Akashi.
He therefore sent a message to his visitor saying:
'Though I am living in a strange land, under circumstances in the highest degree painful and depressing,
from the direction of my own home there does not come
a single message of enquiry or condolence. Here all is
unfamiliar to me; save the stars and sun there is not
one being or thing that recalls to me the life I used to
know. You can imagine then with what joy I saw your
fishing-boat draw near. Tell me, is there not on your
shore some corner where I could hide myself and be at
peace?'

This was just what the old gentleman wanted, and
in high delight he hastened to welcome Genji's suggestion. A great bustle commenced; but before daybreak
all Genji's effects had been stowed away in the boat
and, with his usual band of chosen retainers, he at last
set sail. The wind had veered and was behind them on
the return journey too, so that the little ship flew to
Akashi like a bird. The distance is of course not great and
the voyage does not in any case take more than a few
hours. But so assiduously did the wind follow them on
this occasion that it really seemed as though it were doing it on purpose.

Akashi was evidently a very different sort of place.
Indeed his first impression was that, if anything, it would
be difficult here to find seclusion enough. The ex-
governor's estate comprised not only the fore-shore, but
also a considerable extent of mountain-land behind. And
everywhere, in creeks and hill-folds and on river-shores,

[4] Lao Tzu, say the commentators; but this saying does not
occur in the *Tao Te Ching*.

were felt-roofed huts so situated that the old recluse might not lack an agreeable place of retirement at any season of the year.

On all sides there rose groups of substantial granaries and barns, which looked as though they must contain rice and corn enough to last for the rest of his present existence. But though so careful to provide for his earthly needs, he had by no means forgotten the life to come. On a site which, commanding as it did a magnificent panorama, was calculated to inspire him with the sublimest thoughts, he had built a handsome temple, where part of his time was spent in the performance of penances and mystic meditations.

During the recent storms he had moved his wife and daughter to a lodge on the hillside and was therefore able to place his seaside residence entirely at Genji's disposal. It was still dark when they left the boat; but as they drove along the shore, the growing daylight at last gave him an opportunity of taking a good look at his guest. So delighted was he by the young man's appearance and by the rapid success of his expedition that his usually severe and formidable countenance relaxed into a perfect efflorescence of smiles and affability. But even in this state of preoccupation and excitement he did not forget to offer up a prayer of thankfulness to the God of Sumiyoshi. To the old man it was as though the sun and moon had been taken down from the sky and entrusted to his keeping. It may easily be imagined that he left no stone unturned to make Genji comfortable and contented. Not only was the place one of great natural beauty, but it had been laid out with unusual taste and skill. Copses had been planted, rock-gardens constructed and flower-beds made—all this around the mouth of a little creek that ran in from the sea. The charms of the place were such as a very skilful landscape-painter might possibly manage to convey; to describe them in words would, I fear, be quite useless. The contrast with the uncomfortable quarters where he had been cooped up for months was immense. The house was equipped with every possible elegance and convenience; it scarcely fell short of the great mansions which he had been used to frequent at the Capital; and indeed in many respects surpassed them. Thus admirably served and lodged Genji began to regain some of his equanimity and was soon engaged in writing letters to his friends at the Capital. The messenger who had brought Murasaki's letter was far too much shaken by his previous experiences to be sent back immediately to the City and Genji had left him behind at Suma. He now sent for him and entrusted to him a letter in which he described all that he had recently been through and with many tender messages explained the reasons which had led him to his new abode. He also sent private intimation of his whereabouts and present condition to various holy men who were charged to pray for his welfare. To Fujitsubo he sent an account of the thunderstorm and his own almost miraculous escape from harm. He had tried to write an answer to Murasaki's letter during the melancholy period when he was still at Suma, but had never managed to finish it, for his tears fell so fast that he was for ever putting the letter aside. And it was indeed a piteous sight to see him stop again and again to wipe away the tears that soiled his page. In this letter he said: 'More than once my misery has become so intense that I was fully determined to give up my career and end my days in some cloister cell. But then I always remembered your little poem;[5] and felt that it was impossible to leave the world, at least till I had seen you once again.

> "Swift as before
>   My thoughts fly back to thee,

[5] The mirror-poem, p. 70.

Though now from unknown shore
To stranger and more distant shores I flee. . . ."

Forgive this letter which, written as in a dream, may
well say much which a waking mind can scarcely ap-
prehend.' It was written distractedly and with a shaking
hand: but those who were with him could not forbear
from peeping a little as he wrote, such was their curiosity
to know what he would say to one who held so great
a sway over his affections. And presently, having seen
what they could, his servants too began their own letter-
writing, each of them having some dear one at the City
from whom he was anxious to obtain news.

The bad weather in which for so many weeks there
had not been a single break, had now completely vanished. Out came all the fishing-boats, eager to make up
for lost time. The complete desertedness of Suma, which
apart from a few fishermen who lived in caves under the
cliff, had no inhabitants at all, was very depressing.
Akashi could certainly not be complained of on that
score; indeed, he feared at first that it might prove somewhat too populous. But the beauty of the place was so
great and afforded him so many surprises that he was
soon perfectly contented. His host seemed to be exclu-
sively absorbed in religious exercises. Only one other
matter occupied his thoughts; it was clear from stray
allusions in his conversation that he lived in a state of
continual agitation about his only daughter, to whom
he was evidently attached with an almost morbid degree of concentration. Genji had not forgotten the
favourable account of this lady which had been given
him some years ago. Her presence had of course been
no part of his reason for coming to this place; but the
fact that accident had finally brought him so near her
was in a way intriguing. However, his misfortunes were
still weighing heavily upon his mind and he was in a

mood for prayer and fasting rather than for any gallant diversions. Moreover his thoughts were, for the time being, more than ever turned towards the City, and he would not have dreamed of doing anything that the girl whom he had left in his palace might feel to be a betrayal of his promises. He was therefore careful not to show the slightest interest in the topic to which his host so often returned. But various indications had already convinced him that the lady in question was a person of very unusual and attractive qualities, and despite this assumed indifference he could not help feeling a certain curiosity with regard to her. The ex-governor showed himself to be an ideal host. He stationed himself at the far end of the house, in a wing which was completely cut off from Genji's quarters. Here he was always to be found when wanted, but never obtruded himself. The self-effacement was the more remarkable seeing that he was all the time longing to be in Genji's company, and he was continually praying Gods and Buddhas for guidance as to how he might best win the confidence of his exalted guest. Although he was not much over sixty a constant habit of watching and fasting had told much upon him, so that in appearance he was wizened and almost decrepit. But he was by no means a dull companion, for owing to the influential circles in which his youth had been passed he was extremely well-informed concerning all the principal events of a period which had hitherto lain outside Genji's ken, and his anecdotes were a considerable source of distraction. Genji found indeed that he had started a veritable landslide of information about a generation which his own distractions, both social and political, had never left him time to study. So pleased was he both with his host and with his new place of residence that he thought with horror how easily it might never have occurred to him to pay this visit.

Though he had now become so intimate with his guest, the old man was still daunted by a certain reserve and distance in Genji's manner towards him; and whereas in the first few days of their acquaintance he had sometimes mentioned his daughter, he now hardly ever referred to her. But all the while he was trying to discover some way of unfolding his project and his complete failure to do so distressed him beyond measure. He was obliged at last to confess to his wife that he had made no progress; but she was not able to offer him any useful advice. The girl herself had been brought up in a neighbourhood where there was not a single male of any description whom she could possibly think of as a lover. At last she had a chance of convincing herself that such creatures as men of her own class did actually exist. But this particular one was such an exalted person that he seemed to her in his way quite as remote as any of the local people. She knew of her parents' project, which indeed distressed her greatly, for she was convinced they were merely making themselves ridiculous.

It was now the fourth month. A dazzling summer outfit was supplied for Genji's use; magnificent fresh hangings and decorations were put up in all his apartments. The attentions of his host were indeed so lavishly bestowed that they would have proved embarrassing, had not Genji remembered that he was in the hands of an eccentric, whose exalted notions were notorious and must, in a man of such distinction, be regarded with indulgence. About this time he began to have a fresh distraction; for messengers again began to arrive from the Capital, and came indeed in a pretty constant stream. One quiet moonlit night, when a cloudless sky stretched over the wide sea, Genji stood looking out across the bay. He thought of the lakes and rivers of his native land. This featureless expanse of sea awakened in him only a vague and general yearning. There was no intimate mark

round which his associations might gather, no bourne
to which his eyes instinctively turned. In all the empty
space before him only the island of Awaji stood out
solidly and invited attention. 'Awaji, from afar a speck of
foam,' he quoted, and recited the acrostic verse: 'Oh,
foam-flecked island that wast nothing to me, even such
sorrow as mine is, on this night of flawless beauty thou
hast power to heal!'

It was so long since he had touched his zithern that
there was a considerable stir among his followers when
they saw him draw it out of its bag and strike a few random notes. Presently he began trying that piece which
they call the 'Koryo'[6] and played the greater part of it
straight through. The sound of his zithern reached the
house on the hillside near by, mingled with the sighing
of pine-woods and the rustling of summer waves. The
effect of all this upon the imagination of the impressionable young lady in the house above may well be guessed.
Even gnarled old peasants, whom one would not have
expected to make head or tail of this Chinese music,
poked their noses out of their cottage-doors and presently came to take an airing along the shore. The governor could not contain himself, and breaking off in the
middle of his prayers, hastened to Genji's rooms. 'How
this brings back to me the old days at Court, before I
turned my back on all the pleasures of the world.' He
exclaimed: 'But surely the enchantment of such music as
this is not all earthly! Does it not turn our thoughts towards those celestial strains which will greet us when we
come at last to the place of our desires?' To Genji too the
sound of the zithern brought recollections of many
music-makings at the Capital. He remembered with just
what turns and graces such a one had played the zithern
at a particular banquet or another had played the flute.

[6] Evidently a Chinese tune. Attempts to identify it have
hitherto been very unconvincing.

The very intonations of some singer's voice came back to him from years ago. He remembered many an occasion of his own triumph or that of his friends; the acclamations, the compliments and congratulations of the Court, nay, the homage of everyone from the Emperor downwards; and these shadowy memories imparted to his playing a peculiar tinge of melancholy and regret. The old recluse was deeply moved and sent to his house on the hill for his own lute and large zithern. Then, looking for all the world like a *biwa* priest,[7] he played several very admirable and charming pieces. Presently he handed the large zithern to Genji, who struck a few chords, but was soon overcome by the tender memories which this instrument[8] evoked. The poorest music may gain a certain interest and beauty from the circumstances in which it is performed. It may be imagined then how enchanting was the effect of Genji's touch as the notes sped across the bay. Nor indeed could any flowering groves of spring nor russet winter woods have made a better setting for his music than this huge space of open sea. Somewhere in the region of soft, vague shadows along the shore, shrike were making that strange tapping sound with their bills. It sounded as though someone had been locked out and were rapping, rapping, rapping in the desperate hope that those within might at last relent of their unkindness. The old recluse then played so delightfully on both instruments that Genji was fascinated. 'This large zithern,' he said to the old man presently, 'is usually supposed to be a woman's instrument and requires a very delicate, fluttering touch.' He meant this quite generally, and not as an apology for his own playing; but the old man answered with a deprecatory smile: 'I

[7] Priests who collected money for their community by going round playing the *biwa* at street-corners.
[8] Which he had taught to Murasaki.

cannot imagine a touch more suitable to this instrument than yours. This zithern was originally a present from the Emperor Engi[9] and has been in my family for three generations. Since my misfortunes and retirement I have had little taste for such distractions as this, and have lost what small skill I ever possessed. But in times of great spiritual stress or deep depression I have occasionally turned to this instrument for solace and support. And indeed there is in my household one who from watching me at such times has herself developed a strange proficiency, and already plays in a manner which would not, I venture to think, displease those departed princes to whom the zithern once belonged. But perhaps by now, like the mountain-hermit in the old story, I have an ear that is better attuned to the rushing of wind through the tree-tops than to the music of human hands. Nevertheless I wish that, yourself unseen, you might one day hear this person's playing'; and his eyes moistened in fond paternal recollection. 'I had no idea,' answered Genji, 'that I was in the neighbourhood of genius such as you describe. I fear my playing will have sounded to you indeed as a mere "rushing of wind through the tree-tops,"' and he hastened to put back the zithern in the old priest's hands. 'It is indeed a curious fact,' Genji continued, 'that all the best players of this instrument have been women. You will remember that the Fifth Princess became, under the instruction of her father the Emperor Saga,[10] the most famous performer of her whole generation. But none of her descendants seems to have inherited her talent. Of all the players who in our own time have achieved a certain reputation in this line, there is not one who is more than an intelligent amateur. That in this remote place there should be someone who is really

[9] 898–930. Sixtieth Emperor of Japan.
[10] 810–823. Fifty-second Emperor of Japan.

a skilled performer excites me beyond measure. Do
please lose no time in arranging. . . .' 'As for that,' the
priest answered, 'I do not see why there should be any
great difficulty about it, even if it meant bringing the
player down here to meet you. Was not one that had
sunk into ignominy and made herself a merchant's[11]
drudge once summoned to a great man's side, because
she could still play upon her lute the music that long
ago he had loved? And speaking of the lute, I should
tell you that the person to whom I refer is also a remarkable lute-player, though this instrument too is one
which is very rarely mastered completely. Such absolute
fluency, such delicacy of touch, I assure you! And such
certainty, such distinction of style! Shut away for so
long on this shore, where one hears no sound but the
roaring of the sea, I sometimes fall a prey to dark and
depressing thoughts; but I have only to listen for a while
to this delightful performer and all my sorrows disappear.' He spoke with so much enthusiasm and discern-
ment that Genji was charmed with him and insisted upon
his playing something on the large zither. The old
man's skill was astonishing. True, his handling of the
instrument was such as is now considered very old-
fashioned, and his fingering was all entirely in the discarded 'Chinese' style, with the left-hand notes heavily
accentuated. But when (though this was not the sea of
Ise) he played the song 'Let us gather shells along the
clean seashore,' getting one of his servants, who had an
excellent voice, to sing the words, Genji enjoyed the performance so much that he could not refrain from beating the measure and sometimes even joining in the
words. Whereupon the priest would pause in his playing
and listen with an expression of respectful rapture.

Fruit and other refreshments were then served, all

[11] Po Chü-i. The reference is to his poem *The Lute Girl's
Song.*

with the greatest taste and elegance. The old priest insisted upon everyone present drinking endless cups of wine, though the night itself was of a beauty so intoxicating that the dull realities of life had long ago faded from their minds. As the night wore on a cool wind began to blow among the trees, and the moon, who in her higher course had been somewhat overcast, now at her setting shone out of a cloudless sky. When the company was grown a little quieter, the priest began gradually to tell the whole story of his life on this shore, together with his reasons for settling there and a voluminous account of his vows and religious observances; when without difficulty he led the conversation towards the topic of his daughter. She certainly sounded very interesting, and despite the old man's volubility Genji found himself listening with pleasure at any rate to this part of the discourse. 'It seems a strange thing to say,' his host went on, 'but I sometimes wonder whether, humble old cleric though I be, my own prayers are not really responsible for Your Highness's excursion to these remote parts! You will say that if this is so I have done you a very bad turn. . . . But let me explain what I mean. For the last eighteen years I have put myself under the special protection of the God of Sumiyoshi. From my daughter's earliest childhood I have been very much exercised in mind regarding her future, and every year in the spring and autumn I have taken her with me to the shrine of that deity, where praying day and night I have performed the offices of the Six Divisions,[12] with no other desire at heart save that, whether I myself should be reborn upon a Lotus Throne or no, to her at least all might be given that I asked. My father, as you know, was a Minister of State; while I, no doubt owing to some folly committed in a former life, am become a

[12] A service performed at dawn, sunrise, midday, sunset, dusk and nightfall.

simple countryman, a mere yokel, dwelling obscurely among the hills. If the process continued unchecked and my daughter was to fall as far below me in estate as I am now below my illustrious father, what a wretched fate, thought I, must be in store for her! Since the day of her birth my whole object has been to save her from such a catastrophe, and I have always been determined that in the end she should marry some gentleman of good birth from the Capital. This has compelled me to discourage many local suitors, and in doing so I have earned a great deal of unpopularity. I am indeed, in consequence of my efforts on her behalf, obliged to put up with many cold looks from the neighbouring gentry; but these do not upset me at all. So long as I am alive to do it, I am determined to afford her what little protection my narrow sleeve can give. When I am no longer there to watch over her, she will no doubt do as she thinks best. But I confess I would rather hear she were drowned in the sea than that she had settled herself in the sphere of life to which my folly has for the time reduced her.' He went on thus for a long while, pausing now and again to shed a few tears; but most of what he said would not be worth repeating. Genji was for various reasons also in a very emotional and discursive mood, and presently he interrupted: 'I could never make out why I had suddenly fallen into disgrace and been compelled to live in these remote regions; for I have certainly done nothing in my whole life to deserve so stern a punishment as this. But at last you have furnished me with the explanation, and I am perfectly well satisfied. No doubt it was, as you suggest, entirely in answer to your prayers that all this has happened to me. I only regret that, since you must all the time have been aware of this, you did not think fit to tell me about it a little sooner. Since I left the City I have been so much obsessed by the uncertainty of human life that I have felt no inclination towards any save religious employments. I am now so worn out by months of penance and fasting that no worldly impulse or desire is left in any corner of my being. I had indeed been told long ago that a grown-up daughter lived here with you; but I knew nothing more, and assumed that the society of a disgraced and exiled man could only be distasteful to one of her birth and breeding. But since you thus encourage me, I ask for nothing better than to make her acquaintance as soon as possible. I do not doubt that her company will prove a solace to my loneliness.' His prompt acceptance was more than the old man had dared to expect and in high delight he answered with the verse: 'You too have learnt to know it, the loneliness of night upon Akashi shore, when hour and listless hour must yet be filled before the dawn can come.' 'And when you consider the anxiety in which I have for all these years been living . . . ,' the old man added: and though he trembled somewhat affectedly at the recollection of what he had been through, Genji was willing to concede that to have lived all one's life in such a place must indeed have been very disagreeable. However he would not be too sympathetic and answered: 'You at any rate have the advantage of being used to the coast . . . ,' and he recited the poem: 'What know you of sorrow, who wear not the traveller's cloak, nor on an unaccustomed pillow rest, groping for dreams till dawn?' For the first time Genji was treating him without the slightest formality or reserve. In his gratitude and admiration the old man poured out an endless stream of inconsequent but flattering remarks, which would be wearisome to read. I am conscious indeed that the whole of this section is rather a bundle of absurdities. But how else could I display the vanity and eccentricity of the old recluse?

At last everything seemed to be turning out just as he

desired. He was already beginning to breathe more freely when, to crown his satisfaction, very early on the morning of the next day a messenger from Prince Genji arrived at the house on the hill. The letter which he carried was written with a certain embarrassment, for the lady had grown up in very different surroundings from those whom he was used to address. But the very fact of discovering such talent and charm hidden away in a place where one would least have expected it was enough to kindle his fancy. He took unusual pains with the letter, writing it on a *kurumi-iro*[13] paper from Korea. In it was the poem: 'Long wandered my lonely gaze with nought to rest on save the drifting pathways of the clouds, till the mists divided and I saw the tree-tops by your house.' 'Love has vanquished discretion . . . ,' he ended, quoting from the old song.

Anxious to be on the spot in case such a letter arrived, the old priest had already installed himself in the mansion on the hill before the messenger started. He imagined that his presence in the house was entirely unsuspected. But Genji's man, had he not already been perfectly well aware that the old recluse had preceded him, would certainly have guessed it by the almost embarrassing attentions which were paid to him when he reached the house. Despite the distracting refreshments with which he was being regaled the messenger could not but wonder why the lady was taking such an immense while in composing her reply. The truth was that though her father had gone through into the women's apartments and was giving her all the assistance in his power, she found herself utterly at a loss to frame a reply. Despite the trouble that Genji had taken with his letter, there was an uneasiness about it which made her feel that it was not spontaneous; and even had she known in what terms to reply there was still the question

[13] A double paper; light blue on a white ground.

of handwriting. She guessed that in this matter he would be a severe critic and felt utterly incapable of pleasing him. No! The gulf between them was too great. Pretending that she was unwell she sank helplessly upon a couch. There was nothing for it but to reply in her stead, and the old priest wrote as follows: 'You will think it very peculiar that I should answer your letter in my daughter's stead. Pray attribute her inability to frame a reply not to any want of gratitude or respect, but rather to the bashfulness engendered by country breeding; pray reflect also that she has never yet had the privilege of finding herself in your company. She has however ventured to compose the following poem, which she bids me communicate to you: "That I too for long years have gazed upon these selfsame pathways of the sky is token of some strange kinship in the course of our desires." She is, as you will observe, deeply affected by the arrival of your message. Pray do not think her answering poem impertinently bold.'

This was written on Michinoku paper, and although the style of the writing was quite out of fashion it had a certain dignity and elegance of its own. The poem did strike Genji as somewhat forward in tone, and this surprised him.

He sent back the messenger loaded with handsome stuffs for dresses. Next day he wrote to her again protesting that he was not used to receive, in reply to a private letter, an answer dictated as though to a Palace Secretary. And he added the verse: 'This surely is a dismal and outrageous thing, to greet a passer-by and get no friendly nod nor "Say, how goes the world with you?"' This time he wrote on a very soft thin paper, with great delicacy and care. The appearance of the letter was such that a young girl who did not admire it must needs have been rustic, nay brutish indeed. The lady to whom it was addressed was by no means insensible; but she felt that the writer of it was too far removed from her in rank and influence for any interchange of affection to be thinkable. The discovery that a world existed which was populated by such dazzling creatures, so far from giving her pleasure, merely left her more unhappy and discontented than before. Again she found herself utterly at a loss how to reply, and it was only the persistence of her father which forced her at last to indite the poem: '"How goes the world?" is said to friends. That one whom you have never seen should greet more stiffly, can do small outrage to the feelings of your heart.' It was written in sharply contrasted light and heavy strokes on a deep-brown paper, in a masterly style which would not have disgraced a lady of the Court. Genji was naturally very pleased; but he did not want it to be reported at the Capital that he had committed himself to a fresh entanglement. He was therefore careful henceforward always to leave several days' interval between his letters to her. He wrote in fact only when it chanced that the evening hours hung heavy on his hands, or upon the pretext of some particularly beautiful sunrise or other natural effect; at such times in short as he guessed that she might be under the influence of the same impressions as himself. In such a correspondence it seemed to him that there could not be any impropriety. He had heard so much about her pride that he felt sorely tempted to put it to the test. But he remembered that his retainer Yoshikiyo had spoken of her very much as though she were his own property. Should Genji now by any chance succeed where the devotion of years had brought no reward, he would certainly feel that he had treated his gentleman very badly and suffer the discomfort of remorse. But on reflection he decided that as she had been so reluctantly thrust upon his notice, there could be no harm in pursuing a guarded correspondence with her. She did indeed turn out in the course of this correspondence to be possessed of a pride and aloofness which rivalled that of the greatest princesses whom he had known and, on such occasions as he pitted his own pride against hers, it was generally she who came out on top.

Though now yet another range of hills separated him from the Capital, his mind was more constantly than ever occupied with thoughts of his friends at home. His longing for Murasaki often became unendurable. What was there to be done? In such moments he could not resist making plans for bringing her secretly from the Capital. But quiet reflection would show him that it was unlikely he would go on living for more than a year or two longer at Akashi and no step was worth while which might merely provoke a fresh outburst on the part of his adversaries.

That year the Court was troubled by a succession of disquieting portents and apparitions. On the thirteenth day of the third month, during a night marked by violent thunderstorms and a fierce wind with torrents of rain, the Emperor dreamed that he saw His Majesty the late Emperor standing at the foot of the step before his throne, wearing an expression of extreme displeasure, indeed glaring at him, as it seemed, with an angry and astonished eye. The Emperor having assumed an attitude of respectful attention, the apparition proceeded to deliver a long discourse, part of which was concerned with Genji's present plight. The Emperor was very much frightened, and being in any case somewhat uneasy at Genji's prolonged absence, he hastened to communicate his dream to Kokiden. She was not at all sympathetic. 'These stormy nights are very disturbing,' she said. 'It is quite natural that you should have had bad dreams; the rain alone would have accounted for it. You must not allow such trifles to upset you.' About this time the Emperor began to suffer from a pain in his eyes. Remembering his dream, he could not get out of his head the idea that this pain was in some way caused by the wrathful glance of the apparition which had rebuked him. His sufferings became more and more acute, despite the fact that continual services of intercession were held both in the Palace and at Kokiden's house.

Next came the death of Kokiden's father, the Grand Minister of the Right. There was nothing unexpected in this, for he had reached a very great age. But coming as it did on top of various other public calamities it caused widespread consternation. Kokiden herself, though she had no definite malady, was also very far from well. As time went on she seemed gradually to lose strength. A general gloom spread over the Court. It was felt that if, as was alleged by his friends, Prince Genji had indeed been banished without any sufficient cause, the present misfortunes of the nation might well have been sent as punishment for this injustice. Again and again the Emperor thought of restoring Genji to his previous rank and appointments; but whenever he mentioned this project to Kokiden, that lady would answer: 'To do so would be to incur the public charge of inconsequence and frivolity. He was banished and if, when less than three years have elapsed, he is suddenly recalled to the Capital, a pretty figure you and I shall cut in history!' She spoke with such fierce conviction that the Emperor was completely overawed. So the months went by, and meantime both he and Kokiden were gradually sinking under the burden of their respective maladies.

At Akashi, as frequently happens in autumn, heavy winds were blowing in the bay. Genji began to find the long evenings very monotonous and depressing. Sometimes he would allow the priest to come and talk to him, and in the course of one of these conversations Genji said: 'I am longing for a little diversion. Could you not manage, without attracting too much attention, to bring your daughter here one day to see me?' It seemed somehow to be accepted that for Genji to pay a visit to the house on the hill was entirely out of the question. Unfortunately the lady herself was equally averse to making any move. She knew that gentlemen who visited the provinces on Government business would often take up with some wretched peasant girl and, for so long as they happened to be in the district, carry on a purely frivolous affair with her. The Lady of Akashi was convinced that Genji regarded her in just such a light. To accept his advances could only render her in the end more wretched than before. Her parents, she knew, were still clinging to the idea that all those long years of watchfulness and isolation had at last borne fruit. To them the inevitable disillusion would be a crushing blow. Her mind was quite made up; so long as this prince remained at Akashi she would continue to correspond with him, but further than that she would not go.

His name had been known to her for years past, and she had sometimes wondered whether it would ever fall to her lot to meet, even in the most superficial way, some such magnificent personage as he. Now, astonishing though it seemed, he was actually living a stone's throw away. She could not be said exactly to have met him, but she constantly caught glimpses of him, heard his inimitable zithern-playing, and knew, one way and another, all that there was to know about his daily comings and goings. That such a person should even be aware of her existence was more than, as an inhabitant of this remote fishing-town, she had any right to expect. As time went on it seemed to her less than ever possible that any closer relationship should be established between them. Meanwhile her parents were far less confident about the situation than she supposed. They felt that in their anxiety to see the prayers of half a lifetime at last fulfilled they had perhaps acted somewhat precipitately. If Genji did not after all seem to regard their daughter as 'counting,' her feelings would have been upset for nothing. True he was a great catch and was worth certain risks; but that only made it harder to lose him. They had an uneasy feeling that while they had been placing all their trust in 'Gods whom no eye seeth' they had paid too little attention to the dispositions of the human beings for whose future they had schemed.

'A little music,' said Genji to the old priest one evening, 'would mingle pleasantly with the sound of these autumn waves. It is only as a background to music that the sound of the sea is tolerable.'

The time for action had come. The old priest looked in his calendar, chose a lucky day, and despite the misgivings of his wife began to prepare the house on the hill for Genji's visit. Not even to his most intimate acolytes and disciples did he explain the object of these elaborate preparations. The visit was to take place on the thirteenth day of the month. It turned out to be a resplendent moonlit night. The old man came to Genji's room and recited the line: 'Is this a night to lose?' Genji at once understood that this was an invitation to the house on the hill. Suddenly what had seemed impossible became perfectly simple. He set his cloak to rights and left the house. His host had provided him with a magnificent coach, but the narrow lanes would have made its use inconvenient and Genji preferred to go on horseback. He was accompanied only by Koremitsu and one or two of his other trusted servants. The house stood a little way back from the shore and while he climbed to it he was all the time looking down over the bays that spread out on every side. He remembered the verse: 'Would that to one who loves what I love I now might show it, this moon that lies foundered at the bottom of

the bay!' For the first time since he had agreed to set
out upon this excursion he remembered the lady at his
palace far away, and at that moment he could hardly
resist turning his horse's head and riding straight to the
Capital. 'O thou, my milk-white pony, whose coat is as
the moon-beams of this autumn night, carry me like a
bird through the air that though it be but for a moment
I may look upon the lady whom I love!' So he murmured
as he approached the house, which was thickly girt with
an abundance of fine timber. It was indeed a house im-
pressively situated and in many ways remarkable; but
it had not the conveniences nor the cheerful aspect of
the house on the shore. So dark and shut-in an appearance did it present as he drew near, that Genji
soon began to imagine all its inhabitants as necessarily
a prey to the deepest melancholy and felt quite concerned at the thought of what they must suffer through
living in so cheerless a place. The Hall of Meditation
stood close by and the sound of its bell blent mournfully
with the whispering of the pine-trees that on the steep
uneven ground grew precariously out of a ledge of rock,
their roots clutching at it like some desperate hand. From
the plantations in front of the house came a confused
wailing of insect voices.

He looked about him. That part of the house which
he knew to be occupied by the lady and her servants
wore an air of festive preparation. Full in the moonlight
a door stood significantly ajar. He opened it. 'I wish to
rest for a few minutes,' he said; 'I hope you have no
objection to my coming in?' She had in fact the greatest
objection, for it was against just such a meeting as this
that she had resolutely set her face. She could not
actually turn him away; but she showed no signs of
making him welcome. He thought her in fact the most
disagreeable young person whom he had ever met. He
was accustomed to see women of very much greater

consequence than this girl show at any rate a certain
gratification at being thought worthy of his attentions.
She would not, he felt, have dared to treat him so rudely
but for the present eclipse of his fortunes. He was not
used to being regarded so lightly, and it upset him. The
nature of the circumstances was obviously not such that
he could carry off the situation with a high hand. But
though violence was out of the question, he would certainly cut a very ridiculous figure in the eyes of the girl's
parents if he had to admit that she showed no signs of
wanting to be acquainted with him. He felt embarrassed
and angry. Suddenly one of the cords of the screen-of-
state behind which she was sitting fell across her zithern,
making as it did so a kind of casual tune. As she bent
over the instrument he saw her for an instant just as she
must have looked before his entry had made her stiffen;
just as she must look when carelessly and at ease she
swept an idle plectrum over the strings. He was captivated. 'Will you not even play me something upon this
zithern of which I have heard so much?' he added, and
he recited the poem: 'Were it but from your zithern
that those soft words came which your lips refuse, half
should I awaken from the wretched dream wherein I
am bemused.' And she: 'A night of endless dreams, inconsequent and wild, is this my life; none more worth
telling than the rest.' Seen dimly behind her curtains
she recalled to him in a certain measure the princess[14]
who was now in Ise. It was soon evident that though she
had answered his poem she was no nearer than before
to treating his visit as otherwise than an impertinence.
She had been sitting there so comfortable and happy,
when suddenly this tiresome person burst in upon her
without apology or warning. However, the remedy lay
in her own hands, and rising to her feet she fled into a
neighbouring closet, fastening the door behind her with

[14] Rokujo.

ostentatious care. You might have supposed that this
was the end of the matter, for she had evidently no
mind to return, nor he any intention of forcing bolts and
bars. Curiously enough, however, this was not the end
of the matter. The difficulties that ensued may well be
imagined if we remember the lady's unusual shyness and
pride. Suffice it to say that from this night's meeting,
which seemed at first to have been forced upon him by
chance and other people's intrigues, sprang an intimacy
which was grounded in the deepest feeling. The night,
generally so long and tedious at Akashi, passed on this
occasion all too quickly. It was essential that he should
leave unobserved, and at the first streak of dawn, with
many last endearments and injunctions, he crept stealth-
ily from the room. His next day's letter was sent very
secretly, for he was haunted by the fear that some story
of this adventure might find its way back to the Capital.
The lady for her part was anxious to show that she was
to be trusted, and deliberately treated Genji's messenger
without ceremony of any kind, as though he were bound
on some errand of merely domestic import. He paid
many subsequent visits to the house on the hill, always
with the greatest secrecy. Unfortunately the way there
led nowhere else, and knowing that fisher-folk are notorious gossips he began to fear that his addiction to this
particular road would be noticed and commented upon.
His visits now became far less frequent, and the lady
began to think that her early fears were soon to be fulfilled. The old priest's thoughts were, if the truth must
be told, for the time being much more frequently occupied with the coming of Genji than with the coming of
Amida.[15] He could not make out what had gone wrong,
and was in a terrible state of agitation. To make matters worse he knew that such earthly considerations
ought to leave him quite unmoved and he was ashamed

[15] Buddha.

to discover how little his pious observances had availed
to render him indifferent to the blows of fortune.

Genji would not for all the world have had the news
of his latest adventure reach Murasaki as a piece of current gossip, even though it were represented in the most
harmless light. Her hold upon him was indeed still strong
as ever, and the mere idea of such a story reaching her,
of her feeling that she had been superseded, of a possible
quarrel or estrangement, filled him with shame and dismay. She was not indeed given to jealousy; but more
than once she had shown plainly that his irregularities,
so far from passing unobserved, were indeed extremely
distressing to her. How bitterly he now regretted those
trivial gallantries, so profitless to him, yet to her so
miserably disquieting! And even while he was still visiting the lady of the hillside, since there was no other way
of quieting his conscience concerning Murasaki, he
wrote to the Nijo-in more frequently and more affec-
tionately than ever before. At the end of one of these
letters he added: 'How it grieves me to remember the
many occasions when I have spoilt our friendship for
the sake of some passing whim or fancy in which
(though you could not believe it) my deeper feelings
were not at all engaged. And now I have another matter
of this kind to confess, a passing dream, the insignificance of which you can guess by the fact that I tell
you of it thus unasked. "Though with the shining seaweed of the shore the fisherman a moment toys, yet
seeks he but assuagement of a sorrow that long ere this
has filled his eye with burning tears."'

Her answer showed no resentment and was couched
in the tenderest terms. But at the end, in reference to
his disclosure, she wrote: 'As regards the "dream" which
you could not forbear telling me, I have experience
enough in that direction to enable me to draw several
conclusions. "Too downrightly, it seems, have I obeyed

it, our vow that sooner would the Isle of Pines by the sea-waves be crossed. . . ."' But though her tone was good-humoured, there was in all her letter an undercurrent of irony, which disturbed him. He carried it about with him for a long while and constantly re-read it. During this time his secret nocturnal excursions were entirely abandoned, and the Lady of Akashi naturally imagined that all her fears had now come true. He had amused himself to his fill and had no longer any interest in what became of her. With no support, save that of parents whose advanced age made it improbable that they could much longer be of any assistance, she had long ago given up hope of taking her place in the world with those of equal rank and attainments. But she did now bitterly regret the waste of all those empty months and years during which she had been so conscientiously guarded and kept—for what? At last she had some experience of the usages which prevailed in the 'grand world' outside, and she found them even less to her liking than she had anticipated. She indulged however in no outburst of spleen or disappointment, nor in her letters did she ever reproach him for his long absence. He had indeed as time went on become more and more attached to her, and it was only his desire to be able to allay the anxiety of one who had after all a prior claim upon him that induced him to suspend his visits to the lady on the hill. Henceforward his nights at Akashi were again spent in solitude.

He amused himself by making sketches upon which he afterwards scribbled whatever thoughts happened to be passing through his mind. These he sent to Murasaki, inviting her comments. No method of correspondence could have been better calculated to move and interest her. The distance between them seemed in some sort to have been annihilated. She too, at times when she was feeling out of spirits or at a loss for employment, would also make sketches of the scenes around her, and at the same time she jotted down all that was happening to her day by day in the form of a commonplace book or diary.

What, she wondered, would she have to write in her diary? And he in his?

The New Year had come. At the Palace nothing was now talked of save the Emperor's illness, and the Court was full of restless speculation. The only child of the present Emperor was a boy born to him by Princess Jokyoden, daughter of the new Minister of the Right. But he was only two years old and therefore of no particular account. The Heir Apparent, Fujitsubo's son, was also a minor. The Emperor was fully determined to resign the Throne to him at the earliest opportunity, but should he do so it would be necessary to appoint a regent. There were so few people to whom it would be in any way possible to entrust the affairs of government that it seemed a pity Genji should be out of the running. His presence was indeed becoming in every way more and more imperative, and at last the Emperor decided to recall him, whether Kokiden approved or not. Since the end of the year her illness had taken a more serious turn.[16] The Emperor too—although for a time thanks to the immense efforts made on his behalf in consequence of certain disastrous omens which had engendered something in the nature of a natural panic, although for a time his eyes showed some improvement—was soon in as bad a way as ever, and feeling very uncertain of the future, he dictated an edict in which Genji was commanded to return to the Capital by the end of the seventh month. That sooner or later there would be a turn in his fortunes Genji had always been convinced. But the shortness and uncertainty of life made him little

[16] There is some doubt about the punctuation of this and the following sentence.

inclined to settle down quietly and wait for events to take their course. This swift recall came therefore as an intense relief. And yet, for one reason at any rate, he was by no means anxious to leave the coast so soon. The priest too had never expected that Genji would be with him very long; but the news of his immediate departure came as something of a shock. However, it was a consolation to feel that Genji was now definitely reembarking upon the path of prosperity, and that his partiality, should it continue, would be in the future even more valuable than before. Genji now began again to visit the upper house almost every evening. Since the beginning of the sixth month the Lady of Akashi had been slightly indisposed and it was now certain that she was with child. No sooner had a definite term been put to their friendship than Genji's feeling for her redoubled: surely in those last days she was more charming than she had ever been before! Here indeed, rash though his courtship had been, was one whom under no circumstances he would ever feel that he had loved and cherished beyond her deserts! She for her part sat in absolute silence before him, lost in her own thoughts. Poor soul, he could not blame her.

When three years ago he had set out so reluctantly upon that miserable journey to Suma, his only consolation had been to imagine the joy and excitement with which on some far distant yet inevitable day he would retrace his steps to the City. Now that day had come, and to be returning was indeed very pleasant. But all the while, mingled with delightful anticipations, was the strange fear that he might never be able to revisit the place of his banishment! His servants however were all in high spirits, and this, combined with the bustle of numerous friendly deputations from the Capital, created an atmosphere of general liveliness and excitement, despite the obvious depression that all these signs of departure brought to the host under whose roof the numerous visitors were lodged. The seventh month had begun, and the summer weather was even more delightful than usual. Why, wondered Genji, was he, who took such pleasure in quiet and harmless pursuits, doomed on every occasion to find himself involved in the most harrowing and disastrous situations? It had not indeed escaped the notice of those who knew him best that a fresh complication, of the kind they already knew only too well, had arisen in his life. For several months on end he had never once mentioned the lady's name, and they began to hope that the affair had run its course. But the curiously subdued state of his spirits on the very eve of departure told them only too plainly that this hope was premature. It was whispered that all this trouble had arisen from Yoshikiyo's indiscreet eloquence upon the occasion when after Genji's cure they had climbed the mountain summit and looked down towards the western seas. Yoshikiyo himself, as indeed he had every reason to be, was very much irritated by the whole affair.

Two days before his departure Genji visited the house on the hill some hours earlier than was his wont. He had never before seen the lady by full daylight, and her beauty astonished him. Such dignity of bearing, such an air of proud decision he had not in the least expected. This fresh discovery of her, this last-hour revelation filled him with new longings and regrets. Must he lose her? Could not some excuse be formed for bringing her to the Capital, for installing her at Court? And to ease his feelings he began to discuss with her the wildest plans as though they had been perfectly simple and practicable.

The austerities which he had practised during the earlier days of his exile had left him still looking somewhat worn and thin. Yet such was his beauty that while,

touched by her misery, he sat beside her and with tears
in his eyes whispered the tenderest words of pity and
endearment, for a moment she felt that even if there
had been but one such night as that and after it he had
disappeared for ever, she would still feel his love for her
to have been the greatest happiness of her life.

But for all his kindness he was a prince—the inhabitant
of a world peopled not by creatures like herself, but by
a remote and superior order of beings. Such was the
thought that even at moments like this would obtrude
itself with painful persistency. Oddly enough, though
the promise that she would play to him had been the
excuse for his first visit, she had never once touched her
zithern since he had known her. For this he had often
scolded her, and now he determined to make a last attempt. 'Will you not play one small tune, so that I may
carry it away in my head to remember you by,' he said,
and sent to the lower house for the zithern which he had
brought with him from the Capital. He tuned it with
special care, and the few chords that he struck while he
did so floated with a strange distinctness through the
still midnight air. The old priest heard these sounds, and
unable to contain himself came bustling round to the
women's quarters with his Chinese zithern in his arms
and deposited it in the room where his daughter was
receiving her guest. Then he discreetly withdrew. Genji
now renewed his entreaties and at last she could resist
no longer. He guessed at once, by the way that she
handled and tuned the instrument, that she would prove
to be a remarkable performer. Lady Fujitsubo used generally to be considered the best zithern-player of the
day, and though the applause of the fashionable world
was in part a tribute to her rank and beauty, she was
without question a very fine musician. But the Lady of
Akashi, in addition to a complete command of her instrument, played with an intensity of feeling and a power

of expression utterly unknown to the princess. Such indeed was her playing that even he, who could now so seldom get from music a pleasure that he had not experienced many times before, was utterly taken aback. He could have listened for ever, and his only regret was that he had not forced her to play to him months ago. Of course he must not lose her! And handing to her his own zithern he begged her to keep it for him till they should play together again. She answered with an acrostic poem in which she prophesied that this loan was likely to remain for ever on her hands. And he, in indignation—'Steadfast am I as the middle strings[17] of this my zithern that I leave with you until we meet.' 'Who knows that it may not be soon,' he added. 'Perhaps before these very strings have fallen out of tune.' Thus he sought to comfort her; but to her mind one thought only was present—that he was going away. She began to sob bitterly.

On the day of his departure he was up long before sunrise. The setting out of so large a party (for the house was now full of friends who had come to escort him back to the City) occasioned a tremendous bustle. Genji too was much preoccupied, but in the midst of these distractions he found time to send her a message: 'Because they have left the sea behind them, the rising waves creep listlessly across the sand. But I, a sinking wave, cast back disconsolate thoughts towards the shore whence I retreat.' And she: 'My cabin by the shore the winds have sheltered, and gladly now amid the receding wreckage of the storm would I drift out to sea.' His friends from the Capital noticed that he was in great distress, and could only suppose that, despite the untoward circumstances which had brought him to this place, he had in the course of years become so attached to it that the actual moment of parting was somewhat

[17] Which remained unaltered whatever tuning was adopted.

of a wrench. But they could not help thinking that such
a display of emotion was very excessive. On the other
hand Yoshikiyo and the rest saw their worst fears con-
firmed. This was evidently a serious business, and they
foresaw all kinds of complications that might arise from
it. These gentlemen were delighted to be going home,
but when it came to the actual moment of departure
they felt a certain regret at leaving this extremely agreeable coast, and there were naturally many among them
who had on their own account to face somewhat painful
scenes of farewell. Many affecting poems were written
and tearful speeches made; but what use would it be to
record them all?

In his preparations for the departure of the travellers
the old priest had surpassed himself. For every single
person connected with the expedition, down to the humblest carriers and menials, the most sumptuous equipment was provided. It was indeed hard to imagine how
in these few weeks such elaborate preparations could
possibly have been made. The arrangements for Genji's
own comfort were of the most extraordinary ingenuity;
in fact the luxuries forced upon him filled so many boxes
that it required quite an army of porters to carry all his
luggage. Genji was indeed equipped more like a traveller
setting out from the Capital than like one returning from
the provinces. There seemed to be no imaginable con-
tingency which the old priest had not thought of. To the
travelling cloak which had been specially designed for
that day's journey the Lady of Akashi attached the
poem: 'That this cloak of travel, cut and folded by the
salt seashore, should bear a stain or two of spray, you
will not take amiss!' Despite the noise and confusion of
departure, he found a moment in which to write the answer: 'Though for a while I must wear it in remem-
brance, yet soon as certain days and months are safely
passed, once more no garment shall divide us.' This mes-

sage he sent privately, and when he put on the new
cloak he was at pains to tell those about him that it was a
present from the old priest and worn at his especial desire. The cloak which he had previously been wearing
he sent to the house on the hill, where for long afterwards the sight of it and the smell of the rare scent with
which it was perfumed awakened tantalizing memories
in those from whose thoughts he would in any case
seldom have been absent.

The priest excused himself from accompanying the
expedition even so far as the frontier of the province,
saying that in his present state of grief and agitation he
did not feel equal to so great an exertion. 'Pray do not
think me impertinent,' he added, 'but I ought perhaps
to remind you . . . in fact, we none of us doubt for an
instant. . . . But quite at your own time and convenience, of course!' He did not dare go beyond these brief,
disjointed hints, but Genji, so far from taking offence,
was extremely sorry for the old man, who, it was evident,
had taken the business to heart in the most unfortunate
way. 'There is now a particular reason why I should
cherish and remember her,' said Genji presently; 'you
may be sure that in a very little while I shall see to it
that she has her due. To leave you all at such a moment
grieves me more than I can say. But what would you
have me do?' The lady herself was in a strange state of
mind. She was still convinced that the difference in rank
between them precluded any lasting union and was certain that in the long run she had no more chance of
happiness at the City than she had if left behind here in
the wilds. But when it came to his actually starting, she
could not bear to be left behind. Try as she might, she
could not control herself. His image perpetually haunted
her and every effort to banish it ended in a wild fit of
sobbing. 'It would have saved the poor girl untold misery,' said the mother, having in vain tried every means

to distract her, 'if this wretched business had never begun. And how unnecessary it all is! Nothing of the kind
need ever have entered the child's head, but for the odious and perverse advice which certain people . . .'
'Hold your tongue,' the old priest said angrily. 'This will
all come right in the end; he has told me so himself.
He knows about her condition and will do all that he
can for her.' 'Come, child,' he said, bringing her a basin
of hot water in his own hands; 'you must get up at once
and let yourself be dressed. You really must not go on
like this. It is terrible, you know, terrible,' and he stood
at the corner of the bed looking at her encouragingly.
Not only the mother, but the girl's old nurse and most
of the confidential servants were in a state of indignation against their master and went about saying that his
misguided promptings had brought them all into this
terrible trouble. But the old man's evident misery soon
dismissed their anger. He went about muttering to himself: 'To think that I should have waited all these years
for a chance to do something that would help her! And
just when I thought everything was going so well, I find
I have only made the poor thing unhappy. . . .'

So much did his mistake (for such he was now convinced that it was) afflict the old man that he became
a little queer in the head. During the day he did little
but doze; but at night he would suddenly get up and
seated in an attitude of prayer would fumble with his
hands as though he had forgotten even how to use his
rosary. One night his disciples managed to persuade him
to go for a walk in the moonlight. Mumbling prayers as
he went and quite unaware of his surroundings he stumbled and fell headlong into the moat. He was soon
fished out; but in falling he had caught his leg against a
large stone and done himself considerable injury. During
the illness which followed, his mind, strangely enough,
seemed to be somewhat easier and he appeared to be

worrying less about the unfortunate situation of his daughter.

Meanwhile Genji was on his homeward way. At Naniwa he halted to perform the customary ceremony of Purification. He did not on this occasion go to the Shrine of Sumiyoshi himself but sent a messenger to inform the authorities that he was intending to perform his devotions there quietly on some future occasion. He was now travelling so hurriedly and with so large a retinue that a personal visit was impossible. Apart from the halt at Naniwa he made no unnecessary discursions or digressions, but pressed on with all possible speed to the Capital.

Upon his arrival the Nijo-in presented an extraordinary spectacle. The friends who had accompanied him on the journey were here joined by numerous others who had awaited him in the City. All of them now surged in wild excitement through the Palace, some hurraying lustily, some weeping with joy, and the scene soon became one of indescribable noise and disorder.

And now Murasaki, who at the moment of his departure had vowed in her poem that 'could it but purchase an hour of respite, life itself was a price she would not grudge to pay,' was glad that the gift which in her despair she had bartered so lightly had not indeed been taken from her!

In these three years she had grown even handsomer than before. At first he could not make out in what way it was that her appearance was altered. But when they were alone together he noticed that her hair, which even before he went away had begun to be almost too thick, had been cleverly thinned out. He had to confess that this new way of wearing it became her very well. But suddenly, while he watched her with fond satisfaction, the pleasant thought that she would always be near him was interrupted by a very different image. There rose before his mind the figure of the lady whom he had left behind in that sad mansion above the bay. Plainly as though she were with him he saw her loneliness, her misery, her despair. Why was it that time after time he of all people should find himself in this odious position? Lest Murasaki should feel that things were passing through his mind which he must hide from her, he began telling her about the lady of the shore. But he took such evident pleasure in dilating upon this subject that his frankness had the effect of convincing her that the matter was a far more serious one than she had before supposed. 'It is not for myself I mind,'[18] she quoted, only half meaning him to understand. How terrible that he had lost three whole years of her company, and lost them, too, in punishment for those very infidelities which he would now have given so much to undo!

Soon after his return all his original titles were restored and he was accorded the rank of supernumerary President of Council; while his supporters were re-established in offices equivalent to those of which they had been deprived. Indeed so wide an amnesty was proclaimed that the Court soon wore the aspect of a withered tree that one spring morning suddenly begins to sprout again.

A message came summoning Genji to the Palace. Great excitement prevailed among the Court attendants. It seemed to them that he looked more handsome and flourishing than ever. Had he really spent the last three years under such harrowing conditions as rumour had reported? Among the gentlewomen present were some who had served the old Emperor his father and these old ladies, who had always taken his side, now pressed round him chattering and weeping. The Emperor had

[18] 'It is not for myself I mind; but since the Gods are just, for him who is forsworn I am indeed afraid.' No. 38 of the Hundred Poems; it is by Lady Ukon, 10th century.

been somewhat nervous about this interview. Anxious to make a good impression, he had spent an immense while over his toilet. On this particular day he was feeling somewhat stronger; but for a long while he had been seriously out of health and he was looking sadly altered. They talked quietly till nightfall. It was the fifteenth day of the month. The weather was calm and fine and, as he sat in the moonlight, such a host of memories crowded to the young Emperor's mind that he shed a few tears. He was indeed at that time full of the darkest forebodings. 'Nothing entertaining has happened here,' he said at last. 'I used to like it when you played to me; but of course it is a long time since you did that. . . .' Genji answered with the poem: 'For as many years as the leech-baby[19] could not stand upon its feet have I been set adrift upon the wide plains of the sea.' The Emperor, who felt the sting of this allusion, skilfully parried the thrust with the verse: 'Round the Palace Pillar[20] long enough have we played hide-and-seek; let us forget the rancour of wasted springtimes that we in amity might better have employed.'

After this visit Genji's first care was to perform the ceremonial Eight Readings of the Lotus Sutra in memory of his father the late Emperor. He next visited the Crown Prince and found him grown almost beyond recognition. The child was surprised and delighted to recover his old playmate, whom he perfectly well remembered. Genji was relieved to discover that the boy was unusually quick at his studies and promised, so far

[19] The Royal Gods Izanagi and Isanami bore a leech-child; as at the age of three it could not stand they cast it adrift in a boat.
[20] After a sort of game of hide-and-seek round the Pillar of the Palace of Heaven these Gods met face to face and Izanagi exclaimed: 'I have met a lovely maiden'; whereupon they became husband and wife and bore the leech-child.

as could at present be judged, to make a very satisfactory successor to the Throne.

His agitation upon being admitted to Fujitsubo was not indeed such as it would have been some years ago; but the meeting was an affecting one and they had much to discuss together. One thing I had almost forgotten: by one of the priest's servants who had come with them all the way to the Capital he sent a number of letters to Akashi; among them a long one to the priest's daughter, in which, as he was able to convey it to her secretly, he did his best, by dint of tender messages and allusions, to comfort and console her. In it was the poem: 'At Akashi is all night spent [21] in weeping? And do the mists of morning hide the long-looked-for light of day?'

At last Lady Gosechi,[22] who silently and unknown to all the world had been grieving bitterly at Genji's exile, was able to relieve her feelings by taking action. It was natural and proper that she should write to congratulate him upon his recall. She did so, but left him to guess from whom the letter came. With it was the poem: 'A seafarer that with reluctant heart floated past Suma's shore would fain you saw her sleeve that since that day has never once grown dry.' Her fine handwriting at once betrayed her and he replied: 'With better cause might I make tearful plaint, to whom you steered so close, yet would not stay your course.' Brief as their meeting had been, he still preserved the happiest recollections of it and this sudden reminder of her made him for a moment hope that their friendship might one day be renewed. But what was he thinking of! Now and henceforward there were to be no more frivolities of that kind. Thus he cautioned himself, and the result was that even the lady at the Village of Falling Flowers received

[21] *Akashi* means 'spending the whole night.'
[22] See p. 91.

only a formal intimation of his return. To know that he was to be seen and not to see him was worse than his being utterly out of reach, and the poor lady was unhappier than ever now that he was again at the Nijō-in.

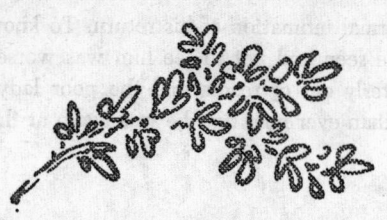

Chapter V

THE FLOOD GAUGE

Since the night of his so vivid and disquieting dream, the late Emperor had been constantly in Genji's thoughts. He longed to succour his father's soul, weighed down as it was (if the words of that nightly apparition were indeed to be trusted) by a load of earthly sin. Now that he was back in the City he was anxious to lose no time, and the great ceremony of the Eight Readings, for which he had begun to make arrangements soon after his return, was duly carried out in the Godless Month.[1] The manner in which this function was attended showed that Genji had fully regained his former ascendancy.

Ill though she was, Kokiden still had sufficient interest in what went on about her to be furious at this recrudescence of a force which she confidently supposed herself to have annihilated. But the Emperor, much as he stood in awe of her, was now obsessed by the idea that if he again disobeyed the late Emperor's injunction some terrible calamity would overtake him. The feeling that he had successfully insisted upon Genji's recall quite braced him, and the pain in his eyes, which had till recently been very troublesome, now began to show

[1] Tenth month. The Shinto gods become inaccessible during this month; but the Buddhas are, apparently, still available.

signs of improvement. But he did not somehow feel that he was likely to be very much longer on the Throne. There were many matters which he desired to see satisfactorily settled while he was still capable of attending to them, and he constantly summoned Genji to the Palace to consult him upon the most confidential affairs of policy and state. In doing so he was but following his real inclination; this was very well understood in the country and the public at large was delighted to see the Emperor once more asserting himself.

As the time drew near when he intended to renounce the Throne, the Emperor became increasingly concerned with regard to the effect that this step would have upon Lady Oborozuki's career. 'My poor grandfather, the late Chief Minister, is gone,' he said to her one day; 'and it does not look as though my mother[2] would be with us much longer. I myself have no intention of remaining on the Throne. I am afraid you will be left in a most tiresome position. I know that there is someone whom you have always liked better than me. But I do not think anyone could possibly be more attached to you than I am, and it distresses me continually to think what will become of you when I am gone. Even if your former friend is willing to look after you again, however kind he is to you, I am quite certain he will take far less trouble about you than I do.' The colour rushed to her cheeks and her eyes filled with tears. He saw that he had wounded her and, moved to sudden pity by the spectacle of her humiliation and remorse, he forgot all her misdeeds and continued in a gentler tone: 'What a pity that we have never had any children! I am sure you and he will have some later on, and it will be a pity that they are his and not mine, because they will only be commoners, you know.' He went on for some while discussing what would happen after he was dead, her distress and

2 Lady Kokiden.

remorse increasing at every word. Her charm was such that, despite his jealousy, the Emperor had grown steadily more attached to her in the years that had passed. But though his partiality had raised her to a position of undisputed pre-eminence at Court, she had not at any time been happy. At first she brooded incessantly upon Genji's comparative indifference towards her, but later, as her sense of responsibility increased, she marvelled more and more at the childish recklessness which had led her into that miserable adventure and, besides destroying her own good name, had reacted so disastrously upon her seducer.

In the second month of the new year the Initiation Ceremony of the Crown Prince was performed. He was only eleven years old but was big for his age, and it was already apparent that he was developing an extraordinary resemblance to his guardian, Prince Genji. In this the world saw nothing to complain of; their future monarch could not, they felt, have chosen a better model. But the Lady Abbess, his mother, watched the growing resemblance with very different feelings and could not but imagine that it was arousing the blackest suspicions.

The Emperor himself was greatly relieved to see that the boy was shaping so well, and he now began to prepare Lady Kokiden for the news that he intended to vacate the Throne. His actual resignation came suddenly, indeed before the end of the second month, and Kokiden was very much upset. To put matters right he assured her that his abdication had but one motive: namely, that he might be free to devote his poor abilities to looking after her. At this she was naturally somewhat mollified.

Fujitsubo's son accordingly became Emperor under the title Ryozen, and Lady Jokyoden's little son became Crown Prince. The new regime bore somewhat the char-

acter of a Restoration and was marked by a return to all
the gaieties and festivities of the old Emperor's reign.
From being President of Council, Genji became Palace
Counsellor; it was intended that he should fulfil the
functions of Chief Minister, and it was only because the
two ministerial posts were already filled that this less
imposing title was given him. Genji however professed
himself quite unable to cope with the duties of so arduous a function, and proposed that Aoi's father, the Minister of the Left, should be asked to assume control. But
the old man pointed out that illness had long ago obliged
him to forgo the executive part of his duties. Since then
he had not grown any younger, and feared that his head
was no longer clear enough to deal with complicated affairs. Genji replied that in the Other Land,[3] at times of
change and uncertainty, even those who had retreated
far away among the hills had sometimes been prevailed
upon to return and lend their aid to a government that
showed itself to be well-disposed. Nor had such men ever
considered that their white hairs constituted a bar, but
had come forward gladly to take office under the new
regime. And indeed for doing so they had always been
deemed true paladins of wisdom. 'It is my desire,' Genji
concluded, 'and that of the Council that you should resume the position which you held before your health
obliged you to withdraw, and we feel that in doing so
you may be sure of incurring no hostile criticism from
any quarter.' It was quite true that retired Ministers had
sometimes been known to resume their functions. The
old man withdrew his opposition and allowed them to
make him Grand Minister with Plenary Powers. He was
now sixty-three. Since the decline of his public influence,
his whole family had lived very much under a cloud.
But now that he was again in the ascendant they began
to resume their old place in society. His sons were soon

[3] China.

once more entrusted with positions of great importance; in particular, To no Chujo became Privy Counsellor of the Second Class. Chujo's daughter, who was now twelve years old, was being trained for the Court, whither she was to be sent as soon as she was old enough. The boy who had sung the Ballad of Takasago so prettily some years ago, was already installed as one of the Emperor's pages and was thought to be doing very well. Besides these he had a number of other children, all of them very promising, and Genji, whose exiguous progeny was of small comfort to him, quite envied Chujo the size and prosperity of his young family.

Yugiri, Genji's son by Aoi, was a fine little fellow. He was already attached to the suite of the new Crown Prince. The princess, Aoi's mother, remained entirely unmoved by the renewed good fortunes of her husband and family. Indeed, this return to happier days only served to awaken fresh memories of the daughter whose loss had marked the beginning of all their troubles. Her one consolation had been that by her death Aoi had been spared the torture which Genji's disgrace and banishment would have inflicted upon her proud and fastidious nature. Now that he was restored to his former glories not even this consideration remained valid. Genji continued to show her the same attentions as before his exile and lost no opportunity of going over to the Great Hall. Yugiri's old nurse and other members of the household had during all these years remained faithfully at their posts, and Genji contrived, in one way and another, to show each of them how much he appreciated her patience and fidelity. The recipients of these small favours were in a state of rapturous gratitude and delight.

He was also deeply touched by the conduct of the gentlewomen at the Nijo-in, in whom he had formerly shown so little interest. He determined henceforward to take more pains about them. He soon found himself so much occupied in paying small attentions to Miss Chujo, Madam Nakatsukasa and other good ladies of his household, that he scarcely ever had time to leave the house. He was also much taken up with the rebuilding of a lodge which stood to the east of his palace, on an estate which had belonged to his father. He took great trouble over the work and had the place put in splendid order, for it was his intention to lend it to unfortunate or unprotected persons, such as the lady at the 'Village of Falling Flowers,' whom he could best assist if he had them near at hand.

Meanwhile he often wondered how the Lady of Akashi was faring, but he was at this time so much occupied both with private and national affairs that he could not get news of her as often as he would have liked to do. He reckoned that her delivery was likely to take place early in the third month, and about that time he contrived to send a secret courier to Akashi and learnt that the event had already taken place sixteen days ago. It was a girl, and everything had gone well. This was Genji's first daughter, and he felt quite excited. But how callous he had been to let her go through all this alone! Why had he not brought her with him to the City and looked after her while this was happening? He felt, indeed, a sudden outburst of tenderness towards her and of remorse at his own hardness of heart.

Astronomers had once told him that he would have three children, of whom the eldest and youngest would eventually ascend the Throne, while the middle one would rise to be Chief Minister. They had further said it would be the lowest-born of the three mothers who would give birth to the future Empress. All that had happened so far fitted in very well with their prognostications. The prophecy that his children would attain Imperial rank and lead the Government of the country had been repeatedly made by sign-readers of all kinds; but during the difficult times from which Genji had just emerged it appeared to be wildly improbable that any of these hopes would be fulfilled. But now the safe accession of Ryozen to the Throne made him feel that everything would happen as the soothsayers had foretold. That he himself was not destined to achieve such honours had been generally recognized and he had long ago given up regarding such a thing as within the bounds of possibility. So well had this been recognized by his father, the old Emperor, that although Genji was his favourite son he had given special instructions that he was to remain a commoner. As regards Ryozen, it was not of course recognized in the world that His Majesty was Genji's son; but that, after all, did not in any way invalidate the truth of the sign-readers' prognostications.

But if this new child were really going to be Empress it seemed almost disrespectful to have allowed her to be born at so strange a place. He must make amends to this future sovereign, and that he might soon be able to lodge both mother and child in proper comfort, he ordered his bailiffs to push through the rebuilding of the eastern lodge as rapidly as possible.

It occurred to him that it would be very difficult for her to secure a suitable wet-nurse at Akashi. He chanced to hear of a young woman, a child of the old Emperor's Lady-in-Attendance, who had recently, under distressing circumstances, been left with an infant on her hands. Both the Lady-in-Attendance and her husband, who had been one of the Royal Chamberlains, were dead, and the girl had been left entirely to her own devices; with the result which I have mentioned above. His informant undertook to interview the girl and, if possible, persuade her to take service at Akashi. She did not in point of fact need very much persuasion. She was young and thoughtless and thoroughly tired of sitting all day in a large tumble-down house with nothing to do but stare in front of her. She could not imagine any service which she would better like to enter than his, and at once agreed to go. Genji was of course delighted; though he felt somewhat uncomfortable at sending away a young girl to a place where she would enjoy so few distractions. There were certain matters which it was necessary to talk over with her, and in complete secrecy, with many precautions against his absence being noticed at home, he contrived to visit the young woman's house. She did not actually withdraw her consent; but she was now feeling very nervous about the whole business. Genji, however, took so much trouble in explaining to her what she had to do and in removing all her doubts and apprehensions that in the end she put herself entirely at his disposal. It happened to be a lucky day, and with many apologies for giving her so little time he asked her to get ready for the journey. 'It seems very hard,' Genji said, 'that you should be packed off to the country like this to look after someone else's child. But I am particularly anxious that someone should be there. I know by experience that it will be rather dull; but you must make up your mind to put up with it for a time, just as I did.' Having thus encouraged her, he gave a detailed description of the place and all that belonged to it.

She had sometimes done service at the Palace and this was not the first time Genji had seen her. But her misfortunes had brought her very low and she looked years older than when he saw her last. The house was in a hopeless state of disrepair and its vast size, together with the carefully planned copses and avenues which surrounded it, made the place only the more depressing. How had she contrived to hold out there so long? His sympathy was aroused. The charm of youth had not after all entirely deserted her, and she was intelligent. He felt inclined to prolong the interview and said laughing:

'Now that it is all arranged I feel quite sorry that you have agreed to go. What do you feel about it?' She felt indeed that if she were destined to enter Genji's service at all, it would have been agreeable to find herself consigned to a rather less remote part of his household. He now recited the verse: 'Can this one moment of farewell indeed have been the sum of all our friendship, whose separation seems now like the parting of familiar friends?' Smiling she answered him: 'Your chagrin, I suspect, is not that I must leave you, but springs from envy that *I* not *you* should go whither your heart is set.' Her quickness delighted him and, whatever truth there may have been in her ironic exposure of his feelings, he was really sorry that she was going.

He sent her as far as the boundary of the City in a wheeled carriage,[4] under the care of his most trusted personal servants, upon whom he had enjoined absolute silence concerning this affair. Among the baggage was a vast number of presents, from the Guardian Sword[5] down to the most trifling articles such as might possibly be useful to the Lady of Akashi at this crisis; upon the young nurse too he lavished every small attention which his ingenuity could devise, determined to mitigate so far as was possible the discomfort of her long journey. It amused him to picture to himself the extravagant fuss which the old priest, at all times so comically preoccupied with his daughter's fortunes, must be making in this latest crisis. Not but what he was himself filled with the tenderest concern for the Lady's welfare. Above all, he must not let her feel at such a minute that there was now or ever could be any obstacle to his fulfilling the promises concerning which she herself had always been so sceptical, and in the letter which he now sent he

---

[4] As opposed to a Sedan-chair. A carriage drawn by oxen is meant; this was a great luxury.

[5] Used at the birth-ceremonies of a princess.

spoke in the most definite manner of his intentions towards the child and his plans for her future life at the Capital.

The travellers proceeded as far as the borders of Settsu by boat, and thence on horseback to Akashi with all possible speed, where their arrival was welcomed by the old recluse with boundless gratitude and delight. With raised hands he solemnly made obeisance in the direction of the Capital, and the mother and child, marked henceforward with this new and unhoped-for sign of princely favour, became invested in his eyes with an almost alarming degree of sanctity. The child was indeed a most exquisite creature, and the young nurse felt, from the moment it was presented to her, that Genji's care and anxiety on its behalf were by no means ill-bestowed. In an instant the discomforts and perils of her long journey seemed like an evil dream, from which she had suddenly awaked to find this pretty and enticing infant lying in her arms. Henceforward she had no thought but how best to tend and succour it.

The mother, it seemed, had for many months past been in very low spirits. Her confinement had left her in a condition of extreme weakness, and she was herself convinced that she would not recover. These fresh tokens of Genji's affection and concern could not fail somewhat to revive her. For the first time she raised her head from the pillows and received the messengers with every sign of interest and delight. They informed her that they had been ordered to return to the Capital without a moment's delay. She contrived to write a few hasty lines, in which little indeed could appear of all that at that moment she was thinking and feeling. Yet these few words made an impression upon their recipient the violence of which surprised and disquieted him.

He had not himself told Murasaki about the birth of his child at Akashi, nor was it likely that anyone else would in so many words have done so. But he feared that some inkling of the matter might reach her, and he finally made up his mind that it would be better for her to know all about it. 'I had far rather that this had not happened. It is all the more irritating because I have for so long been hoping that you would have a child; and that, now the child has come, it should be someone else's instead is very provoking. It is only a girl, you know, which really makes it rather a different matter. It would perhaps have been better from every point of view if I had left things as they were, but this new complication makes that quite impossible. I think, indeed, of sending for the child. I hope that when it arrives you will not feel ill-disposed towards it.' She flushed: 'That is just the sort of thing you always used to say,' she answered. 'It seems to me to show a very strange state of mind. Of course I ought to put up with it, but there are certain things which I do not see how I can be expected to get used to. . . .' 'Softly, softly,' he answered, laughing at her unwonted asperity, 'who is asking you to get used to anything? I will tell you what you are doing. You are inventing all sorts of feelings for me such as I have never really had at all, and then getting cross with me for having them. That is not a very amiable proceeding, is it?' And having gone on in this strain for some while, he became quite cheerful.

She thought of how they had longed for one another during the years of his exile, of his constant letters and messages. This whole affair at Akashi—what had it been but a pastime, a momentary distraction in the midst of his disappointments and troubles? 'You will understand then,' Genji continued, 'that I was anxious to hear how things were going on. I sent to enquire and have just heard that everything is still as well as one can hope for. But if I start telling you about it now I know we shall soon be at cross purposes again. . . .' 'She is of course very charming,' he added presently, 'but I think my feeling for her had a good deal to do with the place and the circumstances. . . .' He began to describe how exquisitely the smoke from the salt-kilns had tapered across the evening sky; he spoke of the poems which they had exchanged, of his first glimpse of her by night, of her delightful playing on the zithern. Upon all these themes he enlarged with evident satisfaction. Murasaki while she listened could not but remember how particularly unhappy she had been just at the very time when the episodes which Genji was now recalling with such relish were taking place at Akashi. Even if this affair were, as he represented it to be, a mere pastime of the moment, it was clear that he had been singularly successful in his search for distraction. 'Come,' he said at last, 'I am doing my best to show you that I am fond of you. You had best be quick, if you are ever going to forgive me at all; life does not last for ever. Here am I trying so hard just now not to give you the slightest cause for one speck of jealousy or suspicion. And now just because of this unfortunate affair . . .' So saying he sent for his large zithern and tried to persuade her to play it with him as they were used to do. But Murasaki could not help remembering his enthusiasm for the playing of the Lady at Akashi. With such virtuosity she did not care to compete, and say what he would he could not persuade her to play a note.

It sometimes happened that her usual good temper and gentleness would thus all at once desert her, giving place to a fit of wild jealousy and resentment. To Genji these outbursts were by no means unattractive.

It occurred to him that the fifth day of the fifth month would be the fiftieth day of the child's life, and he knew that his absence from the Prayers which would be held on that day would be extremely painful to the mother.

If only he had them with him in the Capital, what a delightful affair he could make of this Fiftieth Day Ceremony! It was really too bad that a daughter of his should have come into existence in such an outlandish place as this. He ought never to have allowed it. And this was his first daughter. If it had been a boy he did not think he would have minded nearly so much. But this girl seemed very important, for he felt that in a sense all his misfortunes had come to him as a preliminary to her birth, and had, if one could put it so, no other goal or object. He lost no time in sending a messenger to Akashi with strict injunctions to arrive there on the fifth day without fail. The messenger duly arrived, bearing with him the most touching and gratifying tokens of Genji's anxiety for the welfare of his friends. To the Lady of Akashi he sent an acrostic poem, lamenting that he should have left her to dwell, like the pine-tree that grows beneath the northern cliff, in a place of shadows, to which not even the rejoicings of the Fiftieth Day would bring an altering gleam. 'My anxiety for you both,' his letter continued, 'is becoming too great a torment for me to bear. Things cannot go on like this and I have quite decided to bring you to the Capital. Do not how-ever think that my care for you will end merely with that. . . .' She told her father of Genji's decision, and this time at any rate the old man had good cause for that mixture of joy and weeping to which he was at all times prone. Looking round at Genji's Fiftieth Day pres-ents which lay about in astonishing profusion she real-ized how dark a day this would have been for her but for the coming of this messenger from the City. As a second consolation she had for the first time, in the nurse whom Genji had sent to her, someone to whom she could con-fide the affairs of her heart, and this changed her whole life. Her father had gathered about her, picking them up one by one as opportunity offered, a collection of

dames who, as regards birth and upbringing, were quite
the equals of the new nurse. But the mountain solitudes
of Akashi did not offer much scope for choice and the
poor ladies were one and all the most tottering and
antiquated relics of bygone Courts. Among them the
new arrival felt incredibly brisk and smart and in this
gloomy company her opinion of herself went up by leaps
and bounds. She had endless stories about life at the
Capital; and when these failed, she had only to describe
some occasion at which Genji had figured or some incident showing the affection in which he was held or the
extent of the power which he now wielded (subjects to
which she continually returned with remarkable zest):
at once the Lady of Akashi's cheeks would glow with
pride. She ought indeed to be happy that such a prince
as this should deign even to undo and abandon her,
leaving nothing to show for their love save the child that
had been begotten of it. The nurse was allowed to read
Genji's letters, and though she did so with passionate
interest, she could not but feel somewhat jealous of her
mistress's strange and unforeseen good fortune. At such
times it would seem to the nurse that to her alone of
all mankind nothing good ever happened, till suddenly
in Genji's letter she would come across some reference
to herself: 'What about the nurse? How is she turning
out?' and so forth, or sometimes even more personal
enquiry about her health and spirits. Then for a long
while the girl, usually so despondent, would feel perfectly happy and contented.

To Genji's Fiftieth Day letter the Lady of Akashi sent
the following reply: 'Alas that to the little crane who
calls to you from among the numberless islands of the
deep, you do not come, though the Fiftieth Day[6] be
come.' 'I am for a thousand reasons,' she continued, 'in
great despondency concerning our future; and for that

[6] *Ika*—Fiftieth Day; but also 'Why do you not come?'

very reason occasional kindnesses such as you have to-day shown to me are all the more precious. As for myself I do not rightly know what will become of me. But I earnestly hope that our daughter at any rate may live to be a consolation to you rather than an embarrassment and anxiety.'

Genji carried this letter about with him and constantly re-read it half aloud to himself, pausing over every sentence with fond deliberation; Murasaki could not fail to notice his preoccupation and once, hearing him thus employed, she murmured the song: 'Far from me have you drifted as those boats that, starting from Mikuma shore, now row far out at sea.' She had not meant him to hear. But he looked up and said sharply: 'Do you really think that it is so bad as that! I should have thought you would understand exactly what such a letter as this must mean to me. It is perfectly natural that I should be interested, deeply interested in an occasional budget of news from a place where I spent so long a time, and if in reading it I come across references which remind me suddenly of some interesting event or experience of those days, I think it is quite natural that I should occasionally break out into an exclamation, or something of that sort. It would be much better if you simply pretended not to hear. But here is the letter.' He held it out to her, but in such a way that she could only see the outer fold upon which the address was written. Examining the writing she saw at once that it was a flawless hand, such as the greatest lady in the land would have had no cause to disown. From that moment she knew what was in store for her; this would assuredly prove no fleeting fancy.

In spite of these preoccupations his thoughts sometimes turned towards the lady in the Village of Falling Flowers and he realized with dismay that he had not once been near her since his return to the Capital. For one thing, his new position in the Government had given him so much business to look after and was attended by formalities and restrictions which made it more than ever difficult for him to go about as he chose. Part of the fault however was certainly hers; for, inured to a life that offered few novelties or distractions, she was willing to accept without ill-temper or complaint such treatment as others would have found insufferable. But the fifth month at last brought him a little leisure. Once more he thought of his obligation, and this time he actually managed to slip away and make the long-deferred visit. It was a comfort that here at least he was certain of not being treated to any exhibition of fashionable tantrums, coquettishly withering glances or well-calculated resentment; for he knew that, seldom as she saw him, his interest in her was by far the most important fact in her life, and a visit from him was not lightly to be sacrificed to some useless outburst of jealousy or irritation.

The house had in these last years grown rapidly more and more dilapidated and had indeed become a most melancholy-looking place. After paying his respects to the elder sister he hastened to the main entrance of the western wing and stood in the porch. It was near midnight; the moon had sunk behind a bank of light clouds. It was with feelings of inexpressible joy and agitation that she suddenly saw his figure dimly outlined in the darkness. She had been sitting at the lattice and, in her shyness, did not rise when she saw him. They continued to converse thus, he in the porch and she at her window, but there was in her manner no hint of unfriendliness or reprobation. What a relief to encounter at last a disposition so grateful and unexacting! Some water-fowl were clamouring quite close to the house. She recited the verse: 'Dare I admit you to a house so desolate that even the shy water-birds regard it as their home?' Her voice died away to a whisper as she reached the last words in a way which he found strangely alluring. What a lot of nice people there seemed to be in the world, thought Genji. And the odd part of it was that it was just this very fact which made life so difficult and fatiguing. He answered with the verse: 'If the cry of the water-fowl brings you always so promptly to your door, *some* visitor there must be whom it is your pleasure to admit.' This was of course mere word-play. He did not for a moment suppose that any such agreeable adventures ever fell to her lot; nor indeed that she would welcome them. For though she had had to wait years for this visit, he felt confident that her fidelity had never once wavered. She reminded him of his poem: 'Gaze not into the sky . . .' and of all that had befallen at that farewell scene on the eve of his departure for Suma. 'It seems strange,' she said at last, 'that I of all people should so much have minded your being away, considering how seldom I see you when you are here!' But even this was said with perfect gentleness and good humour. His reply to this charge was, you may be sure, both prompt and conciliatory, and it was not long before he had managed, by kindness of one sort or another, to make her, for the moment at any rate, as happy as it is possible for any woman to be.

He often thought during these days of Lady Gosechi, and would very much have liked to see her again; but the difficulties seemed too great and he did not attempt it. Her parents saw plainly enough that she had not got over her unfortunate attachment and did their best to settle her future in some other way. But she for her part declared she had given up all thought of lovers or marriage. 'If only I had some large convenient building,' thought Genji, 'where I could house these friends of mine and be able to keep an eye not only on them, but on any babies that might chance to get born, how much simpler life would be!' The new eastern wing was indeed promising to prove a very handsome affair and thoroughly in the style of the moment. He was impatient to get it finished, and now appointed special foremen to superintend the different branches of the work and get it put through as quickly as possible.

Not infrequently something would happen to remind him of the Lady Oborozuki and despite all that had happened a fresh wave of longing would beset him. She for her part had not only suffered but learnt her lesson and utterly refused to have any dealings with him, which made him feel very irritated and depressed. Now that the ex-Emperor Suzaku was relieved of the cares of Government, he became somewhat more animated and showed a certain amount of interest in music and other Court diversions. It was curious that among all his Ladies-in-Waiting and Ladies-of-the-Wardrobe it was to Lady Jokyoden, the mother of the Crown Prince, that he paid the least attention. Not even the singular chance which made her mother of the Heir Apparent seemed able to restore to her any particle of the ascendancy which she had lost when Lady Oborozuki was taken into favour. She had indeed left the Emperor's Palace and now lived in apartments attached to those of the Crown Prince, her son. Genji's rooms at Court were in the old Shigeisa; the Crown Prince was occupying the Nashitsubo, which was not far away. Thus Genji, as a near neighbour, was constantly consulted by the prince's staff and was often able to be of considerable assistance to them.

As Fujitsubo had become a nun, her full rank could not be restored; but she received a Royal Grant equivalent to that of an Empress Mother,[7] together with the services of such State officers as usually wait upon an ex-Empress. The whole of these additional resources went in the celebration of those religious functions which

[7] The taxes paid by 2,000 households.

had now become her whole employment in life. For many years she had felt that it was impossible for her to appear at Court and to her great distress her son, the present Emperor, had grown up a stranger to her. Now that he was safely on the Throne she could come and go as she pleased; and indeed her constant presence at Court now became the greatest grievance of her old rival Kokiden, who saw in it the frustration of all the schemes to which her whole life had been devoted. Genji bore Kokiden no malice and, without thrusting his services upon her, did what he could to help her. The fact that these magnanimous overtures were met with unrelenting hostility was observed by all at Court and made a most painful impression.

Prince Hyobukyo had treated Genji with marked coldness in the period before his exile. Now that Genji's fortunes were again on the ascendant he appeared anxious to renew their former friendship; but Genji felt little inclined to do so. That at a time when so many animosities were in abeyance and so many broken friendships had been renewed Genji and her brother should be on these very indifferent terms was to Fujitsubo a source of great disappointment and anxiety.

Power was now pretty equally divided between Genji himself and his father-in-law, the old Minister at the Great Hall. In the eighth month of this year To no Chujo's daughter came to Court. Her grandfather, the old Minister, was a conspicuous figure at the Presentation and saw to it that the ceremony should lack no jot of its traditional grandeur. It was well known that Prince Hyobukyo would very much have liked to see his second daughter in a similar position. But Genji did not feel sufficiently friendly towards him to second this design, particularly as there were many other young ladies who were quite as well qualified to fill the post. Prince Hyobukyo saw nothing for it but to submit.

In the autumn Genji made his pilgrimage to the Shrine of Sumiyoshi, where, as will be remembered, he had various vows to fulfil. The occasion was made one of public importance and the splendour of his cortège, in which all the greatest noblemen and courtiers of the day vied with one another to take part, made a deep impression throughout the kingdom. The Lady of Akashi had been unable to pay her accustomed visit to the Shrine either last autumn or during the spring of this year. She determined to renew the practice, and it so happened that she arrived by boat at Sumiyoshi just as Genji's magnificent procession was passing along the shore. She saw throngs of servitors, laden with costly offerings; she saw the Eastern Dancers,[8] in companies of ten, riding by on horseback, men of picked stature, conspicuous in their strange blue-striped dress. Not a word concerning Genji's visit to Sumiyoshi had reached her, and turning to someone who was standing near she asked what procession this might be. 'What procession?' the man exclaimed in astonishment. 'Why, the Chief Minister's!' and a shout of laughter went up at the notion that there could possibly exist anybody in the world who had not heard of this all-important event, laughter in which a number of rough scallawags who were standing by joined as heartily as the rest.

She was confounded. That after all these long months of waiting it should be thus she met him showed indeed to what a different world he really belonged! Yet after all they were not quite strangers, he and she. She was at least of more account in his eyes than these wretches who had scoffed at her ignorance, than all this rabble who cared nothing for him and had come here only that they might boast of having shared in his triumph. How

---

[8] These men accompanied a Minister of State on pilgrimages to the great Shinto shrines, danced in front of the shrine and afterwards took part in horse-races round it.

cruel an irony that she who thought of him and him only, who painfully gathered together every scrap of intelligence concerning his health and movements, should all unwittingly have chosen this disastrous day for her journey, while all the rest of the world resounded with the news of his coming; she hid her face and wept. The procession moved on its way—innumerable green cloaks, with here and there a scarlet one among them, bright as an autumn maple-tree amid a grove of pines. In cavalcade after cavalcade the varying colours flashed by, now dark, now light.[9] Among the officers of the Sixth Grade there was one whose sheriff's coat of gold and green made him conspicuous; this was Ukon, the gentleman who upon the occasion of Genji's visit to the Imperial Tombs had recited the verse: 'Little, alas, they heed their worshippers. . . .'[10] He had become captain of the Quiver Bearers, and as such was attended by more numerous officers than any other of the sheriffs. Among these attendants was Yoshikiyo, who in a resplendent crimson cloak, worn with an air of the utmost nonchalance, was perhaps the handsomest figure in all the throng.

Here, prosperous and happy, were all the knights and gentlemen whom she had seen at Akashi; then a pitiable band, now scattered amongst a vast cohort of partisans and retainers. The young princes and courtiers who rode with the procession had vied with one another in the magnificence of their accoutrement. Such gorgeous saddles and trappings had rarely been seen; and it may be imagined how they dazzled the eye of a country girl, fresh from her hillside retreat. At last came Genji's coach. She could catch but a momentary glimpse of it; and of the face for which she yearned with so ardent a

[9] The higher officers wore cloaks of deeper hue, i.e. dipped more often in the dye and therefore more costly.
[10] See above, pp. 75–76.

longing she could see nothing at all. Imitating the example of the great Toru[11] he was attended by boy outriders. They were charmingly dressed, their hair looped at the sides and tied with purple ribbons. The ten of them were arranged according to their height, and a very pretty sight they were as they filed past in their dainty costumes. A boy rode by, clad in the dress of a Court page, a person of some consequence evidently, for he was obsequiously watched over and assisted, while a posse of boy grooms, each differently dressed, yet forming between them a carefully designed pattern, rode in his train. She was told that this was Prince Yugiri, Genji's son by Lady Aoi. She thought of her own daughter for whom so different a fate seemed to be reserved, and in sad submission bowed her head towards the Shrine. The governor of the province had now appeared, his arrival being attended by greater pomp than had ever before marked his intercourse with a Minister on pilgrimage. The Lady of Akashi saw clearly that even should she succeed in forcing her way through the crowd, there was little chance that in the midst of all these excitements the God would pay any attention to her insignificant offering. She was on the point of going home again, since there seemed to be no object in staying any longer, when it occurred to her that she might at any rate row over to Naniwa and perform the ceremony of Purification. This she did, while Genji, still unaware that she had been so near him, spent the rest of the evening performing his vows within the Shrine. At last, thinking that by now the God ought to be thoroughly content, Genji determined to enjoy himself a little into the bargain; and the rest of the night was spent by the whole company in the most lively fashion imaginable. Koremitsu and the rest made a mental note

11 For the extravagances of this statesman, see *No Plays of Japan*, p. 293.

that for certain kinds of religious observance there was much to be said. It happened that Genji went outside for a little while and Koremitsu, who was with him, recited an acrostic verse in which he hinted that beneath the pine-trees of Sumiyoshi a less solemn stillness now prevailed than when the Gods first ruled on earth. This could not be denied, and indeed to Genji too a joyful time had succeeded to an age of sadness. He therefore answered with the verse: 'That from wild waves whose onslaught drove me from my course this God delivered me, I shall not soon forget.' Koremitsu then went on to tell him how the boat from Akashi, dismayed by the crowds that flocked the Shrine, had put out again to sea. He hated to think that she had been there without his knowing it; besides, he felt now that it was this very God of Sumiyoshi who had given her to him for a bride. He could not let her go back without a word from him to cheer her. To think that she had come and gone without his even hearing that she was at hand would certainly grieve her worst of all. But for the moment she had gone further up the coast and there was nothing to be done.

After leaving Sumiyoshi he visited several places in the neighbourhood. At Naniwa he too underwent the ceremony of Purification, together with other ceremonies, particularly the Ablution of the Seven Streams. As he passed the estuary of Horiye he murmured, 'Like the tide-gauge at Naniwa . . . ,'[12] hardly knowing why the lines had come into his head. Koremitsu, who was near his coach, overheard these words, and regarding them as a command to him to produce writing materials (a duty for which he was often in request) he whipped out a short-handled pen from the folds of his dress and as soon as Genji's coach came to a standstill

---

[12] 'As to the tide-gauge at Naniwa that now lies bare, so to our love the flood tide shall at last return.'

handed it in to him. Genji was amused by his prompt-
ness and on a folded paper wrote the lines: 'That once
again our love to its flood-mark shall rise, what better
presage than this chance meeting by the tide-gauge of
the shore?' This he sent across to Naniwa by the hand
of an underling who, from conversation with her servants, knew at what address she was to be found. Much
as she had suffered at seeing him pass her by, it needed
only this trifling message to allay all her agitation. In a
flutter of gratitude and pride she indited the answer:
'How comes it[13] that to the least of those who bide as
pilgrims in this town you bear a love that mounts so
high upon the flood-gauge of your heart?' She had that
day been bathing in the Holy Waters at the Shrine of
Rain-coat Island, and she sent him her poem tied to a
prayer-strip which she had brought from the Shrine.
When the message reached Genji it was already growing
dark; the tide was full, and the cranes along the river-
mouth had with one accord set up their strange and
moving cry. Touched by the beauty of the place and
hour, he suddenly lost all patience with the crowds that
surged around him. Could he but banish them all from
his sight and find himself with only the writer of this
diffident poem at his side!

The journey back to the City was enlivened by many
excursions and entertainments, but all the while his
thoughts continually returned to the strange coincidence
of that unhappy meeting. Quantities of dancing-girls
had attached themselves to his retinue. Despite their
total lack of sense or breeding, their company appeared
to afford a vast deal of satisfaction to the hot-blood
young gentlemen who formed Genji's escort. This

---

[13] Pun on Naniwa, name of town and *nani wa* 'How comes
it?' Here and in the preceding poem there is also a play on
miozukushi = tide-gauge, and *mi wo tsukushi* = 'with all
one's heart and soul.'

seemed to him very strange. One cannot enjoy beautiful scenery or works of art in the company of any but the right person; and surely if, in such matters as that, one is so easily put off by commonness or stupidity, it must make some difference *whom* one chooses as partner in these far more intimate associations. He could not indeed contrive to take the slightest interest in these creatures. They on their side quickly perceived that they were not being a success, and at once redoubled their efforts, with the consequence that he found them only the more repulsive.

Next day was marked a 'good day' in the calendar, and Genji's party being safely on its way back to the Capital, the Lady of Akashi was able to return to Sumiyoshi and pursue her devotions in peace, now at last finding occasion to fulfil the many vows that had accumulated since her last visit to the Shrine. Her recent glimpse of Genji in all his glory had but increased the misgivings which day and night beset her: amid such surroundings as that it was impossible that so insignificant a person as herself should not rapidly sink into obscurity and contempt. She did not expect to hear from him again till he was back at Court. She was counting the days, when to her surprise a messenger appeared. In a letter, which had evidently been written during the journey, he named the actual date at which he should send for her to the City. Once more he sought to dispel all her doubts and anxieties; she could rely upon him implicitly; her position in his household would, he besought her to believe, be neither equivocal nor insecure. Nevertheless, she felt that she was embarking upon a perilous voyage under skies which, however promising an aspect they might now be wearing, might at any moment change to the threat of a hideous disaster. Her father too, when it came to the prospect of actually releasing her from his care, was exceedingly perturbed;

indeed he dreaded her departure for the Capital even more than he had feared the prospect of her remaining for ever buried in her rustic home. Her answer to Genji was full of reservations and misgivings concerning her fitness for the position which he promised her.

The retirement of the Emperor Suzaku had necessitated the appointment of a new Vestal at Ise, and Lady Rokujo had brought her daughter back again to the City. Genji had written the usual congratulations and this had given her immense pleasure; but she had no desire to give him the opportunity of once more distracting her as he had done in those old days, and she had answered only in the most formal terms. Consequently he had not, since her return, made any attempt to visit her. He did indeed make some vague suggestion of a meeting; but these hints were very half-hearted and it was a relief to him that they were not taken. He had recently decided not to complicate his life by outside relationships even of the most harmless kind: he simply had not time. And particularly in a case of this sort he saw no object in forcing his society upon someone who did not desire it. He was however extremely curious to see how the Vestal Virgin, now known as Lady Akikonomu, had grown up. Rokujo's old palace in the Sixth Ward had been admirably repaired and redecorated, and life there was in these days by no means intolerable. Rokujo herself had gifts of character and intelligence which the passage of years had not obliterated. Her own personality and the unusual beauty of many of her gentlewomen combined to make her house a meeting place for men of fashion, and though she was herself at times very lonely, she was leading a life with which she was on the whole by no means ill-contented, when her health gave way. She felt at once that there was no hope for her, and oppressed by the thought that she had for so long been living in a sinful place,[14] she resolved to become a nun. This news was a great blow to Genji. That he would ever again meet her as a lover, he had long felt to be impossible. But he thought of her as a friend whose company and conversation would always be among his greatest pleasures. That she should have felt it necessary to take this solemn and irrevocable step was a terrible shock, and on hearing what had happened he at once hastened to her palace. It proved to be a most harrowing visit. He found her in a state of complete collapse. Screens surrounded her bed; his chair was placed outside them, as near as possible to her pillow, and in this manner they conversed. It was evident that her strength was rapidly failing. How bitterly he now repented that he had not come to her sooner; had not proved, while yet there was time, that his passion for her had never expired! He wept bitterly, and Rokujo on her side, amazed to realize from the very intensity of his grief that during all the years when she had imagined herself to be forgotten, she had never been wholly absent from his thoughts, in a moment discarded all her bitterness, and seeing that his distress was unendurable began with the utmost tenderness to lead his thoughts to other matters. She spoke after a while about her daughter, Lady Akikonomu, the former Virgin of Ise, begging him to help her on in the world in any way he could. 'I had hoped,' she said, 'having cast the cares of the world aside, to live on quietly at any rate until this child of mine should have reached an age when she could take her life into her own hands. . . .' Her voice died away. 'Even if you had not mentioned it, I should always have done what I could to help her,' answered Genji, 'but now that you have made this formal request to me, you may be sure that I shall make it my business to look after her and protect her in every way that lies in my power. You need have no

[14] A Shinto shrine, offensive to Buddha.

further anxiety on that score. . . .' 'It will not be so easy,' she answered. 'Even a girl whose welfare has been the sole object of devoted parents often finds herself in a very difficult position if her mother dies and she has only her father to rely upon. But your task will, I fear, be far harder than that of a widowed father. Any kindness that you show the girl will at once be misinterpreted; she will be mixed up in all sorts of unpleasant bickerings and all your own friends will be set against her. And this brings me to a matter which is really very difficult to speak about. I wish I were so sure in my own mind that you would *not* make love to her. Had she my experience, I should have no fear for her. But unfortunately she is utterly ignorant and indeed is just the sort of person who might easily suffer unspeakable torment through finding herself in such a position. I cannot help wishing that I could provide for her future in some way that was not fraught with this particular danger. . . .' What an extraordinary notion, thought Genji. How could she have got such a thing into her head? 'You are thinking of me as I was years ago,' he answered quickly. 'I have changed a great deal since then, as you would soon discover if you knew more about me. . . .'

Out of doors it was now quite dark. The room where he was sitting was lit only by the dim glow that, interrupted by many partitions, filtered through from the great lamp in the hall. Someone had entered the room. He peeped cautiously through a tear in one of the screens which surrounded the bed. In the very uncertain light he could just distinguish Rokujo's form. Her hair was cropped, as is customary with novices before the final tonsure; but elegantly and with taste, so that her head, outlined against the pillows, made a delicate and charming picture. On the far side of the bed he could distinguish a second figure. This surely must be Lady

Akikonomu. There was a point at which the screens had
been carelessly joined, and looking through this gap he
saw a young girl sitting in an attitude of deep dejection
with her chin resting on her hand. So far as he could
judge from this very imperfect view she was exceedingly
good-looking. Her hair that hung loose to the ground,
the carriage of her head, her movements and expression
—all had a singular dignity and grace; yet despite this
proud air there was something about her affectionate,
almost appealing. But was he not already beginning to
take just that interest in her person against which her
mother had a few moments ago been warning him? He
hastily corrected his thoughts. Lady Rokujo now spoke
again: 'I am in great pain,' she said, 'and fear that at
any moment my end may come. I would not have you
witness my last agonies. Pray leave me at once.' This
she said with great difficulty, her women supporting her
on either side. 'How glad I should have been,' said Genji,
'if my visit had made you better. I am afraid it has
only made you worse. I cannot bear to leave you in such
pain. Tell me what it is that hurts so much?' And so
saying he made as though to come to her side. 'Do not
come to me!' she cried out in terror, 'I am grown hideous;
you would not know me. Does what I say seem to you
very strange and disjointed? It may be that my thoughts
wander a little, for I am dying. Thank you for bearing
patiently with me at such a time. I am much easier in
my mind now that I have had this talk with you. I had
meant to for a long time. . . .' 'I am touched,' replied
Genji, 'that you should have thought of me as a person
to whom you could confide these requests. As you know,
my father the late Emperor had a very large number of
sons and daughters; for my part, I am not very intimate
with any of them. But, when his brother died, he also
regarded Lady Akikonomu here as though she were his
own child and for that reason I have every right to

regard her as my sister and help her in just those ways which a brother might. It is true that I am a great deal older than she is; but my own family is sadly small,[15] and I could well afford to have someone else to look after. . . .'

After his return he sent incessantly to enquire after her progress and constantly wrote to her. She died some eight days later. He was deeply distressed, for a long while took no interest in anything that happened and had not the heart to go even so far as the Emperor's Palace. The arrangements concerning her funeral and many other matters about which she had left behind instructions fell entirely upon him, for there was no one else to whom her people could apply. Fortunately the officers who had been attached to Lady Akikonomu's suite while she was at Ise still remained in her service and they were able to give her a certain amount of assistance. Before the funeral Genji called in person and sent in a note to the bereaved lady of the house. A housekeeper (one of the people from Ise) brought back word that her mistress was completely overwhelmed by her loss and could not reply to him. He sent in a second message reminding Lady Akikonomu that her mother had solemnly committed her to his care and begging her not to regard him as an alien intruder into her affairs. He then sent for the various members of the household and gave them their instructions. He did so with an air of confidence and authority which surprised those who remembered for how long he had absented himself from that house. The funeral was carried out with the utmost pomp, the bier being attended not only by her servants, but by all Genji's servants and retainers.

For a long while afterwards he was immersed in prayers and penances and but seldom emerged from the seclusion of a thickly curtained recess. To Lady Aki-

15 Aoi's son Yugiri was his only acknowledged child.

konomu he sent many messages of enquiry, to which she
now answered in her own hand. She had at first been
too shy to do so; much to the dismay of her old nurse,
who explained to her that not to answer letters is considered very uncivil. One day as he sat watching the
wild storms of sleet and snow that were sweeping in a
confused blizzard across the land, he could not help
wondering how Lady Akikonomu was faring in this
rough weather and sent a messenger to her palace. 'I
wonder how you like this storm,' he wrote, and added
the poem: 'I see a house of mourning; dark tempests
threaten it, and high amid the clouds hovers a ghost with
anxious wing.' It was written on light blue paper tinged
with grey; the penmanship and make-up of the note
were indeed purposely intended to be such as would
impress a young girl. So much did this elegant missive
dazzle her inexperienced eye that she again felt utterly
unable to reply, and it was only when one member of
her household after another reproached her for such
rudeness and ingratitude that she at last took up a sheet
of heavily scented dark grey paper and in brush-strokes
so faint as to be scarcely distinguishable wrote the poem:
'Would that like the snowflakes when they are weary
of falling I might sink down upon the earth and end my
days.' There was nothing very remarkable about the
writing, but it was an agreeable hand and one which
bore unmistakable traces of the writer's lineage. He had
formed a high opinion of her at the time when she first
went to Ise and had very much regretted her withdrawal from the world. Now she was an ordinary person again, and, if he wished to cultivate her acquaintance, entirely at his disposal; but this very fact (as was
usual with him) caused a revulsion of feeling. To go
forward in the direction where fewest obstacles existed
seemed to him to be taking a mean advantage. Although
he was, in his attentions to Lady Akikonomu, merely

fulfilling her mother's request, he knew quite well how everyone at Court was expecting the story to end. Well, for once in a way their expectations would be disappointed. He was fully determined to bring her up with the utmost propriety and, so soon as the Emperor reached years of discretion, to present her at Court; in fact, to adopt her as his daughter—a thing which, considering the smallness of his family, it was natural for him to do. He constantly wrote her letters full of kindness and encouragement, and occasionally called at her palace. 'What I should really like,' he said one day, 'would be for you to look upon me, if you will forgive my putting it in that way, as a substitute for your dear mother. Can you not sometimes treat me as though I were an old friend? Can you not trust me with some of the secrets you used to confide to her?' Such appeals merely embarrassed her. She had lived so secluded a life that to open her mouth at all in a stranger's presence seemed to her a terrible ordeal, and her gentlewomen were in the end obliged to make such amends as they could. It was a comfort that many of her officers and gentlewomen were closely connected with the Imperial Family and would, if his project for installing her in the Palace did not come to naught, be able to help her to assert herself. He would have been glad to know more about her appearance, but she always received him from behind her curtains, and he neither felt justified in taking the liberties that are accorded to a parent nor did he feel quite sure enough of himself to wish to put his parental feelings to the test. He was indeed very uncertain with regard to his own intentions, and for the present mentioned his plans about her to nobody. He saw to it that the Memorial Service was carried out with great splendour, devoting to the arrangement of it a care that deeply gratified the bereaved household. Life there was becoming more and more featureless and depressing

as the weeks went by. One by one Lady Akikonomu's
servants and retainers were finding other employment.
The Palace stood at the extreme outer edge of the Sixth
Ward, in a district which was very little frequented, and
the melancholy bells which went on tolling and tolling
in innumerable adjacent temples reduced her every
evening to a state of abject misery. She had always been
used to spend a great deal of time in her mother's company, and even when she was sent to Ise, though no
parent had ever before accompanied the Vestal Virgin,
they still remained unseparated. It can be imagined then
that her mother's loss left her peculiarly helpless and
desolate; and the thought that Rokujo, who had travelled so far for her sake, should now set out upon this
last journey all alone, caused her unspeakable pain.
Many suitors both high and low, under cover of paying
attentions to one or other of her gentlewomen, now began to frequent the house. Genji however had in his best
fatherly style exacted a promise from the lady's old nurse
that she would allow no matchmaking to go on in the
house. Above all he feared that some of her women
might wish for their own ends to keep these gentlemen
hanging about the premises. It soon however became
apparent that there was no danger of this. The ladies
concerned knew that their doings would probably reach
Genji's ears, and they were far too anxious to stand well
with him to dream of abusing their position. The suitors
soon found that their advances were not met with the
slightest encouragement.

It will be remembered that at the time of Lady
Akikonomu's departure for Ise the retired Emperor Suzaku had, when presiding at the magnificent farewell
ceremony in the Daigoku Hall, been greatly struck with
her beauty. This impression had remained with him,
and on her return to the Capital he begged Rokujo to
let her daughter come to him, promising that she should

take her place as the equal of his sister, the former Vestal of Kamo, and the other princesses, his sisters and kinswomen whom he sheltered under his roof. This proposal did not please her. She feared that where so many exalted personages were gathered together her daughter would be likely to receive but scant attention. Moreover Suzaku was at the time in very bad health, and if he should fail to recover, his dependants might be left in a precarious position. Now that her mother was dead it was all the more desirable to establish her in a manner which offered some prospect of security. When therefore Suzaku repeated his invitation, this time in somewhat insistent terms, Lady Akikonomu's friends were placed in an awkward position. Genji's private plan of affiancing her to the boy-Emperor would, now that Suzaku had displayed so marked an inclination towards her, be difficult to pursue without too deeply offending his brother. Another consideration weighed with him: he was becoming more and more fascinated by the girl's beauty and he was in no hurry to commit her to other hands. Under the circumstances he thought the best thing he could do was to talk the matter over with Lady Fujitsubo. 'I am in great difficulties over this business,' he said. 'As you know, the girl's mother was a woman of singularly proud and sensitive temperament. I am ashamed to say that, following my own wanton and selfish inclinations, I behaved in such a way as to do great injury to her reputation, with the consequence that henceforward she on her side harboured against me a passionate resentment, while I on mine found myself branded not only by her but also by the world at large as a profligate and scamp. Till the very last I was never able to recover her confidence; but on her death-bed she spoke to me of Akikonomu's future in a way which she would never have done had she not wholly regained her good opinion of me. This was a great weight off my

mind. Even had these peculiar relations not existed between us, her request was one which even to a stranger
I could hardly have refused. And as it was, you may
imagine how gladly I welcomed this chance of repairing,
even at this late hour, the grievous wrong which my
light-mindedness had inflicted upon her during her lifetime. His Majesty is of course many years younger than
Akikonomu;[16] but I do not think it would be a bad
thing if he had some older and more experienced person
in his entourage. However, it is for you to decide. . . .'
'I am of the same opinion,' Fujitsubo replied. 'It would
of course be very imprudent to offend the retired Emperor. But surely the mother's wishes are a sufficient
excuse. If I were you I should pretend you know nothing
about the retired Emperor's inclination towards her and
present her at the Palace without more ado. As a matter
of fact, Suzaku now cares very little about such matters.
What energy he still possesses is spent on prayers and
meditation. I do not think you will find that he minds
very much one way or the other. . . .' 'All the same,
I think it will be best under the circumstances if the
request for Akikonomu's Presentation came from you,'
said Genji. 'I could then seem merely to be adding my
solicitations to yours. You will think that in weighing the
pros and cons of the matter with such care I am over-
scrupulous; and indeed I fear that you have found me
rather tedious. It is simply that I am extremely anxious
people should not think me lacking in respect towards
my brother. . . .' It soon became apparent that, in ac-
cordance with Fujitsubo's advice, he had decided to
disregard the retired Emperor's wishes. But it was in
Genji's own palace and not, for the moment at any rate,
in the Emperor's household that Lady Akikonomu was
to be installed. He explained the circumstances to

[16] Akikonomu was now nineteen; the boy-Emperor Ryozen,
seven.

Murasaki. 'She is just about your age,' he said, 'and you will find her a very agreeable companion. I think you will get on famously together. . . .' Murasaki at once took to the idea and was soon busy with preparations for the reception of the visitor.

Fujitsubo was all this while extremely exercised in mind concerning the future of her niece, the youngest daughter of Prince Hyobukyo, for Genji's estrangement from the father seemed to block every avenue of advancement. To no Chujo's daughter, as the grandchild of the Senior Minister, was treated on all sides with the utmost deference and consideration, and she had now become the Emperor's favourite playmate. 'My brother's little girl is just the same age as the Emperor,' said Fujitsubo one day; 'he would enjoy having her to play at dolls with him sometimes, and it would be a help to the older people who are looking after him.' But quite apart from affairs of state, Genji had (as Fujitsubo knew) such a multiplicity of private matters to attend to and was plagued from morning till night by such a variety of irritating applications and requests that she had not the heart to keep on bothering him. It was something that a person like Lady Akikonomu would soon be at the Emperor's side; for Fujitsubo herself was in very poor health and, though she sometimes visited the Palace, she could not look after her son's education as she would have liked to do. It was necessary that there should be someone grown-up to keep an eye on him, and though she would dearly like to have seen her niece installed as his playmate, she was extremely glad of the arrangement whereby a sensible creature like Lady Akikonomu was to have him in her constant care.

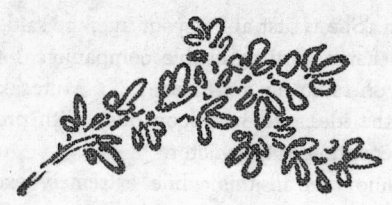

Chapter VI

THE PALACE IN THE
TANGLED WOODS

While Genji, like Yukihira of old, 'dragged his leaky
pails' along the shore of Suma, his absence had been
mourned, in varying ways and degrees, by a very large
number of persons in the Capital. Even those who stood
in no need of patronage or protection and had through
his departure lost only the amenities of a charming
friendship were deeply distressed. For some of them,
such as Murasaki, this sad time was mitigated by constant messages from his place of exile; some were privi-
leged to busy their needles upon such garments as his
altered state prescribed, or were allowed the consolation
of rendering him other small services such as in his present difficulties he was likely to require. But there were
others who, though they had received his favours, had
done so unknown to the world, and these ladies now
learned of Genji's last hours at the Capital from the
casual gossip of some friend who had no idea that the
matter was of any particular concern to them. Needless
to say they feigned a like indifference; but such concealment costs one dear and not a few hearts were broken in
the process.

Among those who fared worst during his absence was

the lady at the Hitachi Palace.[1] During the period after her father's death there had been no one to take care of her and she had for a while led a very wretched existence. But then came the unexpected apparition of Genji. His letters and visits, which to him in the crowded days of his glory were insignificant acts of courtesy, implying no more than a very mild degree of interest and affection, were to their recipient, with her narrow and unvarying life, like the reflection of a star when it chances to fall into a bowl of water. It was but natural, she thought, that when the outcry against him began Genji should no longer find time for an attachment which had in any case played only a very subordinate part in his life, particularly as the attacks upon him were part of a widespread movement which could not but be causing him the greatest anxiety. Then came his exile and at last his triumphant return. But still she heard no word from him.

In old days when she heard nothing from him for a week or two she would become a little tearful it is true, but she still managed to carry on her ordinary existence. Now months, years had passed; long ago she had given up all hope, and sank into a condition of settled apathy and gloom. 'Poor princess!' said the elderly gentlewomen who waited upon her. 'Really she has had the worst possible luck! To see this glorious apparition suddenly descending upon her like a God or Buddha out of the sky—not that he meant very much by it; but she, poor lady, could never get over the surprise of his noticing her at all—and then for him to disappear without a word! She knows of course that it is not from her that he has run away to Suma; it all comes of this new government! But still, one cannot help being very sorry for the poor young creature.' She had indeed during the time after

[1] Suyetsumuhana. See Part I, ch. 6. I shall henceforward call her Suyetsumu.

her father's death become gradually inured to a life of extreme monotony and isolation; but Genji's visits had awakened in her quite new ambitions; for the first time in her life she began to feel herself drawn towards the world of taste and fashion. This made her renewed state of poverty and isolation all the more difficult to bear. The fact that Genji frequented the house had for the time being induced a certain number of other visitors to present themselves. But since his departure one visitor after another, having grown more and more remiss in his attentions, finally ceased to come at all. Her father's ladies-in-waiting were all very advanced in years and every now and then one of them would die; the other servants, both indoors and out, were continually seeking better service, and hardly a month passed but some member of her staff either died or drifted away. The palace grounds, which had for long years past been allowed to sink into a sad state of neglect, had now become a mere jungle. Foxes had made their lairs in the garden walks, while from the ornamental plantations, now grown into dank and forbidding woods, the voice of the screech-owl sounded day and night alike; so little was there now any sign of human habitation in that place, so dim was the daylight that pierced those tangled thickets. The few servants who still lingered on in the midst of all this desolation began to declare that tree-spirits and other fearsome monsters had established themselves in the palace grounds and were every day becoming more open and venturesome in their habits. 'There is no sense in continuing to live like this,' one of these ladies said. 'Nowadays all the government officials are building themselves handsome houses. Several of them have for a long time past had their eye on all your timber and have been making enquiries in the neighbourhood whether you might not be prevailed upon to part with it. If only you would consent to do so, you might with the proceeds easily buy some newer place that would be less depressing to live in. You are really asking too much of the few servants that remain with you. . . .' 'Hush, how can you suggest such a thing!' answered the princess. 'What would people think if they heard you? So long as I am alive no such disrespect to my poor father's memory shall ever be committed. I know quite well that the grounds have become rather wild and dismal; but this was his home, his dear spirit haunts the place, and I feel that so long as I am here I am never far off from him. That has become my only comfort. . . .' She broke off in tears, and it was impossible to allude to the subject again. Her furniture too, though entirely out of fashion, was much of it very beautiful in an old-world way, and enquiries were constantly coming from those who made it their business to understand such matters and had heard that she possessed a work by such and such a master of some particular time and school. Such proposals she regarded merely as an ill-bred comment upon her poverty and indeed complained of them bitterly to the aforementioned gentlewoman. 'But, madam,' the lady protested, 'it is not at all an unusual thing. . . .' And to convince her mistress that funds must somehow or other be procured she began to call her attention to various dilapidations, the repair of which could not safely be deferred for a single day. But it made no difference. The idea of selling any of her possessions seemed to the princess utterly untenable. 'If he had not meant me to keep them, he would not have put them here,' she said; 'I cannot bear to think of them becoming ornaments in ordinary, worldly people's houses. I do not think he would wish me to . . . ,' and that was all that could be got out of her.

Visitors and even letters were now absolutely unknown at the Hitachi Palace. True, her elder brother the Zen priest on the rare occasions when he came up to the

Capital, usually visited the palace. But he did little more than poke his head in and go away. He was a particularly vague and unpractical sort of man, who even among his fellow clerics ranked as unusually detached from all worldly considerations. In fact he was a saint, and consequently very unlikely to notice that the whole place was overgrown with weeds and bushes, still less to suggest any means of clearing them away.

Meanwhile, the state of affairs was becoming very acute. The once elegant courtyard was thickly overgrown with weeds; the lusty hemlock clumps were fast destroying the gables and eaves of the roof. The main eastern and western gates of the park were barricaded by huge masses of mugwort and it was impossible to open them. This might have given the inhabitants of the palace a certain comforting sense of security, had it not been for the fact that the walls which surrounded the estate were everywhere either broken down or upon the point of falling. Horse and oxen from the neighbouring pastures soon found their way through these gaps, and when the summer came they began to make free with the palace lawns in a way which scandalized the little herd-boys who were in charge of them. At the time of the autumn equinox there were very heavy gales, and one day the main roof of the servants' wing was blown right away, leaving only a ceiling of thin match-boarding, a mere shell, which would not have withstood the mildest shower of rain. At this the underservants left in a body. Henceforward the few inhabitants of the palace led a pitiable existence, not even getting enough to eat, for there was no one to make up the fires or prepare their food. Thieves and vagabonds had the place completely at their mercy; but fortunately it never occurred to them to go near it. How could so desolate a ruin contain anything worth meddling with? They shook their heads and trudged on. But strangely enough, had he penetrated those savage thickets, an enterprising burglar would have found, amid a tangled mass of wreckage, a drawing-room[2] perfectly appointed in every detail, each ornament, each screen and article of furniture still standing exactly where the late prince had left it. True, there was no longer anyone to dust this last-surviving room, and it needed dusting badly. Never mind, it was a real room; not just a living-place, but a noble apartment with everything in it handsome and dignified just as it ought to be. And here, year in and year out, her whole life was spent.

Solitary people with a great deal of time on their hands seem usually to turn to old ballads and romances for amusement and distraction, but for such employments the princess showed little inclination. Even in the lives of those who have no particular interest in poetry there are usually periods of inactivity during which they take to exchanging verses with some sympathetic correspondent—verses which, if they are young, generally contain affecting references to various kinds of plant and tree. But the princess's father had imbued her with the belief that all outward display of emotion is undignified and ill-bred; she felt that what he would really have liked best would have been for her to communicate with no one at all, and she had long given up writing even to the few relations with whom she might have been expected occasionally to correspond.

At rare intervals she would open an old-fashioned chest and fiddle for a while with a number of ancient picture-scrolls, illustrations of such stories as *The Chinese Prefect, The Mistress of Hakoya, Princess Kaguya*[3]

[2] Such a term must only be taken as a rough equivalent.
[3] Of these three romances the first is quite unknown; the second must have been a Taoist fairy story, for 'Hakoya' is the 'Miao-ku-she' of Chuang Tzu, Chapter I—a divine mountain inhabited by mysterious sages. The third is either identical with the *Taketori Monogatari* ('The Bamboo-Cutter's Story') or at any rate treated the same theme.

and the like. Then there were some poems which, though all of very ancient date, were excellently chosen, with the names of the poets and the titles of the poems written in a nice clear hand at the side, so that one could really tell what one was reading. They were written on the best Kanya and Michinoku papers, now grown somewhat puffy with age,[4] and though it cannot be supposed that she could derive much pleasure from reading the same familiar pages over and over again, yet it was noticed that in her hours of deepest depression she would often sit with the books spread open before her. As for reading the Sutras or performing those Buddhist ceremonies which have now become so indispensable an element in fashionable life, she would have shuddered at the thought, and would not have dreamed of so much as touching a rosary, even though no one was there to see. Such was the arduous standard of conduct which this lady imposed upon herself.

Of her old servants only Jiju, the daughter of her foster-nurse, had survived the general exodus of the last few years. Jiju's friend, the former Vestal of Kamo, whose company had been one of her distractions, was dead, and the poor lady's existence had become such as no one could reasonably be expected to endure. A sister of the princess's mother had fallen on evil days and ended by marrying a provincial official. She now lived at the Capital, and as she had daughters, together with a bevy of unusually agreeable young waiting-women, Jiju occasionally visited the house, where indeed she was quite at home, for both her parents had been friends of the family. But the princess herself, with her usual unsociability, absolutely refused to hold any communication

---

[4] Kanya River ('Paper-makers' River') is between Hirano and Kitano, near Kyoto. Michinoku paper, from the province of that name, was made of spindle-wood. These stout Japanese papers become thick and fluffy with age.

with her aunt's household. 'I am afraid the princess looks upon me as a very vulgar person,' the aunt said to Jiju one day. 'She still thinks, despite the wretched manner in which she now lives, that to have such relations as we is a disgrace to her. At any rate I suppose that is why she is so careful never to come near us.' It was in this somewhat malicious tone that she always discussed her niece's behaviour.

I have noticed that people of quite common origin who have risen in the world can in a very short time achieve a perfect imitation of aristocratic importance. And similarly, if through some accident an aristocrat falls into low company, he generally exhibits a meanness so thorough-going that it is hard to believe he has been at any pains to acquire it. Of this second tendency the princess's aunt was a good example. She knew that after her unfortunate marriage the people at the Hitachi Palace had regarded her as a disgrace to the family. Now that the prince was dead and Suyetsumu herself was in circumstances of such difficulty, there seemed to be quite a good chance that the princess might eventually have to take shelter under her aunt's roof. This was what the aunt herself was looking forward to. It was her revenge. She saw the princess installed as a dependant, fetching and carrying for her daughters. And what an ideal drudge she would make, being so priggish and strait-laced that it would never be necessary to keep an eye upon her! 'You ought to bring her round to see us sometimes,' the aunt would say to Jiju, 'and if you could get her to bring her zithern, so much the better; we have heard so much about her playing.' Jiju did her best, and the princess, docile as usual, admitted that there was everything to be said in favour of paying an occasional visit. But when it came to the point, panic overwhelmed her. She would do anything, anything that Jiju asked; but she would not make friends.

And so, greatly to the aunt's discomfiture, the matter was dropped.

About this time her uncle was appointed treasurer to a provincial district. He intended to take his family with him, and was anxious to equip his daughters with attendants whom it would be pleasant to name in the ears of provincial visitors. The chance of being able to exhibit a real princess as a member of their staff was not to be thrown away and the aunt returned once more to the attack. 'I am very worried at having to go so far away from you,' she sent word by Jijū. 'We have not had the pleasure of seeing you much lately; but it was a great comfort to me to feel that I was near at hand and could help you if anything went wrong. I am most anxious that, if possible, we should not be separated. . . .' All this had no effect whatever. 'The conceited little fool! I have no patience with her,' the aunt cried out at last. 'She may have these grand ideas about herself if she chooses; but no one else is going to take much notice of a creature that goes on year after year living in the hole-and-corner way that she does; least of all this famous Prince Genji, with whom she pretends to be so intimate.'

At last came Genji's pardon and recall, celebrated in every part of the kingdom by riotous holiday-making and rejoicing. His friends of either sex were soon vying with one another in demonstrations of good will and affection. These testimonies to his popularity, pouring in from persons of every rank and condition in life, naturally touched him deeply, and in these stirring days it would have been strange indeed if many minor affairs had not escaped his memory. But for her the time of his restoration was far harder to bear than that of his exile. For whereas she had before confidently looked forward to his return, counting upon it as we count upon the winter trees to bud again in spring, this glorious home-coming and restoration, when at last they came, brought joy to every hut and hovel in the land, but to her only a hundredfold increase of her former misery. For of what comfort to her were his triumphs, if she must hear of them from other lips?

The aunt had the satisfaction of seeing her prophecies fulfilled. It was of course out of the question that anyone would own to an acquaintance with a person living in such miserable squalor as now surrounded the princess. There are those, says the *Hokkekyo*,[5] whom even Buddha and his saints would have hard work to redeem; and certainly this lady had allowed her affairs to drift into a disorder which the most generous patron would shrink from attempting to set straight. This contempt for all the rest of the world, this almost savage unsociability, was of course no invention of her own; it was merely an attempt to perpetuate the haughty demeanour of the late prince and princess, her parents. But this did not make the young princess's attitude any less irritating and ridiculous. 'There is still time to change your mind,' said her aunt one day. 'A change of scene— a journey through the mountains, for example, is often very beneficial to people who have some trouble on their minds. I am sure you think that life in the provinces is very uncomfortable and disagreeable, but I can assure you that while you are with us you will never have to stay anywhere quite so higgledy-piggledy. . . .' The wretched old women who still dragged on their existence in the palace eagerly watched the princess's face while their fate was being decided. Surely she would not throw away this opportunity of escape! To their consternation they soon saw that her aunt's appeal was not making the slightest impression upon her. Jiju, for her part, had recently become engaged to a young cousin of the provincial treasurer's, who was to accompany him

[5] *The Saddharmapundarika Sutra.*

to his province, and she was therefore pledged to go down to Tsukushi, whether the princess joined the party or not. She was however deeply attached to her mistress and very loath indeed to leave her in her present condition. She therefore discussed the matter with her again, and did everything in her power to persuade the princess to accompany them; only to make the extraordinary discovery that Suyetsumu was still from day to day living in the hope that the visitor from whom she had for all those years had no word would suddenly reappear and put everything to rights again. 'He was very fond of me,' she said. 'It is only because he has been unhappy himself that he has not remembered to write to me. If he had the slightest idea of what is happening to us here, he would come at once. . . .' So she had been thinking for years, and though the general structure of the house fell every day into a more fantastic state of dilapidation, she still persisted as obstinately as ever in retaining every trifling article of furniture and decoration in exactly the place where it had always been. She spent so much of her time in tears that a certain part of her face had now become as red as the flower which the hillman carries over his ear; so that her appearance, particularly when she showed her face in profile, would have struck a casual visitor as somewhat forbidding. But of this I will say no more; it is perhaps always a mistake to enter into matters of that kind.

As the cold weather came on, existence at the Hitachi Palace rapidly became more and more difficult. The princess sat staring in front of her, plunged in unbroken gloom. Meanwhile Genji celebrated the ritual of the Eight Readings, in memory of his father, the old Emperor. He took great trouble in choosing the priests for this ceremony and succeeded finally in assembling a notable band of dignitaries. Among them none was more renowned for the sanctity of his life and the wide range

of his studies than Princess Suyetsumu's brother, the
Abbot of Daigoji. On his way back from the ceremony,
he looked in for a moment at the Hitachi Palace. 'I have
just been celebrating the Eight Readings in Prince
Genji's palace,' he said; 'a magnificent ceremony! It is a
pleasure to take part in such a service as that! I cannot
imagine anything more beautiful and impressive. A
veritable paradise—I say it in all reverence—a veritable
paradise on earth; and the prince himself, so calm and
dignified, you might have thought him an incarnation
of some holy Buddha or Bodhisat. How came so bright
a being to be born into this dim world of ours?' So saying, he hurried off to his temple. Unlike ordinary,
worldly men and women he never wasted time in discussing sordid everyday affairs or gossiping about other
people's business. Consequently he made no allusion to
the embarrassed circumstances in which his sister was
living. She sometimes wondered whether even the Saints
whom he worshipped would, if they had found someone
in a like situation, really have succeeded in behaving
with so splendid an indifference.

She was indeed beginning to feel that she could hold
out no longer, when one day her aunt suddenly arrived
at the palace. This lady was quite prepared to meet with
the usual rebuffs; but having on this occasion come in
a comfortable travelling coach stored with everything
that the princess could need during a journey she did
not for an instant doubt that she would gain her point.
With an air of complete self-confidence she bustled towards the front gate. No sooner had the porter begun
trying to open it than she realized into what a pitch of
decay her niece's property had fallen. The doors were
off their hinges, and as soon as they were moved tottered
over sideways, and it was not till her own men-servants
came to the rescue that, after a tremendous shouldering
and hoisting, a passage was cleared through which she

could enter the grounds. What did one do next? Even such a heap of gimcrack ruins as this presumably had some apertures which were conventionally recognized as doors and windows. A lattice door on the southern side of the house was half open and here the visitors halted. It did not seem possible that any human being was within hail; but to their astonishment, from behind a smoke-stained, tattered screen-of-state the maid Jiju suddenly appeared. She was looking very haggard, but though age and suffering had greatly changed her, she was still a well-made, pleasing woman; 'at any rate far more presentable than her mistress,' thought the visitors. 'We are just starting,' cried out the aunt to the lady of the house, who, as she guessed, was seated behind this sooty screen: 'I have come to take Jiju away. I am afraid you will find it very difficult to get on without her, but even if you will not deign to have any dealings with us yourself, I am sure you will not be so inconsiderate as to stand in this poor creature's way. . . .' She put in so moving a plea on behalf of Jiju that there ought by rights to have been tears in her eyes. But she was in such high spirits at the prospect of travelling as a provincial governor's wife that a smile of pleasant anticipation played upon her lips all the while. 'I know quite well,' she continued, 'that the late prince was not at all proud of his connection with us, and I am sure it was quite natural that when you were a child you should pick up his way of thinking and feeling. But that is a long time ago now. You may say that it was my fault we did not meet. But really while celebrities such as Prince Genji were frequenting the house I was not at all sure that humble people like ourselves would be welcome. However, one of the advantages of being of no importance is that we humdrum creatures are not subject to the same violent ups and downs as you exalted people. I for my part was very sorry to see your fortunes declining so rapidly as they have done of late, but so long as I was near at hand I was quite happy about you and did not consider it my duty to interfere. But now that I am going away to another part of the country, I confess I feel very uneasy. . . .' 'It would be delightful to go with you. Most people would be very glad indeed. . . . But I think that as long as the place holds together at all I had better go on as I am. . . .' That was all that could be got out of her. 'Well, that is for you to decide,' said the aunt at last, 'but I should not think that anyone has ever before buried himself alive in such a god-forsaken place. I am sure that if you had asked him in time Prince Genji would have been delighted to put things straight for you; indeed, with a touch here and there no doubt he would soon have made the place more sumptuous than the Jade Emperor's[6] Palace. But unfortunately he is now entirely preoccupied with this young daughter of Prince Hyobukyo, and will do nothing for anyone else. He used to lead a roving life, distributing his favours in all sorts of directions. But now that has all stopped, and under these circumstances it is very unlikely to occur to him that a person living buried away in the middle of such a jungle as this, is all the time expecting him to rush round and take her affairs in hand.' The princess knew that this was only too true and she now began to weep bitterly. Yet she showed no signs of changing her mind, and the Chancellor's wife, after wasting the whole afternoon in tormenting her, exclaimed at last: 'Well then, I shall take Jiju. Make haste, please, please; it is getting late!' Weeping and flustered Jiju drew her mistress back into the alcove: 'I never meant to go,' she whispered, 'but this lady seems so very anxious to take me. I think perhaps I will travel with them part of the way and then come back again. There is a great deal of truth in all that she has been

[6] The sovereign divinity of the Chinese Taoists.

saying. But then, on the other hand, I do not like to
upset you by leaving. It is terrible to have to decide so
quickly. . . .' So she whispered; but though the princess loved her dearly and was stung to the quick that
even this last friend should be making ready to desert
her, she said not a word to encourage Jiju to stay, but
only sobbed more bitterly than before. She was wondering what she could give to her maid to keep in remem-
brance of her long service in the family. Perhaps some
cloak or dress? Unfortunately all her clothes were far
too worn and soiled to give away. She remembered that
somewhere in the house was a rather pretty box containing some plaited strands of her own hair, her fine
glossy hair that grew seven feet long. This would be her
present, and along with it she would give one of those
boxes of delicious clothes-scent that still survived from
the old days when her parents were alive. These she
handed to Jiju together with an acrostic poem in which
she compared her departure to the severing of this
plaited tress of hair. 'Your Mama told me always to
look after you,' she said, 'and whatever happened to me
I should never dream of sending you away. I think however that you are probably right to go, and only wish
that someone nicer were taking charge of you. . . .' 'I
know Mama wished me to stay with you,' said Jiju at
last through her tears. 'But quite apart from that, we
have been through such terrible times together in these
last years that I cannot bear to go off heaven knows
where and leave you here to shift for yourself. But,
madam, "By the Gods of Travel to whom I shall make
offering upon my way, I swear that never can *I* be shorn
from you like this tress of severed hair."' Suddenly the
voice of the aunt broke in upon them shouting im-
patiently: 'What has become of Jiju? Be quick, now, it is
getting quite dark!' Hardly knowing what she did, Jiju

climbed into the coach and as it drove away stared helplessly at the dilapidated house.

So at last Jiju had left her; Jiju who for years past,
though in sore need of a little pleasure and distraction,
had never once asked for a single day's holiday! But this
was not the end of the princess's troubles; for now even
the few old charwomen who still remained in the house
—poor doddering creatures who could never have per-
suaded anyone else to employ them—began threatening
to leave. 'Do you think I blame her?' said one of them,
speaking of Jiju's departure. 'Not I! What had she to
stay for, I ask you. And come to that, I should like to
know why we go on putting up with it all.' And they
began with one accord remembering influential patrons
who had at one time or another promised to employ
them. No, decidedly they would not stay in the place
any longer.

These conversations, which took place in the princess's
hearing, had the most disquieting effect upon her. The
Frosty Month[7] had now come. In the open country
around, though snow and hail frequently fell, they
tended to melt between-whiles. But in the wilderness
that surrounded the Hitachi Palace vast drifts of snow,
protected by the tangled overgrowth from any ray of
sunlight, piled higher and higher, till one might have
fancied oneself in some valley among the Alps of Koshi.
Through these arctic wastes not even the peasants would
consent to press their way and the palace was for weeks
on end entirely cut off from the outer world.

The princess sat staring at the snow. Life had been
dull enough before, but at any rate she had someone at
hand whose chatter at times broke in upon her gloom.
But now Jiju's laughter, Jiju's tears were gone, and as
she lay day and night alike behind her crumbling
curtains-of-state the princess was consumed by a lone-

[7] Eleventh month.

liness and misery such as she had never known before.

Meanwhile, at the Nijo Palace, Genji remained wholly absorbed in the girl from whom he had so long been separated, and it was only a few very particular friends who heard any news of him at all. He did sometimes think of the Hitachi Palace and wondered whether the princess could still be living there all alone. But he was in no great hurry to discover, and the New Year passed without his having taken any steps about her. In the fourth month he decided to call upon the ladies in the Village of Falling Flowers, and having obtained Murasaki's permission he set out one evening, clad in his usual disguise. For days it had rained unceasingly. But now, just at the moment when the heavy rain stopped and only a few scattered drops were falling, the moon rose; and soon it was one of those exquisite late spring nights through whose moonlight stillness he had in earlier years so often ridden out on errands of adventure. Busy with memories of such excursions he had not noticed where he was driving, when suddenly looking up he saw a pile of ruined buildings surrounded by plantations so tangled and overgrown that they wore the aspect of a primeval jungle. Over a tall pine-tree a trail of wisteria blossoms was hanging; it quivered in the moonlight, shaken by a sudden puff of wind that carried with it when it reached him a faint and almost imperceptible odour of flowers. It was for orange-blossom that he had set out that night; but here too was a flower that had a fragrance worth enjoying. He leaned out of the carriage window. They were passing by a willow whose branches swept the ground; with the crumbling away of the wall which had once supported it the tree had fallen forward till its trunk was almost prostrate. Surely he had seen these grounds before? Why, yes, this must be—suddenly it all came back to him. Of course it was that strange lady's house. He was driving past the Hitachi Palace. Poor creature, he must discover at once what had become of her; and stopping his carriage and calling to Koremitsu, who as usual on occasions of the kind was in attendance upon him, he asked him whether this was not indeed Princess Suyetsumu's place. 'Why certainly!' said Koremitsu. 'In that case,' said Genji, 'I should like to find out whether the same people are still living there. I have not time to pay a personal visit now, but I should like you to go in and enquire. Make sure that you discover exactly how things stand. It looks so silly if one calls on the wrong people.'

After a particularly dismal morning spent in staring blankly in front of her the princess had fallen asleep and dreamed that her father, the late prince, was still alive and well. After such a dream as that she woke up more miserable than ever. The window side of the room had been flooded in the recent rains; but taking a cloth she began mopping up the water and trying to find a place where she could put her chair. While she did so the stress of her sufferings stirred her to a point of mental alertness which she did not often reach. She had composed a poem, and suddenly she recited the lines: 'To the tears I shed in longing for him that is no more, are added the ceaseless drippings that patter from my broken roof!'

Meanwhile Koremitsu had made his way into the house and was wandering this way and that looking for some sign of life. He spent a long while in poking into all sorts of corners and at last concluded that the place had been abandoned as uninhabited. He was just setting out to report this to Genji when the moon came out from behind a cloud, lighting up the front of the house. He then noticed a trellis roll-door which was half pulled up. A curtain behind it moved. It almost seemed as though someone were there. Koremitsu, feeling oddly enough quite nervous, turned back and approached this door, clearing his throat loudly as he did so. In answer to this signal a very aged, decrepit voice answered from within the room. 'Well, what is it? Who are you?' 'It is Koremitsu,' he answered, 'could you tell Jiju that I should like to speak to her?' 'Jiju?' the aged voice answered, 'you cannot speak to her, she has gone away. But would not I do just as well?' The voice was incredibly ancient and croaking, but he recognized it as that of one of the gentlewomen whom he used to meet here in former days. To those within, inured as they were to years of absolute isolation, the sudden apparition of this figure wrapped in a great hunting cloak, was a mystery so startling and inexplicable that for a while it did not occur to them that their visitor could be other than some fox-spirit or will-o'-the-wisp masquerading in human form. But the apparition behaved with reassuring gentility and coming right up to the doorway now addressed them as follows: 'I must make it my business to find out exactly how matters stand. If you can assure me that, on your mistress's side, nothing has changed since the time when we used to come here, then I think you will find His Highness my master no less ready to help you than he was in days gone by. Can I trust you to let her know that we halted here tonight? I must be able to report to my master that his message is in safe hands. . . .' The old lady and her companions burst out laughing. 'Listen to him!' they cried, 'asking whether Madam has altered her way of life, whether she has taken to new friends! Do you suppose, young man, that if she were not waiting day and night for this famous prince of yours, she would still be living in this wilderness? Why, if there had been a soul in the world to help us, we should have shifted from these tumble-down quarters a long while ago. Just let Prince Genji have a look at the place for himself; he'll soon know how things stand! Yes, and we have been living like this for years;

I shouldn't think anyone in the world has ever been through such times as we have in this house. I tell you it's a wonder we've been able to bear it for so long, such a life as we and our poor young lady have been leading. . . .' They soon got launched upon a recital of their sufferings and misfortunes, which wandered so far from the purpose in hand that Koremitsu, growing impatient, at last interrupted them. 'Enough, enough,' he cried; 'that will do to go on with. I will go to Prince Genji at once and tell him of this.'

'What a long time you have been!' exclaimed Genji, when Koremitsu finally reappeared. 'Are things in the palace much as they used to be? The whole place is so overgrown with creepers and bushes that I hardly recognize it.' Koremitsu described how he at last discovered signs of life in the house and finally recognized the voice of Shosho, Jiju's old aunt, who had told him the lamentable tale which he now repeated.

Genji was horror-stricken at what he heard. How she must have suffered, buried away month after month amid all this disorder and decay! He was appalled at his own cruelty. How was it conceivable that he should have left her all this while to her own devices? 'Now then, what am I to do?' he said at last. 'If I am to visit the poor lady I had much rather it was not at this time of night; but if I do not go in now, I may not get another chance for a long while. I am afraid that what the old ladies said is only too true; if she were not counting upon my return, she would scarcely have gone on living such a life as you have just heard described. . . .' He was about to go straight into the house, but suddenly he hesitated. Would it not be better first of all to send in a very nice friendly note and discover whether she really insisted upon seeing him? But then he remembered the extraordinary difficulty with which she penned an answer. If she had not very much improved in this respect since his last dealings with her, he might easily spend the rest of the night waiting for his messenger to return with her reply. He had just dismissed that idea as impracticable when Koremitsu broke in: 'Pardon me, you have no notion how difficult it is to force a way through the brambles. Let me go first and shake the dew off the long branches. Then you will not get quite so wet.'

Accordingly Koremitsu went in front lashing the bushes with his riding-whip. But when they got under the trees such showers shook down on them from the branches (for the woods were still wet with the recent rains) that Koremitsu was obliged to go and fetch his master's umbrella, quoting as he held it aloft the old song about the dense forests of Miya-gi-no, where 'the drippings from wet boughs are worse than rain.' Even so, the ends of Genji's trousers became dripping wet before he reached the house. It was by no means easy even in old days to distinguish which was supposed to be the front door. By now such architectural features as doors and lobbies had long ago become merged in the general dilapidation. Genji's entry, though effected by a somewhat undignified scramble, had at any rate the advantage of being completely private and unobserved. At last, just as she had always predicted, Genji had come back! But in the midst of her elation a sudden panic seized her. How could she meet him in the miserable dress that she was wearing? All seemed lost, when she remembered the clothes that her aunt had brought for her to travel in. She had thought at the time that her father would have considered them very unsuitable and had put them aside after a mere hasty glance. The servants had packed them in a scented Chinese trunk and now brought them out, smelling deliciously fragrant. She could not receive him in what she was wearing and she had nothing else to change into. Much as she disapproved of her aunt's taste, what could she do but let them dress her in these new-fangled clothes? Thus equipped she took her seat behind the smoky curtains-of-state and waited. Presently Genji entered the room. 'It is a long time since we have held any communication, is it not?' he said. 'But on my side at any rate that does not mean that there has been any change of feeling. I was all the while expecting to hear from you and was determined that I would not be the first to give a sign of life. At last however the sight of the familiar tree-groups by your gate overcame this resolution and I could not forbear. . . .' So saying he lifted one corner of the curtains that surrounded her daïs and peeped in. As in old days she was utterly overcome by confusion, and sat for some while unable to make any kind of re-joinder. At last, almost inaudibly, she murmured some-thing about its being 'kind of him to have found his way . . . through all those wet bushes . . . such a scramble!'

'I am afraid you have been having a very dull time,' he went on; 'but pray give me credit for tonight's per-sistence. It showed some devotion, did it not, that I should have forced my way into the heart of this tangled, dripping maze, without a word of invitation or encouragement? I am sure you will forgive me for neglecting you for so long when I tell you that for some while past I have seen absolutely no one. Not having received a word of any kind from you, I could not sup-pose that you were particularly anxious to see me. But henceforward I am going to assume, whether you write to me or no, that I shall not be unwelcome. There now! After that, if I ever behave badly again you will really have some cause to complain.' So unhappy was he at the thought of all that she must have suffered during those years of penury and isolation that, in his desire to make amends, he soon began saying things which he did not quite mean. He even had thoughts of giving up his intended excursion and staying here for the night. But the princess seemed to be so painfully conscious of the deficiencies in her domestic arrangements and in general so completely overwhelmed by the presence of a visitor, that after passing some time in rather unsuccessful efforts to make further conversation, he began looking for an opportunity to slip quietly away. There came into his mind the old song: 'The tree I planted spreads its boughs so high.'[8] He had not indeed planted those great pine-trees that closed about the ruined palace on every side, but it seemed to him that they had shot up surprisingly since he first visited the place. How quickly the years had sped! And from the thought of what she must have been through during all this time he passed naturally to the recollection of his own misfortunes and adventures. 'Yes, when one comes to think of it, it is indeed a long time,' he said at last. 'At Court there have been great changes, many of them for the worse. Some day when I have plenty of time I must tell you of my exile and the strange outcast life we led on those deserted shores. You too, no doubt, have much to tell of all that has befallen you in these last dull and dreary days. I could wish indeed that you had many friends to whom you could confide your sorrows. But if for the moment I am the only one, make what use of me you can. You will find that, whatever my faults may be, as a listener I have much to recommend me.'

The moon was now sinking. The main western door stood wide open, and as the covered gallery which had formerly run along that side of the house had now completely crumbled away, the moonlight streamed unimpeded into the room where they were sitting. Looking

---

[8] 'I knew it not; but an old man must I be indeed; the pine-tree that with my hands I planted spreads its boughs so high.'

about him he recognized one after another the familiar fittings and ornaments. Not a thing was missing from its place. It was strange indeed to contrast the absolutely unchanged aspect of this corner of the house with the surrounding wreckage and desolation. He remembered the old story of the unfilial son who so much enjoyed pulling down the pagoda which his poor father had erected. The princess could not indeed prevent the outward fabric of her father's palace from falling into decay; but it was astonishing how little trace the passage of time had left upon the inner room in which he had once taken such pride.

Genji's thoughts returned to the princess herself. She was the shyest, the most awkward creature he had ever met; and yet there was something extraordinarily distinguished about her movements and bearing. She interested him, as indeed she had always done; so much so that he had fully intended not to lose sight of her. How should he ever forgive himself for allowing her affairs to drift into this deplorable condition? The truth was, he had been entirely absorbed in his own troubles and projects. But that was no excuse.

Had his ultimate destination that night been some scene of lively modern entertainment, the contrast would have been fatal. But the Village of Falling Flowers struck him on this occasion as particularly staid and dreary, and he left with the impression that the latter hours of the night had been by no means more agreeably spent than the former.

The time of the Kamo Festival had come. On the eve of the festival-day Genji was to undergo the ritual of Purification and the presents which are customary in connection with this occasion began pouring in thick and fast. Much of his time was spent in acknowledging them; but he did not forget his promise to the lady at Hitachi. The first thing to do was to make her palace habitable;

and sending for his most reliable bailiffs he explained to them what he wanted done. Soon a host of workmen were clearing away the undergrowth, while carpenters went round with planks and stays, here patching a hole, there shoring up a tottering wall or replacing some rotten beam, till at last all was tolerably weather-tight and secure. The mere fact that Genji's men were at work upon the building at once set the gossips talking and the most absurd stories were circulated. Somewhat embarrassed by all this Genji himself remained at a distance, but he wrote a long letter to the princess, telling her of the new rooms which he was now adding to his palace and offering her accommodation in them, so soon as the place was ready. 'You had better be looking round for a few nice young maids and pages to bring with you,' he told her. Nor did he forget to enquire individually after each of the queer old waiting-ladies, an attention which put them into such high spirits that the old palace had hardly room enough to hold them, as now gazing up at the sky, now staring in the direction from which the messenger had come, they gave unbridled vent to their gratitude and admiration. It was well known in society that Genji took little interest in the common run of women. Even the mildest flirtation with such persons seemed to hold no attraction for him; their conversation would have bored him and indeed he scarcely seemed to notice their existence. Those few favoured persons with whom he was generally known to have been on terms of intimacy were in every case women of entirely exceptional qualities. That one who in general showed such discrimination should single out as the recipient of his attentions a creature who could not lay claim to a single merit either of person or intellect, caused universal astonishment. This much at any rate was agreed, that though no one had heard anything about it, the affair must in reality be of very long standing.

The retainers and dependants who, thinking that the Hitachi Palace would never see better days, had a short while ago been in such a hurry to seek other employment, now one after another came begging to re-enter the princess's service. She at any rate knew how to behave towards those who waited upon her—treated them even with perhaps an exaggerated consideration. Whereas in the houses to which they had betaken themselves, belonging for the most part to wholly uncultured and undistinguished members of the petty bureaucracy, their experiences had been such as they would never have imagined to be possible; and they made no secret of the fact that they heartily repented of their recent experiment.

Prince Genji's influence was now greater than it had ever been in the days before his disaster. The mere fact that he was known to take an interest in the Hitachi Palace was enough to invest the place with a certain glamour. Visitors began to make their appearance, and soon the once deserted hills presented quite a busy and animated scene. One thing which had made the house so depressing was the fact that it was wholly shut in by bushes and trees. This jungle Genji now ordered to be reduced to tolerable dimensions; he had the ponds cleared and pleasant streams were made to run in and out among the flower-beds. All this work was performed with remarkable despatch, for even the lowest labourers and serfs knew that it was in their interest to please a lady who, for whatever reason it might be, evidently stood high in Genji's esteem.

She lived for two years more in the old palace, at the end of which time she moved into the new Eastern Wing that Prince Genji had been building. He did not spend much time in her company, but she was well content merely to feel that they inhabited the same domain, and whenever he had occasion to visit that part of the house he would look in upon her for a few minutes, that she might not feel she was wholly neglected. Her aunt's astonishment when in due time she returned to the Capital—Jiju's delight at her mistress's good fortune and shame at the thought that she had not held out a little longer in the princess's service—all this remains yet to be told. I would indeed have been glad to carry my story a little further, but at this moment my head is aching and I am feeling very tired and depressed. Provided a favourable opportunity presents itself and I do not forget to, I promise I will tell you all about it on some future occasion.

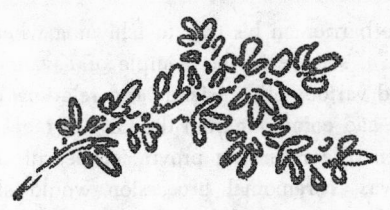

Chapter VII

A MEETING AT THE FRONTIER

It will be remembered that the year after the old Emperor's death Iyo no Suke[1] was sent as governor to a distant province and that his wife, the lady of the Broom-tree episode, was prevailed upon to accompany him. Vague rumours reached her concerning Genji's banishment; it was said that he was in disgrace and was living somewhere along the shores of Suma. Though obliged to feign indifference, she was indeed naturally very much distressed and longed to write to him. But though 'the wind sometimes blew across the Tsukubane hills'[2] she dared not trust her secret to so fickle a breeze, and while she waited for some securer messenger the months and years went swiftly by. It had at one time seemed as though Genji's banishment might last indefinitely, far longer in any case than Iyo no Suke's short term of office. But in the end it so turned out that Genji had already been back in the Capital for a year when Iyo's governorship expired. By an odd chance it happened that on the very day when the ex-governor and his party were to enter the Barrier at Osaka, Genji was to pass through

1 Utsusemi's husband. See Part I, chapters 2 and 3.
2 'The wind that blows across the ridge, that blows across the hills would that it might carry a message to him that I love.'

this same barrier on his way to Ishiyama where he was to attend a service in the Temple of Kwannon. Ki no Kami and various other friends and relations of the ex-governor had come out from the City to meet him, and from them the returning provincials learnt that Genji with a vast ceremonial procession would shortly be passing along their road. Iyo no Suke, wishing to reach the Barrier while things were still quiet, set out with his party long before daylight. But his wagons crowded with women and their luggage jolted along so slowly that when daylight came they were still trailing along the coast-road at Uchi-ide. News now came that Genji's procession had crossed the Awata Road. Already his first outriders were in sight. So dense was even this vanguard of the great procession that to press past it was out of the question. Accordingly, at the foot of the Frontier Hill Iyo called a halt. The wagons were drawn up along the wayside, and the oxen released from the yoke were soon browsing here and there among the fir-trees. Meanwhile the travellers sat in the shelter of a neighbouring copse, waiting for the procession to pass.

Although this was but a portion of Iyo no Suke's train, for he had sent some wagons on in advance while others were still to follow, it seemed a very large party; no less than ten coaches, with such a blaze of shawls, scarves and gaily coloured favours protruding from their windows that they looked more like the coaches from which ladies of fashion view the departure of Vestals to Ise or Kamo than the workaday vehicles in which rustic persons are usually conveyed to the Capital.

In honour of Genji's return to public life the pilgrimage to Ishiyama was on this occasion carried out with unusual solemnity, and at the head of the procession rode vast throngs of noblemen and courtiers, most of whom stared with considerable curiosity at this cluster of gay equipages drawn up along the roadside.

It was the last day of the ninth month, and autumn leaves in many tints of red and brown stood out against a dull background of colourless winter grass. Suddenly from behind the frontier guardhouse there burst forth a blaze of many-coloured travelling cloaks, some richly embroidered, some batik-dyed, of every pattern and hue. Genji's coach was passing. He too scanned the party by the roadside, but instantly lowered the carriage blind. He had recognized, among those who had come out to meet the travellers, his page and message-carrier, Utsusemi's brother—a child in those old days but now Captain of the Guard. He bade one of his equerries call this young man to his side and when he arrived said to him laughingly: 'I hope your sister notices how attentive I am to her. It is not often that I go all the way to the Barrier to meet my friends!' He spoke lightly, but his heart beat fast and there rose up in his mind a host of tender memories to which in this hasty message it would have been useless to allude.

It was years since Utsusemi had spoken of Genji; yet she had never forgotten what had passed between them and it needed only these few words from him to renew all the misery in which her yearning for him had plunged her long ago.

When Genji returned from Ishiyama, Utsusemi's brother, the Captain of the Guard, came out towards the Barrier to meet him and made his excuses for having taken a day's leave in honour of his sister's return. As a boy he had been very good-looking and Genji had taken a great fancy to him. But despite the fact that he owed everything to Genji, without whose patronage he would never have been able to enter the Imperial Guard at all, still less to obtain promotion, no sooner had his master's fortunes begun to decline than this young man, fearing to offend those in power, entered the service of his brother-in-law, the provincial governor. Genji, though he showed no resentment at the time, found this dereliction very hard to forgive. Their old relations were never resumed; but the Captain was still numbered among the favourite gentlemen of his household. Iyo no Suke's son, Ki no Kami, had become governor of Kawachi and was consequently no longer on the spot. The younger son, Ukon no Jo, had, as will be remembered, followed Genji into exile and now stood very high in his favour. His position was envied not only by this young Captain of the Guard but by many another who in the days of Genji's adversity had thought it wiser to leave him to his fate.

Soon after this Genji sent for the Captain[3] and gave him a letter to be taken to his sister. 'So was this affair, which he thought had come to an end long ago, still dragging on after all these years?' the young man asked himself as he carried the letter to Iyo no Suke's house. 'Did not our meeting of the other day seem almost as though it had been arranged by Fate? Surely you too must have felt so.' With the letter was the acrostic poem: 'Though on this lake-side Fate willed that we should meet, upon its tideless shore no love-shell[4] can we hope to find.' 'How bitterly I envied the Guardian of the Pass,'[5] he added.

'I hope you will send an answer,' said the Captain. 'He has got it into his head that I behaved badly to him some time ago. I should be very glad if I could get back on to the old terms with him. I do not myself see much point in correspondences of this kind; but when anyone writes to me such a letter as I suppose this to be, I take care to write a civil answer. No one blames me for that; and still less is a woman thought the worse of for show-

---

[3] Utsusemi's brother; the 'boy' of Part I, ch. 3.
[4] *Kai-nashi* = 'no shell'; but also 'no profit.'
[5] I.e. Iyo no Suke.

ing that a little harmless flattery does not altogether displease her.'

She was still the same shy, inexperienced girl of years
ago; her brother's tone profoundly shocked her and she
had no intention of carrying on a flirtation for his benefit.
But naturally enough she *did* feel flattered at the reception of such a note and in the end consented to reply.
With her letter was an acrostic poem in which she said
that the Barrier of Osaka had been no barrier to her
tears, nor the Hill of Osaka a true hill of meeting.[6]

She was connected in his mind with the most delightful and also perhaps the most painful moment in his life.
Hence his thoughts tended frequently to recur to her,
and he continued to write to her from time to time.

Meanwhile Iyo no Suke, who was now a very old man,
began to decline in health, and feeling that his end was
near, he called his sons to him and discussed with them
the disposition of his worldly affairs. But what evidently
concerned him above all was the future of his young
wife. They must promise him to yield to her wishes in
everything and to treat her exactly as they had done
during his lifetime. Still unsatisfied by their assurances
he sent for them over and over again at every hour of
the night and day and exacted fresh promises. But
Utsusemi, after all that she had suffered already, could
not believe that happiness of any kind could ever be in
her fate. She saw herself, so soon as her husband was
dead, bandied about unwanted from one relation's house
to another, and the prospect appalled her. Iyo knew
only too well what was passing in her mind. He desired
so persistently to comfort and protect her that, could life
be prolonged by mere anxiety to live, he would never
have deserted her. For her indeed he would gladly have
foregone the joys of Paradise that his ghost might linger

[6] O-saka means 'Hill of Meeting'; *seki* means a barrier,
but also a flood-dam.

on earth and keep her from all harm. Thus, profoundly distrusting the intention of his sons and full of the blackest forebodings, he died at last after a bitter struggle against fate, and only when his will could no longer hold out against the encroachments of sickness and old age.

For a while, with their father's dying injunctions fresh in their ears, the stepsons treated her with at any rate superficial kindness; but this soon wore off and she began to find her position in the house exceedingly unpleasant. This no doubt lay rather in the nature of the circumstances themselves than in any particular ill will on the part of her guardians. But she felt herself to be the object of a deliberate persecution and her life became one continual succession of tears and lamentations. The only one of the brothers who seemed to have any sympathy with her was Ki no Kami: 'Please keep nothing back from me,' he said. 'My father was so anxious that I should help you and how can I, unless you entrust your secrets to me?' Then he took to following her about. She remembered how amorous he had always been. Soon his intentions became perfectly apparent. She had suffered enough already in her life; why should she sit down and wait quietly for the fresh miseries which fate had now in store for her? Without a word to anybody she sent for her confessor and took the vows of a nun. Her waiting-women and servants were naturally aghast at this sudden step. Ki no Kami took it as a personal affront. 'She did it simply to spite me,' he told people; 'but she is young yet and will soon be wondering how on earth she is going to support such an existence for the rest of her life'—sagacity which did not impress his hearers quite as he intended.

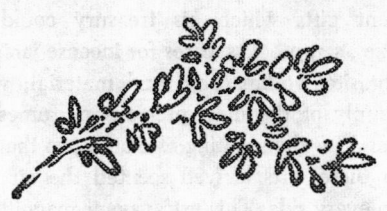

Chapter VIII

THE PICTURE COMPETITION

It will be remembered that after Rokujo's death Genji
decided that her daughter, Princess Akikonomu, had
best come and live with him till the time came for her
Presentation at Court. At the last minute, however, he
altered his mind, for such a step seemed too direct a
provocation to Princess Akikonomu's admirer, the young
ex-Emperor Suzaku. But though he did not remove her
from her palace in the Sixth Ward he felt his responsi-
bilities towards this unfortunate orphan very keenly and
paid her many lengthy visits. He had now definitely
arranged with Fujitsubo that Akikonomu was soon to
enter the Emperor's Palace; but he was careful not to
betray in public any knowledge of this plan, and to the
world at large he seemed merely to be giving the girl
such general guidance and support as might be expected
from a guardian and family friend.

Suzaku was indeed bitterly disappointed at the intelligence that the princess had been handed over to a mere
infant such as the present Emperor. He often thought of
writing to her but at the same time dreaded the scandal
which would ensue if his attachment became known.
When however the day of Presentation at last arrived
his caution suddenly deserted him, and he sent to
Akikonomu's palace an assortment of the most costly and

magnificent gifts which his treasury could supply—comb-boxes, scrap-boxes, cases for incense-jars; all of the most exquisite workmanship and material; with these was a supply of the most precious perfumes both for burning and for the scenting of clothes, so that the bales in which these gifts arrived scented the air for a full league on every side. This extravagant magnificence, besides relieving Suzaku's feelings, had another very definite object. It was particularly intended to annoy the lady's guardian, to whom, as Suzaku very well knew, the contents of these packages would immediately be shown. It so happened that Genji was actually at Akikonomu's palace when the scented bales arrived; her servants at once showed them to him and told him whence they came. He picked up at random one of a pair of comb-boxes; it was a work of fascinating elegance and delicacy. Near it was a box for combs such as are worn in the hair, decorated with a pattern of flowers. In the very centre of one petal was an inscription. Looking closer he read the poem:

'Come not again!'[1] Because it fell to me,
   Who least would have it so,
At Heaven's command your exile to ordain;
To others, not to me who bade you go,
   You come again!

Somehow or other, in cases of this kind, Genji could never help imagining what he himself would feel if he were in the same position. Supposing that he had fallen in love with someone all those years ago and that the beloved person had gone away immediately to some far-off place; and suppose that he, instead of forgetting all about her as might have been expected, had waited patiently year after year and, when at last she returned,

[1] The formula with which the Emperor despatches the Vestal of Ise.

had been told that she was to be handed over to someone else—he saw on reflection that the situation was
really very painful. Judging from his own experience he
knew that Suzaku's complete lack of employment, now
that he had resigned all his official duties, would gravely
aggravate the case. Yes, he must indeed be passing
through a period of terrible agitation! He was now extremely sorry that he had ever suggested the Presentation of the young princess. He had indeed in the past
good reason to resent his brother's conduct towards him.
But lately Suzaku had shown nothing but affability.
. . . He stood for a long while lost in thought. It was
all very perplexing. Turning at last to Akikonomu's
gentlewomen who were inspecting these magnificent
presents, he asked whether their mistress had already
composed her answering poem. 'And surely a letter must
also have come with these things?' he added. There was
indeed a letter and the gentlewomen had read it, but
they very much doubted whether it was fit for Genji's
eyes and made no offer to produce it. The princess herself was distressed by this exhibition of devotion on the
part of one with whom she could no longer have any
dealings. What answer could she possibly contrive? But
her maids were pressing round her, insisting that it
would be intolerably rude to allow the messengers to
depart without handing to them a word of thanks, and
Genji was telling her that not to reply was out of the
question; a few words would suffice. No doubt they were
right. She felt very much embarrassed by Suzaku's attentions; but she remembered distinctly how handsome,
how distinguished he had seemed to her on that day of
the farewell ceremony. There had been tears in his eyes,
and though it all happened so many years ago she could
recall as distinctly as if it were yesterday the vague feelings of childish sympathy and admiration which her
meeting with the young Emperor had aroused in her on

that last morning when she went to the Palace for her Crowning. With these memories were blended others; thoughts, for example, of her mother Lady Rokujo and of the long exile which they had shared. She wrote no letter, but only the poem:

'Come not again!' I wept to hear those words,
Thinking you willed it so,
When Heaven's command my exile did ordain;
Now hearing that it grieved you I should go,
I weep again.

The messengers who had brought the presents were richly rewarded and sent upon their way. Genji would very much have liked to see her reply, but she refused to show it to him.

She was small and frail. How well Suzaku, with his almost girlish beauty, would have suited her; while as for the Emperor, he was years her junior, scarcely out of the nursery. Did she too (though she certainly breathed no word of complaint) secretly resent the steps which he had taken for her worldly advancement? This idea troubled him sorely; but it was by now far too late to undo the arrangement, and the best he could do was to stay with her for a little while and advise her as kindly and discreetly as possible how to conduct herself in the new life that was before her. He then interviewed the Court chamberlains who were to arrange her Presentation, and having settled everything satisfactorily with them he made his way to the Inner Palace. He did not wish it to appear that he was himself standing sponsor for the new arrival nor that he was in the Palace as her relative or guardian. He therefore gave his coming the appearance of an ordinary ceremonial visit.

Princess Akikonomu's palace was famous for the unusual number of good-looking gentlewomen who were in service there. Many of these had recently been living at their homes, but they now assembled in full force, and arriving with their mistress at Court created a most dazzling impression. Were Rokujo alive, with what solicitude would she be watching over that day's momentous proceedings, thought Genji, as he saw the procession arrive; and remembering her singular gifts and lively intelligence, he felt how great a loss she was not to himself only, but to the whole life of the Court. So rare indeed (as it now seemed to him) was her perfection both of mind and person that he seldom encountered among his acquaintance talent or accomplishment of any kind without immediately recalling how slender these attainments would seem if set beside those of Lady Rokujo.

On the day of the Presentation Fujitsubo was at the Palace. When she told the Emperor that someone new was coming to see him, he listened very earnestly and attentively. He was an intelligent and lively child, very forward for his age. After telling him all about the princess, 'So you see she is rather an important lady,' Fujitsubo continued, 'and when she comes this evening you must be very polite to her and not play any of your tricks. . . .' The Emperor said nothing, but he thought to himself that if the lady were indeed so grown-up and so important, far from wanting to tease her he would be very frightened of her indeed. Great was his delight then when very late that evening there arrived at the Palace a very shy, shrinking girl, very small and fragile, not indeed looking like a grown-up person at all. He thought her very pretty; but he was much more at his ease with Chujo's little daughter, who had lived at the Palace for some while and was very sociable and affectionate, while the new princess was terribly silent and shy. Still, though he found her rather difficult to get on with, he felt, partly owing to the deference with which, as Prince Genji's ward, she was treated by everyone else at Court, and partly owing to the magnificence with which she was served and apparelled—he felt that she was in some way which he did not understand a person of very great importance. In the evenings indeed he allowed the one to wait upon him as often as the other; but when he wanted a partner in some game or someone to amuse him in the early part of the day, it was seldom Akikonomu for whom he sent.

To no Chujo had presented his daughter at Court with the express intention that she should one day share the Throne. The presence of this formidable rival at the Palace could not fail to cause him considerable anxiety.

The poem with which Princess Akikonomu had acknowledged the ex-Emperor's gifts had but served to increase his agitation. He knew that he must now banish all thought of her from his mind; but it was hard indeed to do so. He was brooding now over his loss, when Genji arrived on a visit. They talked for a long while about many different matters, and in the course of this conversation mention was made of the ceremonies upon the occasion of Lady Akikonomu's departure for Ise. This was a subject which they had often discussed before; but now, as on previous occasions, the conversation terminated without Suzaku making the slightest allusion to the real reason why this topic so much interested him. Genji naturally did not betray his knowledge of the secret; but he was envious to know exactly how far this mysterious passion went, and he could not restrain himself from experimenting upon his brother with various anecdotes concerning the lady in question and her recent admission to the Emperor's suite. It was apparent in a moment that Suzaku suffered acutely while these subjects were being discussed, and Genji, ashamed of his unkindness, hastily turned the conversation to other matters.

At such a ceremony as that of the crowning of the

Vestal the Emperor meets the lady whom he is to initiate face to face and during the whole proceedings no curtain or screen divides them. Suzaku must therefore at least know what Princess Akikonomu looked like; which was more than Genji did, for she had till this day never received him except in an unlighted room or behind her curtains-of-state. In what exactly did her charm consist? What was it that had kindled in the ex-Emperor's heart a passion that had survived the lapse of so many years? The problem intrigued him and he almost envied his brother the knowledge which he must possess on the subject. She was indeed evidently of a very melancholy, indolent disposition. If only she would sometimes forget herself, show a little of the impetuosity of youth, then in course of time he might hope for a moment to catch a glimpse of her as she really was! But while her gravity and reticence seemed to become every day more pronounced, all his dealings with her tended only to confirm his conviction that underneath all this reserve was concealed an interesting and admirable character.

Now that all the Emperor's time was divided between the two princesses of his retinue, Prince Hyobukyo had given up all idea of presenting his second daughter at Court. Perhaps an opportunity would occur later on when the Emperor was of an age to perceive for himself that such a match was by no means to be despised. Meanwhile his favour seemed to be pretty equally divided between the two existing claimants. He was particularly interested in pictures and had as a result of this taste himself acquired considerable skill. It happened that Lady Akikonomu painted very charmingly, and so soon as he discovered this the Emperor began constantly sending for her to paint pictures with him. Among the serving-women in the Palace he had always taken an interest in any who were said to be fond of pictures; and it was natural that when he discovered painting to be the favourite occupation of the pretty princess he should become very much attached to her. Hers were not solemn pictures, but such clever, quick sketches; so that just to watch her do them was an exciting game. And when, sitting so charmingly beside him on the divan, she paused and held her brush in the air for a moment wondering where to put the next stroke, she looked so daring that the little Emperor's heart was completely captivated. Soon he was going to her rooms at all hours, and To no Chujo became seriously alarmed lest his own daughter should lose her primacy. But he was determined not to be outdone, and being of an extremely ingenious and resourceful nature he soon had a plan for putting an end to this menacing situation. He sent for all the most skilful painters in the land and under strict bond of secrecy set them to work upon a collection of pictures which was to be like nothing that had ever been seen before. They were to be illustrations to romances, which would be preferable to purely ingenious subjects, the significance being more easily grasped by a young mind and all the most interesting and exciting stories were chosen. In addition to these illustrations there was to be a set of 'Months,' a very attractive subject, with texts specially written for the occasion. In due time Princess Chujo[2] showed them to the Emperor, who was naturally very much interested and soon afterwards asked for them again, saying that he thought Princess Akikonomu would like to see them. At this Princess Chujo began to make difficulties, and though His Majesty promised to show them to no one else and carry them with the greatest care straight to the other prin-

---

[2] Chujo's daughter. Actually she is called Kokiden, but this is a name of another character in the book, and as the use of it would lead to confusion, I have given her a name which links her to her father.

cess's apartments, she refused to part with them. Genji heard of this and was amused to see that To no Chujo could still throw himself into these absurd conspiracies with the same childish excitement as in their young days. 'I am very sorry,' he said to the Emperor, 'to hear that Princess Chujo hides her pictures from you and will not let you take them away and study them at your ease. It seems, too, that she was quite cross and quarrelsome about it, which was most reprehensible. But I have some very nice pictures, painted a long while ago. I will send them to you.'

At the Nijo-in there were whole cupboards full of pictures both old and new. Taking Murasaki with him he now inspected their contents and together they went through the whole collection, putting on one side those which were most likely to appeal to modern taste. There were naturally many illustrations of the *Everlasting Wrong*[3] and the story of Wang Chao-chün,[4] both of them very interesting and moving subjects, but unfortunately quite inappropriate to the present occasion. These therefore had to be excluded. But it occurred to Genji that his own sketches made during his sojourn at Suma and Akashi might be of interest, and sending for the box in which they were kept he took advantage of this occasion to go through them with Murasaki. Even someone seeing them without any knowledge of the circumstances under which they were painted would, if possessed of the slightest understanding of such matters, have at once been profoundly moved by these drawings. It may be imagined then with what emotion they were examined by one to whom each scene came as an answer to the questionings and anxieties of some evil dream

[3] The story of Ming Huang and Yang Kuei-fei; a long poem by Po Chü-i.

[4] A Chinese princess given to a Tartar king in marriage and carried away into the north.

from which it seemed there could be no awakening. She told him more of what she had suffered in those unforgettable days than she had ever done before. Why had he not sometimes sent such pictures as these? How they would have comforted and reassured her! And she recited the verse: 'Better had it been for me when I was alone to look at pictures of the realms where fishers dwell, than stare at nothing, as I did all day long!' Genji was deeply moved and with tears in his eyes he answered with the verse: 'It was an evil time; yet never once in all those days was my heart sore as now when, hand in hand, we view the pictured past.'

To one other person only had he shown them—the ex-Empress Fujitsubo. Going through the whole collection sketch by sketch, in order to choose out the best and also to give as good an idea as possible of the different estuaries and bays, he could not help wondering all the time how things were faring in the house of his host at Akashi.

On hearing of the preparations that were taking place at the Nijo-in, To no Chujo went through his pictures again and had them all fitted out with the most elegant ivory-rollers, backings and ribbons.[5] It was about the tenth day of the third month. The weather was delightful, things were looking at their best and everyone was in a good temper; moreover it was a time at which no particular fêtes or ceremonies occupied the Court, so that uninterrupted attention could be now given to those lighter pastimes in which the Emperor so much delighted, and whole days were spent unrolling painting after painting. The one ambition of everyone at Court was to rout out and bring to the Palace some picture which should particularly catch the young Emperor's fancy. Both Akikonomu's partisans and those of Lady

[5] For tying up the rolls.

Chujo had brought forward vast numbers of scrolls. On the whole, illustrated romances proved to be the most popular. Akikonomu's side was strongest in ancient works of well-established reputation; while Lady Chujo patronized all the cleverest modern painters, so that her collection, representing as it did all that most appealed to the fashionable tastes of the moment, made at first sight a more dazzling impression. The Emperor's own ladies-in-waiting were divided in opinion. Some of the most intelligent were on the side of the ancients; others favoured the present day. But on the whole modern works tended to win their approval.

It happened that Fujitsubo was paying one of her periodical visits to the Court, and having given a casual inspection to the exhibits of both parties she decided to suspend her usual religious observances and devote herself to a thorough study of all these works, for painting was a matter in which she had always taken a deep interest. Hearing the animated discussions which were taking place between the supporters of modern and ancient art, she suggested that those present should be formed into two teams. On Lady Akikonomu's side the principal names were Heinaishi no Suke, Jiju no Naishi, Shosho no Myobu; on Lady Chujo's—Daini no Naishi no Suke, Chujo no Myobu and Hyoye no Myobu. These were considered the cleverest women of the day, and Fujitsubo promised herself very good entertainment from such an interchange of wit and knowledge as their rivalry was likely to afford.

In the first contest that archetype and parent of all romances, *The Bamboo-Cutter's Story*,[6] was matched against the tale of Toshikage in *The Hollow Tree*. The

[6] A 9th-century story about a fairy who was found in a bamboo-stem, set various fantastic ordeals to her lovers and finally disappeared in the Land Above the Sky. It is written in a rather disjointed style. Translated by Victor Dickins in *Japanese Texts*.

partisans of antiquity defended their choice as follows:
'We admit that this story, like the ancient bamboo-stem
in which its heroine was found, has in the course of ages
become a little loose in the joints. But the character of
Lady Kaguya herself, so free from all stain of worldly
impurity, so nobly elevated both in thought and conduct,
carries us back to the Age of the Gods, and if such a
tale fails to win your applause, this can only be because
it deals with matters far beyond the reach of your frivolous feminine comprehensions.' To this the other side
replied: 'The Sky Land to which Lady Kaguya was removed is indeed beyond our comprehensions, and we
venture to doubt whether any such place exists. But if
we regard merely the mundane part of your story, we
find that the heroine emanated from a bamboo joint.
This gives to the story from the start an atmosphere of
low life which we for our part consider very disagreeable. We are told that from the lady's person there
emanated a radiance which lit up every corner of her
foster-father's house. But these fireworks, if we remember aright, cut a very poor figure when submitted to the
august light of His Majesty's palace. Moreover the episode of the fireproof ratskin ends very tamely, for after
Abe no Oshi[7] had spent thousands of gold pieces in
order to obtain it, no sooner was it put to the test than
it disappeared in a blaze of flame. Still more lamentable
was the failure of Prince Kuramochi[7] who, knowing that
the journey to Fairyland was somewhat difficult, did not
attempt to go there but had a branch of the Jewel Tree
fabricated by his goldsmith; a deception which was exposed at the first scratch.'

The picture was painted by Kose no Omi[8] and the

---

[7] One of the suitors.
[8] Also called Aimi. Successor of Kose no Kanaoka, who
founded the Kose school in the 9th century.

text was in the hand of Ki no Tsurayki.[9] It was on Kanya paper backed with Chinese silk. The cover was of a reddish violet tinge, the rollers being of sandalwood—by no means an extraordinary get-up. The moderns then proceeded to defend their own exhibit; 'Toshikage,'[10] they said, 'though buffeted by wind and wave, pitched headlong into a stormy sea and in the end cast up upon an unknown shore, pursued, undaunted by suffering and disaster, the purpose which he had set before him, and succeeded at last in displaying, both at the foreign court[11] and in our own country, the marvellous talent which it had cost him so much to acquire. The adventures of so dauntless a character, affording as they do a comparison between the manners of the Land Beyond the Sea and of our own Land of Sunrise, cannot fail to be of interest; moreover the same contrast has been maintained in the style of the pictures as in the matter of the text.'

It was painted on thick white paper such as poem-slips are made of, the outer cover was of blue paper and the roller of yellow jade. The artist was Tsunenori;[12] the scribe, Ono no Michikaze[13]—a combination that could hardly have been more dazzling in its fashionableness and modernity. Against such claims as these the partisans of the antique were quite unable to prevail and Lady Chujo's side scored the overwhelming victory.

[9] 883–946 A.D. Editor of the *Kokinshu,* the first official anthology of poetry.

[10] Having set out from Japan to China he was wrecked on the coast of Persia, where he acquired a magic zithern and the knowledge of unearthly tunes, armed with which he won great fame as a musician in China and Japan. See Aston's *History of Japanese Literature,* p. 76.

[11] China.

[12] Asukabe Tsunenori, flourished about 964 A.D.

[13] Also called Ono no Dofu, the most celebrated calligraphist of Japan.

In the next contest the *Tales of Ise*[14] were pitted against the story of Sho Sammi.[15] A long discussion ensued; but here again the fact that *Sho Sammi* deals with persons in a comfortable and prosperous situation, presents scenes of court life and shows the world as we know it today could not fail to render this work far more attractive to the majority of these young critics. An opposite opinion was voiced by Heinaishi, who recited the verse: 'Shall we leave the deep heart of Ise's waters unexplored till time shall have effaced their secret, like a footprint that the tide washes from the shore?' 'Shall the fame of Narihira,'[16] she added, 'be eclipsed by modern tittle-tattle dressed up in the finery of a specious style?' To this Daini no Naishi no Suke replied with the verse: 'Upon the topmost regions of the sky[17] our hero's heart is set; with scorn he views your shoals, upon which, heavy as a thousand watery fathoms, the ages rest.'

'Well,' said Fujitsubo, 'ambition such as that of Prince Hyoye[18] is no doubt a very valuable quality; but I sincerely hope that admiration for him and his like will never cause us to let the fame of Captain Laigo[19] sink into decay!' And she recited the verse: 'Has the old fisherman of Ise shore, like seaweed that the ebbing tide reveals, so long been flattered by the public eye, only to sink at last beneath the rising sea of scorn?'

These feminine discussions are capable of continuing, more or less at cross-purposes for an indefinite length of time. It would indeed be impossible to record all the

---

[14] A collection of short love-episodes, each centring round a poem or poems. See Aston's *History of Japanese Literature*, p. 80.

[15] Already lost in the 15th century.

[16] Hero of the *Tales of Ise*.

[17] I.e. upon promotion at Court. Courtiers were called 'men above the clouds.'

[18] Presumably the hero of the tale of Sho Sammi.

[19] Narihira, hero of the *Tales of Ise*.

arguments and counter-arguments that were expended over even one of these pictures. Moreover the younger and less considered of the gentlewomen present, though any one of them would have given her eyes not to miss any of the paintings that were being unrolled, were hustled into the background, even though they belonged to the Emperor's own or to Lady Fujitsubo's household, and were scarcely able to see anything at all. This occasioned much jealousy and heart-burning.

Presently Genji arrived at the Palace and was greatly diverted by the spectacle of this disorderly and embittered combat. 'If you will get up another competition,' he said, 'I will arrange for the Emperor to be present and will myself make the awards.' In preparation for this event, which he had indeed been contemplating for some time, he made a further selection from the pictures which he had recently put aside, and having done so he could not resist inserting among them the two scrolls of his sketches made at Suma and Akashi. To no Chujo meanwhile, determined not to be outdone, was straining every nerve in preparation for the new contest. It was indeed a moment in the history of our country when the whole energy of the nation seemed to be concentrated upon the search for the prettiest method of mounting paper-scrolls. In arranging the conditions of the contest Genji had said: 'My idea is that it should be confined to paintings already in existence; we do not want a lot of new work hurriedly executed for this special purpose. . . .' But To no Chujo could not resist the temptation to set some of his favourite masters to work, and improvising a little studio with a secret door he strove to steal a march on his rivals. The secrecy was not however as well maintained as he could have desired; even Suzaku, in his secluded apartments, heard the story and determined to put his own collection at the service of Princess Akikonomu. He had a series of 'Festi-

vals All the Year Round,' painted by various famous old
masters; texts explaining these pictures had been added
by no less a hand than that of the Emperor Daigo.[20]
Why should he not order a series of paintings illustrating
the principal events of his own reign? Among these subjects one would naturally be the crowning of the Vestal
at the Daigoku Hall upon the day of her departure for
Ise. He entrusted this scene to Kose no Kimmochi[21] and
it may be imagined with what care and insistence he
discussed every detail of a work so dear to his heart. It
was encased in a delicately fretted box of aloeswood.
The pattern on the wrappings and decorations of the
roll was a heart-shaped crest formed by leaves of the
same tree. Nothing could have been more delightfully
up-to-date. He sent it by the hand of the Captain of the
Senior Bodyguard, who was one of his retainers. There
was no message, save for a poem written on the picture
just by where the Vestal was shown arriving in her litter
at the Daigoku Hall: 'Though I no longer within the
Circle of the Gods a place may take, yet unforgotten is
the concourse which in those hours with bright Divini-
ties I held.'

To return no answer would show too great a disrespect
towards one who had once occupied the Throne, and
though these attentions distressed her she broke off a
piece of the ritual comb which he had fastened in her
hair on that day long ago, and tying to it the verse, 'Not
yet forgotten is that high converse, and once again
within the Precinct of the Gods oh were it but my lot to
stray!' she wrapped the broken comb in Chinese paper
of deep colour and gave it to the messenger, whom she
rewarded with many handsome presents. The ex-Em-

[20] 898–930, a great patron of literature, and himself an important poet and calligrapher.
[21] Grandson of the great Kose no Kanaoka. Flourished
about 960 A.D.

peror when he opened the packet was deeply moved, and for the first time regretted that he had so soon resigned the Throne. Not unnaturally he was feeling somewhat bitterly against Prince Genji; but he realized that he had himself, in past days, deserved none too well at his brother's hands. Most of the ex-Emperor's pictures had belonged to his mother, the Empress Kokiden; unfortunately a considerable part of her collection had however come into the possession of Lady Chujo, who was her granddaughter.

The ex-Emperor's wife, Lady Oborozuki, was also extremely interested in painting and had shown the utmost discrimination in forming her collection.

When the great day came, though there had not been much time for preparation everything was arranged in the most striking and effective manner. The ladies-in-waiting belonging to the two sides stood drawn up in line on either side of the Imperial Throne; the courtiers, very much on the alert, were ranged up in the verandah of the small back room. Lady Chujo's party (the left) exhibited their pictures in boxes of purple sandalwood mounted on sapanwood stands, over which was thrown a cover of Chinese brocade worked on a mauve ground. The carpet on which the boxes stood was of Chinese fine-silk, dyed to the colour of grape-juice. Six little girls were in attendance to assist in handling the boxes and scrolls; they were dressed in mantles with white scarves lined with pink; their tunics were of scarlet, worn with facings blue outside and light green within.

Akikonomu's boxes were of aloeswood arranged on a low table of similar wood, but lighter in colour. The carpet was of Korean brocade on a blue-green ground. The festoons hanging round the table and the design of the table-legs were carefully thought out and in the best taste. The little girls in attendance wore blue mantles, with willow-coloured scarves; their tunics, brown outside and yellow within. When all the boxes were duly arranged on their stands, the Emperor's own ladies took up their places, some with Lady Chujo's supporters, some with the opposing side. At the summons of the herald Genji and To no Chujo now appeared and with them Genji's half-brother, Prince Sochi no Miya, who among the various arts which he cultivated was particularly fond of painting. He had received no official summons on this particular occasion, but had in the end yielded to Genji's entreaties that he would come and help him in his difficult task. Prince Sochi was at once called to the Emperor's side and appointed part-umpire in the coming contest. An amazing collection of paintings had been assembled and assuredly the task of the judges was no light one. A great impression was made when Akikonomu's side produced the famous series of 'Four Seasons' by noted masters of antiquity. Both the charming fancy displayed in the choice of episodes for illustration and the easy, flowing character of the brush-strokes rendered these works highly attractive; and the modern paintings on paper, being necessarily limited in size, sometimes, especially in landscape, made a certain impression of incompleteness. Yet the far greater richness both of brushwork and invention gave even to the more trivial of these modern works a liveliness which made them compare not unfavourably with the masterpieces of the past. Thus it was very difficult indeed to reach any decision, save that today, as on the previous occasion, both sides had produced many works of absorbing interest.

The sliding-screen of the breakfast-room was now pushed aside and Lady Fujitsubo entered. Remembering how learned she was in these matters Genji felt somewhat shy, and contented himself henceforward as exhibit after exhibit was produced with an occasional comment or suggestion, discreetly thrown in only when some point of especial difficulty threatened an indefinite delay. The contest was still undecided when night fell.

At last the moment arrived when there was only one more picture to show on each side. Amid intense excitement Princess Akikonomu's side produced the roll containing Genji's sketches at Suma. To no Chujo was aghast. His daughter's side too had reserved for their last stroke one of the most important works at their disposition; but against the prospect of so masterly a hand working at complete leisure and far from the distracting influences which beset an artist in town, Lady Chujo's supporters at once knew that they could not hope to prevail. An additional advantage was given to Genji's paintings by the pathos of the subject. That during those years of exile he had endured a cheerless and monotonous existence those present could well conjecture. But when they saw, so vividly presented, both the stern manner of his life and in some sort even the feelings which this rustic life had aroused in one used to every luxury and indulgence, they could not but be deeply moved, and there were many (Prince Sochi no Miya among them) who could scarcely refrain from tears. Here were presented in the most vivid manner famous bays and shores of the Suma coast, so renowned in story yet to these city folk so utterly unknown and unimagined. The text was written in cursive Chinese characters, helped out here and there with a little native script, and unlike the business day-to-day journals that men generally keep it was varied by the insertion of an occasional poem or song. The spectators now clamoured only for more specimens of Genji's handiwork, and it would have been impossible at that moment to interest them in anything else. It seemed to them as though all the interest and beauty of the many pictures which they had been examining had in some strange manner accumulated and attached themselves to this one scroll. By universal and ungrudging consent Princess Akikonomu's side was awarded the victory.

It was already nearing the dawn when Genji, feeling somewhat discursive, sent round the great tankard and presently began telling stories to the company. 'From my earliest childhood,' he said at last, 'I have always been fond of books; and my father the late Emperor, fearing that I might become wholly absorbed in my studies, used to say to me: "Perhaps learning carries with it inevitably so great a share of the world's esteem that, to redress the balance, the scholar, once he advances beyond a certain stage of learning, is doomed to pay for his enviable attainments either by ill health or poverty. Those who are born to greatness may be certain that, whether they exert their minds or not, the advantages of noble birth will suffice to distinguish them from their fellows; and for you of all men the acquisition of such ill-starred accomplishments would be entirely superfluous. I sincerely hope that you will not allow them to occupy too much of your time." He arranged that most of my lessons should be in practical subjects connected with national administration and economy. I got on fairly well, but there was no branch in which I showed any particular aptitude. It was only in painting, which my preceptors considered a very trivial and unbecoming pastime, that I displayed any unusual talent. Often I used to wonder whether I should ever get the chance of using this gift to the full, for the time allotted to these lighter distractions was very short. At last, with my unexpected retirement to a remote shore, the longed-for opportunity arrived. On every side the great sea spread about me; I began to learn its secrets, became so intimate with its every mood and aspect that where these sketches fail it is not for lack of understanding, but because there came at last a point where my brush could no longer keep pace with the visions that beset my brain.

Not having previously had any opportunity of showing these sketches to His Majesty, I took advantage of this occasion to display them. But I fear that my action in using them for this competition will when reflected upon provoke very unfavourable comments. . . .' The conversation was carried on by Prince Sochi no Miya: 'I know, of course,' he said, 'that mere industry will not carry one far in any art; his heart must be in the matter. But all the same there is a great deal which can simply be learnt from masters; so that a man, without any understanding of what is really important, will often easily succeed in imitating the outward forms and procedures of an art. But painting and draughts demand an extraordinary degree of natural equipment and also furnish us with the strangest surprises; for some apparently half-witted fellow, who does not seem capable of any useful activity, will turn out to be a genius at draughts or painting! On the other hand I have occasionally come across instances where intelligent children of good family have possessed what I may term a general superiority, showing an unusual capacity in every form of art and learning.

'My father the late Emperor gave personal attention to the training of all his children, both girls and boys, in every imaginable art and accomplishment. But it was in your education, Genji, that he took by far the greatest interest, and it was to you, whom he considered most likely to profit by it, that he was at pains to hand on the great store of information which in the course of his long life he had here and there acquired. In literature of course you were far ahead of any of us; just as you were in other less important matters, such as playing upon the zithern, which was indeed perhaps your principal accomplishment. But I remember that, in addition to this, you played reasonably well on the flute, guitar, and great zithern; as indeed your father often mentioned with wonder. These talents of yours were well known at Court, and I for my part had heard that you occasionally amused yourself with brushes and paints. But I had always supposed that this was a mere pastime, and I confess that the masterpieces which you have exhibited before us today took me completely by surprise. I assure you that even the great ink-painters of antiquity would feel no small uneasiness should their works be set beside these sketches of yours. You are indeed a prodigy!' He spoke rather thickly and indistinctly, for he was already a little bit fuddled with wine; and being for the same reason somewhat lachrymose, when mentioning his late father's name he suddenly burst into tears.

It was towards the end of the month and the late moon had at last risen. The rooms where they were assembled were still dark, but the sky outside was already aglow with dawn. The Keeper of Books and Instruments was asked to bring out the zithers. To no Chujo took the *wagon*,[22] which he played, if not so well as Genji, at any rate in a very distinguished manner. Sochi no Miya took the great zither and Genji the *kin*.[23] The lute was played by Akikonomu's gentlewoman Shosho no Myobu. There was a certain courtier who had a genius for beating time; he was now sent for and a most agreeable concert ensued. Dawn was spreading fast. Colour began to come into the flowers, and the features of those sitting by became dimly discernible in the growing light. The birds were singing lustily; a pleasant morning had begun.

Presents were now distributed to the guests by Lady Fujitsubo on behalf of the Emperor; Prince Sochi no Miya received in addition the special tribute of a cloak from the wardrobe, in recognition of his services as umpire.

Genji gave instructions that the Suma scroll should be

22 Japanese zither.
23 Chinese zither.

left with Fujitsubo. Hearing that it was only one of a series, she begged to be shown the rest. 'You shall see them all in good time,' Genji said; 'there are far too many of them to go through at one sitting.' The little Emperor, too, seemed to have thoroughly enjoyed the proceedings, which was a great comfort to those who had engineered them.

When To no Chujo saw with what zest Genji supported his ward Princess Akikonomu even in such trifling matters as this contest he again became a little uneasy about Lady Chujo's position. But observing the situation closely, he noted that the young Emperor, who certainly began by being very deeply attached to his little play-mate, after the first excitement of recognizing this new companion with her interesting grown-up accomplishments had passed away, settled down again quite happily to his old love. For the present at any rate there was no need for anxiety.

Genji had a strong presentiment the Court ceremony and festivals of the reign were destined to be taken as a model in future times. It was for this reason that even in the matter of private pastimes and receptions he took great pains that everything should be carried out in the most perfectly appropriate and pleasurable manner. Hence life at Court during this period became one long series of exquisitely adjusted pomps and festivities.

Genji was still haunted by the impermanence of worldly things, and now that the Emperor was beginning to reach years of discretion he often thought quite seriously of embracing a monastic life. It seemed to him that in history one so often reads of men who at an immature age rose to high position and became conspicuous figures in the world only to fall, after a very short time, into disaster and ignominy. With regard to himself he had felt since his exile that if the position in which he now found himself was beyond that to which he was

properly entitled, this was only fate's kind compensation
for the indignities to which in his early life he had suddenly been exposed. But now the debt which fortune
owed him was fully discharged and he could not believe
that he was far from the brink of some fresh disaster.
He would have liked to shut himself away in some
retired corner and devote himself to meditations upon
the life to come; he did indeed choose a quiet site on a
hill near the City and build a hermitage there, which he
even went so far as to furnish with images and holy
books. But so many questions arose concerning the education of his children and their future at Court that there
could be no question of his actually taking his vows, at
any rate for some considerable time; and what exactly
he had in mind when he began building this hermitage
it would be hard to say.

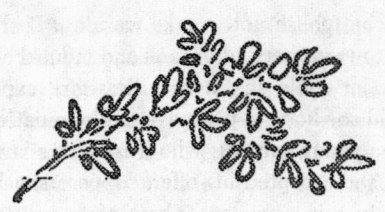

Chapter IX

THE WIND IN THE PINE-TREES

The new quarters which Genji had built to the east of his palace were now ready and the lady from the Village of Falling Flowers was duly installed there. The western wing and connecting galleries of the Nijō-in had been arranged in offices for the clerks whom he employed in his capacity as Grand Minister. In the eastern wing he intended to establish the Lady of Akashi. The women's quarters at the back of the palace he enlarged considerably, making several sets of very agreeable and comfortable apartments; these he destined for those ladies who having in the past received some mark of favor which, though fleeting, had generally been coupled with handsome promises, now looked to him for recognition and support. He kept the Grand Bedchamber of the Palace open, and though he lived chiefly in the new building, he continued to use the other from time to time and none of the necessary furniture was removed.

He wrote frequently to Akashi and many times begged her to come up to the Capital. But she had heard so many stories of how others had suffered at his hands—how he had again and again toyed with the affections not only of humble creatures such as herself, but of the greatest ladies in the land, only to cast them aside a few months later with the most callous indifference. Surely it would be foolish not to take warning. If this was his conduct towards persons of rank and influence, what sort of treatment could she, a friendless girl, expect? What part could she hope to play save the humiliating one of a foil to the young princess who was Genji's lawful bride? Suppose she accepted his offer, suppose she let him install her in this new house, how often would he come near her? Sometimes perhaps on his way to Murasaki's room he might look in casually for a moment; more she could not expect. She saw herself the butt of every lewd wit in his palace. No; she would never consent.

But there were other considerations. Should she continue to bring up her baby daughter in this sequestered spot, how could the child ever hope to take its place among the princes and princesses of the Blood? Little as she trusted Genji, she must not cut off her child from all possibility of an ultimate transference to the Capital. Her parents too realized with dismay that her prospect at the City was none too bright; but on the whole they inclined towards a move.

There was a certain estate near the Oi River[1] which her mother had inherited (it had belonged to Nakatsukasa no Miya, the mother's paternal grandfather). Successive heirs failed to claim it and for two years the place had been falling into decay. A fresh plan had occurred to the old recluse and his wife. They summoned the caretaker of the place, a descendant of the man whom Nakatsukasa had originally left in charge and said to him: 'We had intended to quit the world for ever and end our earthly days in this inaccessible retreat. But certain unexpected events in our family have made it necessary that we should again seek a residence within easy reach of the Capital. After our long absence from the Court we should feel utterly lost and bewildered were

[1] Also called the Katsura River. Runs near Saga (to the east of Kyoto) where Genji was building his hermitage.

we to plunge straight into the bustle of the town, and it occurred to us that while we are looking for some quiet, old house to live in permanently, it might be a good thing to use this place at Oi which you have been looking after for us!' 'I am afraid you will be very disappointed when you see it,' said the man. 'For years past no one has been in possession and everything is tumbling to pieces. I have been making shift myself to live in a room which has indeed a kind of ceiling, but no roof! And since the spring they have been building this new hermitage for Prince Genji close by, and this has changed the whole character of the district. The place is crowded with workmen; for the hermitage, by what I can make out, is going to be a very grand affair. If what you are looking for is a quiet, unfrequented spot you will certainly be badly disappointed.' His remarks had the opposite effect to that which he had intended. To learn that at Oi they would be living as it were under Genji's very wing was an astonishing piece of news. He ordered the man to put the large repairs in hand at once; what wanted setting to rights indoors they could see to at leisure later on. This did not at all suit the caretaker. 'If you want to know,' he said sulkily, 'I reckon this place belongs to me as much as to anyone. I have been living there quietly all these years and this is the first I have heard of anybody putting in a claim to it. When I first took things in hand the pastures and rice-fields were all running to waste, and his lordship Mimbu no Tayu told me before he died that I could have them for my very own and do what I could with them as payment of certain sums which he then owed me.' What he was really frightened of was that, if the family came into residence, they would lay claim to some of the livestock and grain that their land had produced. He had suddenly grown very red in the face, his voice quivered with anger and his whole aspect was so grim and even

menacing that the old recluse hastened to reassure him:
'I am not in any way interested in the farm or its produce,' he said; 'with regard to them please go on just as
before. As a matter of fact I *have* got the title-deeds
somewhere here, but it is a long time since I attended to
business matters of any kind and it might take me a long
while to find these papers. I will remember to look into
the question and see how it stands. . . .' The steward
soon cooled down. He noted that the old priest was
evidently on friendly terms with Genji. This decided him
to be civil. And after all, even if the presence of his masters might for the moment be rather inconvenient, he
would later on have plenty of opportunities for reim-
bursing himself. Mollified by these reflections he set the
repairs in hand at once.

Genji meanwhile had no notion of what was afoot and
could not understand why, after all his entreaties, the
Lady of Akashi still hung back. He did not at all like
the idea of their child being brought up amid such uncivilized surroundings. Moreover, if the story afterwards
became known, it would certainly seem as though he
had been reluctant to acknowledge the child and had
behaved with great heartlessness in making no proper
provision for it or for the mother.

But at last the house of Oi was ready and a letter
came from Akashi describing how, with no idea that he
was building in the district, they had suddenly remembered the existence of the place and were making plans
for living there. He understood quite well the object of
this move. The Lady of Akashi was determined that if
their intercourse was to be resumed it must be in a place
where she would not be subjected to a humiliating contact with her rivals. To avoid this she was evidently
prepared to make every conceivable sacrifice. He was
curious to know more about her future plan of retreat
and sent Koremitsu, who was always employed in con-

fidential missions of this kind, to investigate the place a
little and let him know if there was anything he could
do to assist the newcomers at Oi. Koremitsu reported
that the house was in a very agreeable situation which
somehow reminded one of the seaside. 'It sounds just the
place for her,' said Genji. The hermitage which he was
building was to the south of Daikakuji, which temple,
in the beauty of its groves and cascades, it even bid fair
to rival. The house where the family from Akashi was
coming to live was right on the river, among the most
delightful pine-woods, and the unpretentious way in
which it was planned, in one long building without galleries or side-wings, gave it rather the air of a farmhouse
than of a gentleman's mansion. As regards furniture
Koremitsu told him what was most needed and he saw
to it that these wants were supplied.

A number of Genji's personal servants now arrived at
Akashi to assist the family in their removal. When she
found herself actually faced with the prospect of leaving
these shores and inlets, near which so great a part of her
life had been spent, the Lady of Akashi was filled with
consternation. The present plan was that her father
should stay on at Akashi alone, and the idea of leaving
him made her very unhappy. Looking back over the
whole affair, with all its consequences, she was amazed
to think that she had ever drifted into this miserable
union, which had brought nothing but trouble and confusion upon herself and those for whom she cared. She
found herself envying those whose fortune it had been
never to cross this prince's path. Her father, seeing the
house full of the servants and retainers whom Genji had
sent from the Capital, could not deny to himself that
here indeed was the fulfilment of his every dream and
prayer. He had secured his daughter's future. But what
about his own? How would his life be endurable without her? He brooded on this night and day, but never

showed what was passing in his mind, save for saying once or twice to his wife: 'Do you think even if I went with you I should see much of the little girl?'[2] The mother was also much distressed. For years past her husband had slept in his little hermitage and had lived an entirely separate life, engrossed in his meditations and devotions. There was little reason to suppose that, even should she stay behind, he would give her very much of his society, and virtually she would be living without any companionship or support. But though he was a spectator of their lives rather than a participator in them, his casual exits and entrances had become the rock in which her whole existence was rooted; the prospect of separation appalled her. He was a strange creature; but she had long ago given up expecting him to play in any sense a husband's part. His odd appearance, his eccentric opinions, their lonely life—all these she had learnt to tolerate in the belief that this at any rate was the last stage of her disillusionment, the final and unalterable ordeal which death alone would end. Suddenly she found herself face to face with this undreamed-of parting, and her heart shrank. The wet-nurse and other young persons whom at the time of the child's birth Genji had sent from the Capital were beginning to become very restive and the prospect of the coming journey delighted them. Yet even the most frivolous among them could not leave these creeks and sandy bays without a pang; and there were some who, knowing that it might never be their lot to visit such scenes again, came near to adding the salt of tears to sleeves already splashed by the breakers of the rising tide.

Autumn had begun and the country was at its loveliest. At dawn upon the day fixed for their departure a chill wind was blowing and insects filled the air with their interminable cry. The Lady of Akashi, already

[2] The Lady of Akashi's child.

awake, kept going to her window and looking out across
the sea. Her father had returned early from celebrating
the night service in his chapel; it was with trembling lips
that he had performed the familiar ceremonies. But now
that the day of parting had come no words of sorrow or
ill-omen must be spoken. So each was determined, but it
was no easy matter to keep things going. The child was
brought in, its infant beauty shining like a jewel in the
greyness of the dawn. The grandfather never wearied of
holding it in his arms and, young as it was, an understanding seemed to have grown up between them. He
was indeed astonished by the readiness with which
the child accepted a companion whose appearance and
manners, so different from those of its regular attendants,
might have been expected to have alarmed it in the
highest degree. Moreover there seemed something inappropriate, almost sinister in their alliance. Yet for long
he had scarcely let it be a minute out of his sight. How
should he live without it? He did not want to spoil the
journey by an outburst of unrestrained grief; yet utterly
silent he could not remain, and reciting the verse:
'While for good speed upon their road and happiness to
come I pray, one thing the travellers will not deny me,
an old man's right to shed a foolish tear or two,' he tried
to hide his tears with his sleeve, exclaiming: 'No, I ought
not to; I should not do it!'

His wife stood weeping at his side; there was one
thing that she could not disguise from herself; after long
years both of his life and her own that had been spent
in an unceasing protest against the pleasures and frivolities of the world, it was to those same frivolities and in
pursuit of the most worldly ambitions that her husband
was sending her away from him: 'Together we left the
City,' she cried; 'how all alone shall I refind the paths
down which you led me over heath and hill?' The Lady
of Akashi also recited a poem in which she said that even

to those who seem to have parted for ever, life with its turns and chances brings strange reunions to pass. She besought her father to come at least part of the way with them; but he seemed to regard it as utterly impossible that he should venture away from his seaside retreat, and it was evident that he regarded the negotiation even of the short road down to the sea as the most venture-some and nerve-racking business.

'When I first put worldly ambitions aside,' said the old man, 'and contented myself with a mere provincial post, I made up my mind that, come what might, you, my dear daughter, should not suffer from my having sacri-ficed my own prospects; and how best, despite the re-moteness of our home, to fit you for the station of life to which you properly belonged became my one thought and care. But my experience as governor taught me much; I realized my incapacity for public affairs, and knew that if I returned to the City it would only be to play the wretched part of ex-governor. My resources were much diminished and were I to set up house again at the Capital it would be on a very different scale from before. I knew that I should be regarded as a failure both in my private and public life, a disgrace to the memory of my father who occupied the highest station in the State; moreover my acceptance of a provincial governorship had everywhere been regarded as the end of my career, and as for myself, I could not but think that it was indeed best it should be so. But you were now growing up and your future had to be thought of. How could I allow you to waste your beauty in this far corner of the earth like a brocade that is never taken from the drawer? But no better prospect seemed to pre-sent itself, and in my despair I called upon Buddha and all the gods to help me. That, living as we did, any fresh acquaintances should ever be formed by us seemed out of the question. Yet all the time I believed that some strange chance would one day befall us. And what indeed could have been more utterly unforeseen than the circumstance which at last brought so distinguished a guest to our home? In this I could not but see the hand of Heaven, and my only anxiety was lest too great an inequality of rank should divide you. But since the birth of this child, that fear has not so much troubled me, for I feel that your union is fated to be a lasting one. A child of Royal Blood cannot, we must allow, pass all its days in a village by the sea, and though this parting costs me dear I am determined never again to tamper with the world that I have renounced. Princes are the lamps that light this world, and though they may for a time be destined to cast confusion upon the quiet of rusticity, soon they must perforce return to their true firmament; while those whom they have left smile back, as I do now, into the lowly Sphere[3] from whence they sprang. Should you hear that I am dead, do not tease yourselves concerning the welfare of my soul, and above all, while less than death divides us, do not worry over what may be befalling me.' Thus he poured out all that was passing through his mind and at last he added in conclusion: 'You may be sure that each of the six times of Prayer, till the day when the smoke rises from my pyre, I shall pray with all my heart for the happiness of the little princess. . . .'

Hitherto he had spoken with great self-possession; but now his face began to pucker.

There was so much baggage to be transported that a vast quantity of wagons would have been required had the whole party proceeded by road. To send some of the stuff by road and the rest by sea was in many ways inconvenient; moreover Genji's retainers did not wish to be recognized on the journey, and for all these reasons it

[3] The metaphor is of souls sinking back into lower incarnations.

seemed best that the whole party should proceed by water. They set sail at the hour of the Dragon, and soon their ship, like that of the old poet's story,[4] was lost amid the morning mists far out across the bay. The old priest stood gazing after it lost in a bewildered trance of grief from which it seemed as though he would never awake. The wind was fresh and favourable, and they arrived at the City punctually at the hour they had announced. Wishing to attract no notice they left their large baggage on board and travelled inland as quickly as possible. The house at Oi at once took their fancy and was, as Koremitsu had noticed, in some curious way very reminiscent of the seaside, so that they soon felt quite at home. The mother had known this place as a girl and moving recollections crowded to her mind at every turn. By Genji's orders a covered gallery had been added to the house, which was a great improvement, and the course of the stream had also been very successfully altered. Much still remained to be done, but for the most part only such small jobs as could easily be finished off later on, when they had got things straight and settled in. On their arrival they found that entertainment had been prepared for them at Genji's command by one of his confidential servants. He intended to come himself at the earliest opportunity, but many days passed before he could contrive an excuse for slipping away. The Lady of Akashi had made sure that he would be there to welcome her. She therefore spent the first days at Oi in the deepest depression, regretting her old home and quite at a loss how to occupy her time. At last she took out the zithern which Genji had given to her at Akashi. She was feeling at the moment particularly desperate, and as she had the part of the house where she was sitting entirely to herself she gave vent to her feelings in a somewhat wild improvisation, which

[4] See Waley, *Japanese Poetry* (Oxford, 1920), p. 56.

soon startled her mother from the couch where she was lying and brought her to the player's side. With the music of the zithern was blended the sighing of the wind in the great pine-woods that lay behind the house. 'An altered and a lonely woman to this my native village I return. But still unchanged the wind blows music through the trees.' So the mother sang, and the daughter: 'Far off now is the dear companion of my happier days, and none is here who comprehends the broken language of my lute.'

While things were going thus dismally at Oi, Genji was feeling very uneasy. To have established the people from Akashi so close to the Capital and then neglect them entirely was indeed a monstrous way to behave; but circumstances made it very difficult for him to escape unobserved. He had not said anything to Murasaki about the move to Oi, but such things have a way of getting round, and he decided that it would be better not to explain his absence in a note. He therefore wrote to her one morning as follows: 'There are various matters at Katsura[5] which I ought to have looked into a long while ago; but I did not at all want the bother of going there and have kept on putting it off. Some people whom I promised to visit have settled near by and I am afraid I shall have to go and see them too. Then I ought to go over to my hermitage at Saga and see the Buddha there before it is painted. So I am afraid I shall have to be away for two or three days.'

Some faint echo of the business at Oi had reached her, but in a very garbled form. She heard that Genji was hurriedly building a large new mansion on his estate at Katsura. This was of course quite untrue. Murasaki at once concluded that the mansion at Katsura was intended for the Lady of Akashi and depressed by this she wrote in answer: 'Do you know the story of the wood-

[5] Where Genji had an estate.

man[6] who waited so long that leaves sprouted from the handle of his axe? Do not imagine that I shall be quite so patient as that. . . .' It was evident that she was out of humour with him! 'How crotchety you are!' he said. 'In the past you did indeed have some excuse; but now I have entirely changed my habits. Anyone who knows me would tell you as much.' It took the whole morning to coax her back into a reasonable frame of mind. At last very secretly, with no outriders of any kind save for a few intimate personal attendants, and taking every precaution lest he should be spied on or followed, he set out for Oi and arrived there just as it was growing dark. Even when dressed in the plain hunting clothes that he wore at Akashi he had seemed to the Lady of the Shore a figure of unimaginable brilliance; and now when he appeared in full Court dress (he had indeed made himself as splendid as possible for the occasion) she was completely overwhelmed by his magnificence and soon, in contemplating this dazzling spectacle, the whole household recovered from the gloom into which they had been plunged. The little princess had of course to be fetched and it was naturally with considerable emotion that he now saw his child for the first time. It was indeed a pity that he should make its acquaintance in this belated manner. What nonsense people talk about children, he thought. Everyone used to make such a fuss about Yugiri, Princess Aoi's child, and pretend it was so remarkably handsome. Such people were mere time-servers and flatterers. If it had not been the Prime Minister's grandchild no one would have seen anything remarkable about it at all. But here was a very different

[6] A Chinese named Wang Chih. He watched a couple of hermits playing chess in a cave. The game absorbed his attention so completely that it seemed to him to last only a few minutes; but when it was over he found that years had elapsed and leaves had actually sprouted from the wood of his axe.

story. If this little creature did not grow up into a woman of quite exceptional beauty, he was indeed very much mistaken. The child smiled at him with such innocent surprise and had such a perfect little face and air that he at once took an immense fancy to it. The nurse who when he had first sent her to Akashi was already losing her looks, had now grown quite middle-aged. He asked her many questions about her experiences in these last months, to which she replied frankly and without any shyness. He felt sorry that he had sent her to waste the last hours of her vanishing youth in so dull a place and now said sympathetically: 'Here too you are a long way from everything and it is not at all easy for me to come over. I wish you would persuade your mistress to make use of the apartments I originally offered her. . . .' 'We must see how we get on,' the Lady of Akashi interposed.

That night at least she had no reason to complain of neglect and day came only too swiftly. During the morning he gave fresh instructions to the retainers who were responsible for the redecoration of the house, and presently a number of people who farmed on and around his Katsura estate came to pay their respects, having heard beforehand that he was about to visit his properties in this neighbourhood. As they were there, he thought he had better make them useful and set them to work repairing some places in the Lodge where the shrubs had been trodden down. 'I see,' he said, 'that some of the artificial rocks have rolled over and almost disappeared under the grass. I must get my people to hoist them up again into some position in which they will not look quite so pointless. However this is not the kind of garden that looks the better for too much trouble being taken with it; and you may not be staying here very long. It will not do to make everything here too nice or it will soon be as hard to go away from here as it was to leave Akashi.' Soon they fell to talking of those old days, now laughing, now weeping, but all the time divinely happy. Once her mother came and peeped at them as they sat talking and the sight of their happiness made her forget that she herself was old, was wretched. Wreathed in smiles she hobbled away from the room. A little later she was watching him standing in his shirt-sleeves instructing the workmen how to utilize the little spring of water that issued near the gallery of the eastern wing. He had no idea that he was being watched, till happening to come across a tray for flower-offerings and other religious gear lying about the house, he suddenly thought of the pious old lady and said to his companion: 'By the way, did your mother come with you? I had quite forgotten she might be here or I should not be going about the house dressed in this fashion.' He sent for his cloak and going up to the curtains-of-state behind which he was told the old lady would probably be sitting, he said in a gentle tone: 'Madam, I have come to thank you; for it is your doing that the little girl thrives so well. Your prayers and devotions it is that have lightened the load of her *karma* and caused her to grow up so fine and healthy a child. I know well enough what it must have cost you to leave the house which had become your sanctuary and mingle once more with the follies of this transitory world. I know too what anxiety you must be in concerning the husband whom you have left. . . . For this and much else, madam, I have come to thank you. . . .' 'That you should guess how dear it cost me to come back to the turmoil of the world, and that in these kind words you should tell me my exertions have not been made in vain, is in itself sufficient reward for all that I have endured, and justifies a life drawn out beyond the allotted span.' So the pious old lady spoke and then continued, weeping: 'I have been in great anxiety concerning this "twin-leaved pine,"[7] and

[7] Two-year-old child.

while we dwelt under the shadow of those wild cliffs I scarce dared hope that it would at last find room to spread and grow. But now I pray more confidently—though still afraid that from roots[8] so lowly no valiant stem can ever spring. . . .'

There was in her speech and bearing a courtly dignity which pleased him, and he led her on to talk of the time when her grandfather, the old Prince, was living at the house. While she spoke the sound of running water reached them. It came from the buried spring near the eastern wall of the house; the workmen had just finished clearing it. It seemed like the voice of one suddenly aroused from lethargy by the mention of old familiar names. 'I, that was mistress here, scarce know the way from room to room; only this crystal spring remembers still and meditates the ancient secrets of the house.' She murmured this poem softly to herself and did not know that he had heard what she said. But it had not escaped him; indeed, he thought it by no means lacking in beauty and power of expression.

As he stood looking down at her, full of interest and compassion, the aged lady thought him more beautiful than anything she could have ever dreamed would exist in the world. He now drove over to his hermitage at Saga and arranged for the Reading of the *Samantabhadra Sutra* and the meditations on Amitabha and Shakyamuni to take place every month on the fourteenth, fifteenth and last days respectively, together with other rituals for which he now made the final arrangements. The decoration of the Buddha Hall and the provision of the necessary altars and furniture were then discussed and various duties assigned to those in charge of the place. He returned to Oi by moonlight. It was strangely like those nights of old when he used to visit

8 Referring to the Lady of Akashi's comparatively humble birth.

her at the house on the hill. It seemed natural enough that, as in those days, she should bring out a zithern (it was indeed his own, which he had given her), and soon, stirred by his presence and the beauty of the night, she began to finger the instrument. He noticed at once that true to her promise she had not altered the tuning since that last night at Akashi, and it seemed as though all that had happened since were obliterated and he were still listening to that farewell tune.

He was conscious of no inequality between herself and him. Despite her mixed descent and rustic upbringing there was about her an air of personal distinction which made ample amends for her lack of breeding and worldly experience. Her looks had indeed greatly improved since he knew her, and as he gazed, now at her, now at the lovely child, he felt that both of them were destined to occupy henceforward a very large share of his attention. But what was he to do? It would indeed be a great pity that the child should grow up in an obscure country-house. Most people would no doubt think him perfectly justified in taking it away with him to the Nijo-in and bringing it up in whatever way he chose. But he knew that this would be a terrible blow to the mother and could not bring himself to suggest it. He sat watching the two of them with tears in his eyes. The little creature had at first been rather shy with him. But now it was quite at its ease, prattled and laughed in his face and in fact showed every sign of wanting to make friends with him. The infant in this expansive mood seemed to him more entrancing than ever. He took it up in his arms, and watching the tenderness with which he held it the mother felt that its fortunes were indeed secure. Next day he was to return to the Capital. He therefore returned to rest for a while; but the news that he was shortly to leave this house spread with disconcerting rapidity to his tenants at Katsura and the ante-rooms

were soon full of visitors waiting to escort him on his
journey. A number of courtiers had also discovered his
whereabouts and were waiting to pay their respects.
While he was being dressed, Genji said petulantly: 'This
is intolerable. If I am being tracked down even to such
a place as this, where can I ever hope to hide my head?'
And with a mob of visitors pressing round him he was
swept away to his carriage. At a window by which they
had to pass, stationed there as though by accident, was
the child's nurse with the infant in her arms. Stroking
its face tenderly as he passed, Genji said to her: 'I should
have been sorry not to see this child. But it has all been
so hurried. . . . Better than nothing perhaps. . . . But
"your village is so far away . . ."9 'We shall expect
rather more from Your Highness than we did in the old
days when we really were a long way off,' the nurse replied. The little princess stretched out her hand as
though trying to hold him back. Pausing for a while he
turned and said: 'It is terrible to have such a sentimental
disposition as mine. I cannot bear to part from those I
am fond of even if it be only for a single day. But where
is your mistress? Why did not she too come to bid me
good-bye? Tell her that it is barbarous. . . .' The nurse
smiled and withdrawing into the house delivered the
message. But so far from being unconcerned at his departure, the Lady of Akashi was so much agitated that
she had sunk helpless upon her bed, and it was some
while before she could muster enough strength to rise.
At last, after Genji, not knowing what was amiss, had in
his heart passed severe censure upon her coyness, she
arrived in the front-room supported by her ladies and
sank into a seat where, though she was partly hidden
by a curtain, he got a fair view of her face. Such delicacy

9 Quoting the old song: 'Your village is so far away that I
must go back almost as soon as I come. Yet short as our meetings are perhaps we should be still unhappier without them.'

of feature, such distinction, such grace would not he thought have done discredit to an Emperor's daughter. He went up to the window, pulled aside the curtain and whispered a few words of farewell. Then he hastened to rejoin his companions; but looking back for an instant over his shoulder he saw that, though all this time she had remained motionless and silent, she was following him intently with her eyes. He had in old days been somewhat too slender for his height; now he had filled out a little and she found this slightly robuster air very becoming. He must indeed have expended considerable thought upon his appearance, every detail down to the elegantly adjusted billowing of his wide, puffy trousers being calculated with the nicest eye for effect. Such at any rate was her impression as he passed out of sight that morning—a view perhaps somewhat coloured by partiality.

Ukon, the brother of Ki no Kami, had relinquished his office of Treasurer, and having been appointed Quiver-bearer to His Majesty had this year been formally invested as an officer of the fifth rank. He now came to relieve Genji of his sword, and looking in the direction from which his master had come saw the Lady of Akashi's form dimly outlined at the window. He had himself formed some slight acquaintance with her during the period of Genji's exile and wished to discover whether she still had a liking for him. He therefore drew one of her maids-of-honour aside and said: 'I have not forgotten those hours of pleasant intercourse, but fear to give offence. Sometimes when, waking before the dawn, I hear the rustling of the wind among the trees, I think for a moment that I am back at Akashi, or listening again to the waves that beat upon the shore. At such moments I long to break the silence with some message or token; but till now no proper means has come to hand. . . .' He purposely spoke in such a way that she might not understand him unless she were already aware of his feelings towards her mistress. 'The clouds that hang eightfold about this lonely hillside screen us from the world no less securely than the mist-wreaths of that sequestered bay. I for my part thought that of my friends in those days "none save the ancient pine-tree"[10] remembered me, and it is good news indeed to hear that by you at least . . .' She could not have been wider of the mark![11] He was now very sorry that he had in old days so scrupulously avoided all reference to this attachment. He would have explained himself further, but Genji was waiting; and calling out with an assumed cheerfulness, 'Let us talk of this another time,' he hastened to rejoin his master. Already the outriders were clearing intruders from the road and amid great clatter and bustle the procession started on its way. Two officious gentlemen, the Captain of the Guard and a certain Hyoye no Kami, rode at the back of Genji's coach. 'I object to being tracked down like this,' said Genji wearily, 'when I go to pay a quiet visit to private friends.' 'The moonlight was so exquisite last night,' they said in self-defence, 'that we could not bear having been left behind, and this morning we groped our way through the early mist to find you. The maple-leaves in the Capital are not yet quite at their best; but in the open country the colours are marvellous. We should have been here sooner, had we not become involved in a hawking party that one of the chamberlains had got up.' 'I must go back to Katsura first,' said Genji; and accordingly the party set out in that direction. It was no easy matter on the spur of the moment to provide entertainment for so

[10] Allusion to an old poem.

[11] The lady was unaware that he had been in love with her mistress and imagined it was of his feelings for herself that Ukon was speaking.

large a number of persons. However, the cormorant-
fishers who ply their trade on the Katsura River were
hastily sent for, and promised to secure food enough for
the whole party. Their strange, clipped talk reminded
Genji of the fishermen at Suma and greatly diverted him.
The falconers, who had decided to camp in the open
country, sent a present of small snipe, each bird tied to a
bunch of sedge-leaves. They played at the game[12] of
floating wine-cups down the stream. So many times were
the cups set afloat and so steep were the banks of the
stream that the game proved somewhat dangerous. But
the wine made them reckless and they were still shouting
out their couplets long after it grew dark. At last the
moon rose and it was time for the music to begin. The
most skilful performers on zithern, lute, *wagon,* and
various wind instruments were called upon and were
soon playing such tunes as were best suited to the place
and hour. A gentle breeze blew down the stream blend-
ing its whisperings with a music of pipe and string.
Higher and higher the moon rose above them; never had
night been so radiant and still. It was already very late
when a band of four or five courtiers made their appearance. They had come straight from the Palace
where the Emperor had been giving a concert. 'This is
the first of the Six Fast Days,' His Majesty had suddenly exclaimed. 'I expected that Genji would be here.
What has become of him?' Someone then informed His
Majesty of Genji's present whereabouts and messengers
were at once despatched to Katsura bearing a letter in
which the Emperor declared himself envious of the
pleasant excursion in which his Minister had found time
to indulge. With this letter was the poem: 'How pleasantly the shadow of the laurel-tree must fall upon the

---

[12] Each competitor had to improvise a verse before the cup
reached him.

waters in the village beyond the stream!'[13] Genji answered with due humility and respect. The messengers found this moonlight concert even more agreeable than the one which they had left and had soon settled down to drink and listen for the second time that night. When at last they rose it was proper that they should not be sent away empty-handed. As there was nothing here to give to them Genji sent a note to Oi: 'Have you anything that would do to give to some messengers from the Court?' After looking round for a little they sent such objects as they could lay hands on. There were two boxes full of clothes. For the chief messenger, who was now anxious to return to the Palace, he selected a lady's dress of very handsome stuff.

The company now became extremely animated. Poem followed poem in a swift exchange, and even Genji's conversation, usually equable and restrained, began to take so extravagant a turn that his hearers would gladly have kept him talking thus till the end of the time. As for things at home, he reflected—the harm was already done. The rishi's axe must by now have blossomed, aye, and withered too. Why not one more day? But no; that would never do; and the party broke up hastily.

They set out for the Capital, each wearing on his head the bright-coloured scarf with which, according to his rank and station, he had been presented the night before and with these gay patches that bobbed up here and there in the morning mist blended the colours of the flowers in the gardens through which they passed.

There was with them a certain member of the Night Watch famous for his singing of ancient ballads, and to cheer the company he now sang with great spirit the ballad 'Ho, my pony'; whereupon his companions doffed their scarves and wound them round the singer's head.

---

[13] Many puns. *Katsura* = 'laurel.' Also, a *katsura*-tree was supposed to grow in the moon.

The wind fluttered through the many-coloured ends that dangled about his shoulders, weaving as gay a brocade as that with which the storms of autumn carpet a forest floor.

The news of his swift return or at least some faint echo of it reached the Lady of Akashi in her chamber, making her feel more than ever desolate. To Genji it suddenly occurred that he had never written the customary[14] letter. Other things had indeed been occupying his attention; but he wished he had remembered.

On his return to the Nijō-in he rested for a little while and then went to tell Murasaki about his country visit. 'I am very sorry that I was away longer than I led you to expect,' he said; 'those wretched fellows hounded me down and, try as I might, I could not get rid of them. I am very tired this morning. I think, if you will excuse me, I must get some more sleep,' and so saying he retired to his own room. When they met later he saw that things were not going well, but for a time pretended not to notice. At last she became so tiresome that he said somewhat sharply: 'This is ridiculous. You know quite well that there can never be any comparison between her position and yours. Surely you had better drop this absurd affectation and make the best of me now I am here.'

He had promised to be at the Palace before nightfall, and now rose to go. But before he left the room she saw him go into a corner and scribble a hasty note. She guessed at once to whom it was addressed. What a long time it was taking! He seemed to have a great deal to say. Her women saw him giving it to a messenger with many whispered instructions and they were duly indignant.

He was supposed to be on duty all night at the Palace. But he was impatient to put matters right, and though

14 The 'next morning' letter.

it was very late indeed before he could get away he hurried back to Murasaki at the first opportunity of escape. While he was with her, the messenger returned from Oi with an answer in his hand. Genji read it without any attempt at concealment, and finding it to be of the most harmless description, he handed it to her saying: 'Please tear it up when you have read it, and do not leave the pieces lying about; pieces make such a bad impression! In my position one has to be so careful.'

He came and sat by her couch; but he was thinking all the time of the Lady at Oi and wishing he could be with her. For a long while he sat gazing into the lamp and did not speak a word.

The letter which he had handed to Murasaki was spread open before her; but she was not reading it. 'I am sure you have been peeping,' he said at last. 'That way of reading letters is very tiring,' and he smiled at her with such evident affection that the tears welled to her eyes. 'There is something I want to talk to you about,' he said, bending over her; 'I have seen the little girl and, as a matter of fact, taken a great fancy to her. I naturally want to do as well for her as I can, but under the circumstances that is far from easy, and I am rather worried about it. I want you to think about the matter a little, and see if you cannot help me. What can be done? For example, would you be willing to have her here and bring her up as your own child? She is almost three years old, and at that age they are so pretty and innocent that it is very hard indeed to harden one's heart against them. It is getting to be time that she came out of her long clothes. Would you be very much upset if I asked you to take charge of the ceremony?'[15] 'I was cross just now,' she said; 'but I knew you were thinking all the while about other things, and there seemed to be no use in pretending we were friends if we were not. I should

[15] The *mogi* or 'First Putting On of the Skirt.'

love to look after the little girl. She is just the age I like best.' She laughed with joy at the thought of having such a creature in her arms, for she was passionately fond of children. Should he try to secure the child? Genji was still very doubtful. Visits to Oi were very difficult to arrange, and he seldom contrived to get there except on the two days in each month when he went over to hear the service at his chapel near Saga.

Thus though the Lady of Akashi fared considerably better than the Weaving Lady[16] in the story and though her expectations were of the most modern description, it would have been strange had these hurried visits contented her.

[16] The two stars, Weaving Lady and Plough Boy, meet only on the seventh day of the seventh month.